HARD *hart*

HART'S BAY

E. DAVIES

Hard Hart / E. Davies. – 1st ed.
ISBN: 978-1-912245-35-2

To all of us who take the plunge. May a wave always catch you and sweep you to a place of your own.

1

JESSE

"Wait 'til you get a load of this."

Jesse Stone's fingers were nearly crushed by Finn's grip as the stranger pulled him over the crest of the hill.

"A load of what?" Jesse responded innocently and then met Finn's look with a sly smirk. They both knew exactly what he was implying. The best day of Jesse's life was about to get even better.

"A load of *this*."

Oh, that view wasn't bad. Almost as good as the view of Finn's ass that Jesse had enjoyed on their way out of the bar, until Finn grabbed his hand to lead him along the unmarked coastal path toward the cliffs.

They stepped over the grassy hill and those very cliffs crashed into sight: they were just entering a shallow, curved bay tucked away in the crook of the coast. Beyond it, the gravel beach turned to towering rocks. The deep blue of evening cast its filter across the blue of the sea, and green trees crammed onto the shore all the way up to the cliff's edge.

"Wow," Jesse breathed in, turning on the spot to take in the sight. He was so glad he'd accepted the stranger's invitation. They'd met just minutes earlier at the one tiny bar in town—Cher's End Table.

It had seemed like winning the lottery when he'd looked up from the bar to see a hunky guy about his own age, with soft grayish-blue eyes and a boyish grin, smiling at him. An outright miracle when he'd asked him to walk to the coast with him so he could show off his hometown.

"Told you so." Finn grinned down at him. "I love watching people see this spot for the first time."

"Do you often pick up strangers from the bar and bring them here?" Jesse was still very aware of the warm, broad fingers jammed around his own. His body prickled with a pleasant heat, the tension steadily building between them.

It was very clear that they were alone. The path itself didn't look like it was used too often.

"A gentleman doesn't kiss and tell," Finn answered, winking through the gloom of early evening in the forest. Then he leaned down to whisper, his breath hot on Jesse's neck. "But the answer is no. I'm a big fan of bedrooms."

"Me too." Jesse dropped Finn's hand and stepped closer, running his hands up his thighs to grip his hips. Wide, strong, solid. Exactly his type.

After all the weeks of stress and work it had taken to move to Hart's Bay, he wasn't looking a gift guy in the mouth. It looked like he was going to remember his first trip to the bay with a whole different kind of warmth than he'd expected.

Jesse stretched up on tiptoes, and Finn leaned in to kiss him. This was no innocent peck on the lips for their first kiss, either. Their lips crashed together hard and fast.

This kiss said *I want you tonight and only tonight*, and that suited Jesse just fine.

Strong hands skimmed up Jesse's back until one cupped the back of his head, hauling him in to deepen the kiss. As he stumbled, the stranger's other arm looped around his waist and easily supported his weight like he was made of nothing.

And then Finn scooped him off his feet.

"Oop!" Jesse's voice squeaked as he gasped for breath. He grabbed the first thing at hand—Finn's shirt. As much as he wanted to protest, he was rock-hard at the show of strength. Finn was sweeping him off his feet in every which way.

"There's a private spot I like nearby," Finn murmured. "I'd like to show you."

"I'll show you mine if you show me yours," Jesse said.

He was rewarded with a rich laugh as they stepped off the path. Although he curled into Finn's chest and held his breath, the hold on him never faltered. His feet didn't even brush against tree trunks or bushes as they descended the slope onto a rocky beach.

Moments later, they were in a little cove tucked into the rocky shoreline. Finn set Jesse down and swept a hand around the inlet, which was big enough for perhaps three people at most. But it only needed to be big enough for two, the way this was going. "It's like a bed, but not."

Jesse looked around, then crouched to scoop up a handful of colorful rocks. He let all but one drop, a piece of sea glass—a smooth, hazy piece of green glass turned into a stone by the wash of water over time. It was pretty enough that he pocketed it. Driftwood lay around, too. Lots of stuff that could be used in art. He'd have to come back here.

But right now, he had another priority.

"It's perfect," Jesse said. His voice dropped to a low growl that surprised even himself as he said, "You wanna come here?"

"That's the plan, yeah. But you're gonna come first," Finn told him, his voice steady and certain. He stepped closer, backing Jesse up against the rock face of the cliff. "I want to kiss you."

Jesse's knees melted. "Yes," he whispered. There was nothing hotter than a confident guy who wanted to get him off, and who asked before kissing. It was like Finn was tailor-made to check all of his boxes.

Finn pressed Jesse up against the rock face, grinding against him in a slow, rippling roll of his body. His hot, wet lips caught Jesse's in a dirty, openmouthed kiss. The firm bulge of his cock pressing into Jesse's thigh made it clear what he was after.

And Jesse's body responded in kind, suddenly hotter and tighter. His chest swelled with passion just like the rest of him. Jesse's nails dug into Finn's shoulders as he clung to him.

When Finn finally pulled back, Jesse gasped for breath. His lips were swollen and he was dizzy already with desire, desperate for release from the prison of his too-tight jeans.

Finn looked him up and down like the tastiest morsel in a five-star restaurant. He ran his hand from Jesse's shoulder over his chest.

"Fuck," Jesse gasped when his palm grazed his nipple. Even through his shirt, it was impossible to miss the lightning bolt of sensation that went straight to his dick.

But Finn didn't linger—his hand swept down to the catch of his jeans, and then Finn paused and looked up at Jesse. He raised his eyebrow to ask the question he didn't need to put out loud.

"Please," Jesse gasped, pushing into Finn's hand. A little lower and he could grind against that hand. But Finn denied him, unbuttoning his jeans instead.

And then, thank God, that hand slid into his jeans and curled around his hard shaft, sliding up and down with practiced ease. The hot, strong fingers curved around him. He held on firm enough not to tickle, but not so hard as to hurt all those nerve endings that were so on edge.

Jesse whimpered and spread his legs, rolling his head back against the face of the rock. The slight breeze of cool outdoor air and the murmuring, ever-present wash of the sea reminded him of their daring choice to do it outside.

He felt naughty, and his nerves were on fire with how much he loved it.

"Can I fuck you?"

"Fuck, I hope so," Jesse whispered and gave Finn another cheeky grin. "It would be a waste of a great inlet otherwise."

"Are you talking about yourself or the scenery?" Finn added an extra squeeze around Jesse's cock, making his whole body tighten and vibrate with pleasure that verged on pain. Slowly, his fist slid down all the way to the base of Jesse's shaft as he waited for an answer.

Jesse barked out a laugh when his sex-addled brain understood. "Both. I like a good, long outlet in my inlet."

With his free hand, Finn grabbed Jesse's hand and moved it to the bulge in his crotch. Jesse knew his eyes must have widened with surprise. Oh, Finn was so turned on already.

Jesse didn't need any more prompting to start rubbing along the length, pressing the heel of his palm in with each stroke until Finn's breathing went ragged.

"Fuck, that's it," Finn murmured. He groaned, the rocks under them clicking softly as he shifted his weight from foot to foot. "You're so damn hot."

"You're not bad yourself, as far as eye candy goes," Jesse responded with a teasing little grin. "I can put up with—

oof!" Finn just squeezed him firmly, and he jolted and shivered.

"Cheeky little one, aren't you?" Finn's breath was hot as it ghosted across his jawline. He pressed kisses from Jesse's throat to his ear, each hot touch of his lips making Jesse's toes curl.

"I think you like me that way." Jesse worked his fingers into the tight space under the waist of Finn's jeans, sliding them down across soft curls until the tips of his fingers brushed the end of the hard shaft. "With a smart mouth and a smart ass."

"I'll make your ass smart," Finn teased, pressing Jesse against the wall of rocks until they dug into him. But the pricks of pain that flashed through him only made him burn all the more for Finn.

"You better." Jesse hauled Finn's pants down and grinned at the line of his hard cock pressing through his underwear. "I'm counting on it."

Finn growled under his breath. He kissed Jesse again, his mouth hot and demanding as he peeled Jesse's shirt off and tossed it aside. The corner caught on a rocky outcropping, and it dangled there like a clothes hook.

Gravel shifted underfoot as Jesse spun around to face the rock. He hauled down his pants, then braced his forearms on it and bent over to make it clear what he wanted.

"Fuck, that's a hot sight." Finn's breath was hot on the back of Jesse's neck. He smacked Jesse's ass lightly, sending a tingle through Jesse's body as blood gathered down south. Finn nipped along the back of his neck around to his ear, his body sinuously grinding against Jesse's back in slow waves.

All Jesse could concentrate on was the hard cock against his ass, with just one layer of underwear in the way.

It didn't take long before Finn shifted, reaching between

them to haul that down. The smooth heat of skin on skin ignited a need deep inside Jesse—the need to be filled, claimed, fucked until he couldn't think straight.

All he wanted was to be covered by Finn's weight, wrapped in his arms, underneath him, his cock surging into his tight body until he was so filled he couldn't take another inch.

"Fuck me," Jesse growled. "I've got a condom. Here."

He fumbled to pass it back to Finn and listened to the packet ripping open over the sound of waves lapping the shore. The breeze cooling his skin only excited him more, his hardness jutting up toward his own chest as he braced himself on the wall again.

Finn spat on his fingers, and then those wet fingers pressed against and into Jesse. He moaned, biting his lip.

"Don't be quiet," Finn urged, his voice low and desperate. "We're all alone. I want to hear you."

When Jesse moaned, his voice echoed off the rock walls of the little inlet before ghosting away across the nearby ocean. It was so strange hearing, smelling, and feeling nature all around him instead of bedroom walls.

But it felt so fucking hot, too.

Jesse had expected to spend months sex-starved and single when he'd moved here, but instead, he was starting his new life in style. He'd never fucked outside, and here he was, bold and brash and naughty with a man who was hot as sin itself.

So there, Dominic. Jesse grinned to himself. His cheating bastard of an ex would never have dreamed of sex this hot. Really, he'd been doing Jesse a favor. And technically, Jesse wasn't breaking his promise to the friends he'd moved here with. *No romance* was the rule, not *no hookups.*

Strictly hookups could be really fucking good, apparently. He'd never been more glad that his friends had ditched the plan to come out and explore the town's bar tonight. This could be Jesse's little secret.

Jesse gasped as heat crawled through his body, pushing back against Finn's fingers when he found the spot inside. "Yes! There!" Finn had better hurry up, or Jesse was going to come right here and now, with his fingers alone.

"Can I fuck you now?" Finn murmured. He pressed a kiss on top of Jesse's shoulder. "You're too hot to resist."

"Please," Jesse begged. He whimpered when those fingers pulled out, pressing back against Finn in desperate search of the suddenly missing sensation. "Need you now."

Finn shushed him with a nip on the back of his neck and pressed his tip against Jesse. Then he was sliding inside, inch by hot inch.

Jesse whimpered at how fucking big he was. It was a beautiful pain, but it made his knees shake.

Finn slid a strong arm around his waist and pulled Jesse against his body, going still for a moment. "You all right?"

That second was more care than his ex had ever shown him. From a total stranger. Jesse's mind was blown. "Yeah, fine," he grunted, squeezing his eyes shut and pressing his forehead against the rock face.

Gravel shifted again as Finn kept his hold around Jesse, his palm flat against Jesse's chest as if to steady and keep him still. He pulled out and thrust again, opening Jesse up inch by inch. Every thrust, he worked his way a little deeper.

It didn't take long before Jesse's body relaxed. He gasped for breath as Finn's nails dug into his hip, his balls slapping against sensitive, hot skin.

"Fuck," Jesse panted. "Harder."

Finn's chuckle was low, and with his body pressed tightly

against Jesse's back, Jesse felt it reverberate through his chest. "I don't want to hurt you."

"Can't get pleasure without a little pain." Jesse gasped when Finn's answer was to start thrusting in sharp, quick pushes of his hips. "Yes!"

Finn's grunts joined Jesse's whimpers, the sharp clicks of rocks underfoot punctuating each thrust. The smell of salt air mingled with sex and Finn's own musk, teasing Jesse's nose as he pressed his lips together tightly. His nails caught on the rocks and dragged, instantly ragged and scuffed.

He felt small and vulnerable in Finn's arms, but in the best possible way. Finn was wrapped around and deep inside him, every muscle hard as he gasped for breath.

Jesse pushed back against Finn, keeping up the rhythm and matching it where he could. His knees were weak, but he leaned heavily on the rocks, letting them take their combined weight.

"Yes... oh, fuck." Jesse bit his own lip hard. Finn shifted his angle, and his cock slid into Jesse just right. The ridge of his cock head already did exquisite things to Jesse's body.

If only he weren't so busy these next few months. He hadn't left his whole life in Portland behind and moved to a tiny town of a thousand only to let a guy distract him.

However high that guy was making him float, however much his skin vibrated with pleasure, however close he quivered to the edge of orgasm. He shifted his weight against one forearm and reached down to stroke himself, but Finn gently flicked his hand away.

"Oh!" Jesse groaned when Finn's broad, hard palm grazed his shaft. It was excruciatingly pleasurable to feel the tight grip of his fingers around his sensitive shaft. And when Finn started stroking? Oh, he could hardly hold on, his body clenching around the length deep inside him.

Every thrust seemed to hit deeper inside Jesse, making him press harder against Finn, desperate for more and more. He couldn't stop himself silently begging for it, and Finn sensed it. His touch might have been gentle, but his hips weren't. Exactly like Jesse wanted it: hard and fast.

There was no restraint now. Finn almost crushed him into the rock face as he thrust hard and fast, both men in silent agreement that they needed more right now.

Well, not quite silent.

"Yes, yes, yes!" Jesse gasped. "Fuck me, Finn. You're so fucking big and hard. I need to come with you inside me."

Finn's teeth closed around Jesse's earlobe, surprisingly gentle considering how hard and fast he was going. "I can do that," he hissed into Jesse's ear. "I can come with you wrapped around me. All day long. I'm so close. You want me to come in you?" Finn squeezed Jesse's cock for emphasis, making him whimper.

"Yes!" Jesse's thighs shook, his body tensing up. He reached back to Finn, grabbing his hips to push as deep as possible. The words settled deep in his brain and belly, stoking the barely contained inferno.

"Come for me," Finn growled. "I'm about to fill you up, baby. About to blow my load in you, right here." The noises of their bodies slapping together began to drown out the lapping of the waves and seagulls crying in the distance. Every other sense seemed to disappear in turn.

Until there was only the two of them, locked together in ecstasy as they came in shuddering thrusts, gasps, nails digging into each other's skin, and growled approximations of each other's names.

"Fuck." Jesse tried to catch his breath when he finally came down from his high. He melted against the rock, clinging to it for support now as Finn softened and slid out of him.

Rational thought was slow to return. Instead, a wave of contentment swept through him first, making him want to press his nose into Finn's chest and cuddle the evening away.

But—no, he reminded himself. Tonight wasn't about that.

Finn's arm swept around his shoulder and pulled him away from the rocks. Jesse's one-night partner spun him around, then pulled him in for a crushing hug. It was like he'd somehow known what Jesse needed.

Jesse leaned into Finn, his arms around his waist, pressing his face into his shoulder as the strangely intense desire to cuddle Finn ebbed from him. Satisfaction set in, a need scratched that he hadn't even realized he'd had.

At last, he was left with just the reality: he was hugging a near-stranger for dear life. Jesse laughed sheepishly and pulled away from Finn's hold, blinking up into his face.

"You all right?" Finn murmured. He raised a hand to brush Jesse's cheek and forehead where he'd pressed against the rock face. "You've got a dent or two."

"Don't we all?" Jesse smiled and found his footing again, wriggling until he could pull his underwear back up. He was pretty fucking proud of himself for taking it like a champ. He'd clearly impressed Finn, and even that thought pleased him.

Finn would remember this, he was sure of it.

The next thought was *I wonder if I'll see him around again.*

"I'd better get going home," Jesse murmured before he could let other, related, more dangerous thoughts creep in— like whether they could sleep together again. Or kiss. Finn was a good kisser.

For God's sake, Jesse, he lectured himself. *You didn't move to Hart's Bay to kiss men.*

That slow smile, the flash of perfect white teeth, nearly did him in. "I'll walk you back," Finn told Jesse as he pulled off the condom and found a tissue to wrap it up.

Fuck, he was sweet. He'd make someone a great boyfriend. Just not Jesse.

"No, no." Jesse grabbed his shirt and pulled it on. "I've got it." The path had been pretty straightforward, after all.

Before he scampered away, though, he paused to lay a hand on Finn's shoulder. When Finn looked at him again, Jesse leaned in and up for one bold kiss. "Thanks."

"No," Finn murmured, laying a hand over Jesse's hand. "Thank you."

As Jesse climbed the path back to the grassy hill and into the town square, his fingers slid over the piece of smooth green glass in his pocket. He took a moment to pause and look over his shoulder at the coast that stretched from horizon to horizon, the flat line of the sea stretching out before him.

Something deep inside him—and quite different from the spot deep inside him that had approved so recently—told him he'd made the right choice in moving here.

Hart's Bay was going to treat him well.

2

———————

FINN

Finn Hart brushed off the familiar flush of embarrassment as he looked out the open truck window toward Hart Square.

It was nearly deserted. All that remained of the once-vibrant downtown was the grocery store on one side and a bar opposite that was only occasionally open. In the middle of the square of shabby buildings was a run-down patch of dead grass with a single wooden bench. A couple of storefronts were boarded up, the for-sale signs long since faded.

The grocery store was only open until early evening, and as for the bar? Well, there was no point in calling the bar or checking online for hours. Cheryl proudly ignored the phone, opened the bar when and as she wanted to, and welcomed everyone in. So last night, Finn had been in the mood for a drink after a long day of talking to people who never listened. He'd walked from his house down to the square he was now surveying from his truck window like some lost territory.

And thank goodness Finn *had* gone out last night. Jesse—his gorgeous eyes and slender body and smart mouth—had been in his dreams all last night.

13

He couldn't remember the last time he'd had such a great hookup. He figured Jesse was a tourist. After all, if new residents were rare in Hart's Bay, new gay residents were practically unicorns. So he wasn't exactly going to get his hopes up that he'd see Jesse ever again.

Most tourists kept their windows rolled up and sped through Hart's Bay when they caught a glimpse of the boarded-up downtown. They favored hotspots like Cannon Beach. But Cheryl, the owner of Cher's End Table, sometimes got the adventurous tourists, or those who were more interested in a Bud Light than a lighthouse.

It was rare that Finn got a chance to blow off steam so close to home. He was used to having to drive to Portland to find a one-night stand. In a town of a thousand, a gay bar was out of the question, and Grindr was about as useful as a Blockbuster card.

Cheryl didn't mind who came into her bar, but eligible men usually simply didn't. It was the first time Finn had met someone so cute and adventurous and strangely captivating in Hart's Bay.

It wasn't even just that living in a small town meant you knew all your neighbors, and none of them were gay. Finn was also a Hart.

Once, being a young Hart in this town would have meant going into the family business—Hart Fisheries. By now, at twenty-nine, Finn would be a respected member of the business and the town. But that had all ended two decades ago, when the fishery and the Hart family collapsed.

As far as he was concerned, anyone who was nice to him because of his name was just underscoring the embarrassment of what the *other* half of the Hart family had done. He'd been too young to know the full extent of what was going on, so he was hardly guilty of anything. Even so, Finn had grown up in the shadow of that history.

Thank goodness Jesse hadn't been one of those to treat him differently because of what his name was. They'd just been two guys filling a need on a deserted rocky beach.

As much as Jesse had intrigued him, maybe it was better he didn't get to know the guy. Nobody ever turned out to be who they said they were.

"Hey, man."

Finn flinched and looked across the car to the guy scrambling into his passenger seat. "Hey, there you are."

"Sorry. I couldn't find my lunch." Justin, the newbie on the construction crew, needed a ride, and Finn sympathized. Until Justin got his first paycheck and could buy his own car, he was happy to give the guy a ride to their jobsites.

It was rare that the crew worked here in the town. As much as the buildings here needed refurbishment, the other half of the Hart family refused to maintain them. Which was weird, really. Finn would have thought they'd want to keep their property values up, if nothing else.

"Where was it?" Finn bit back his amusement. Justin was the kind of person who could forget his own head, but he was one of their hardest workers already.

"Uh, top of the fridge."

"Not in the fridge?"

Justin gave an elaborate shrug. "Probably no room in there. Fridge is full of beer for the game this weekend."

Finn swallowed a sigh. He looked like a guy who liked sports, so he'd learned to have conversations about it without ever expressing much of an opinion. "Yeah? You got friends over, or do you need an intervention?"

Justin laughed. "Friends," he told Finn. "You wanna come?"

"Nah, I can't. I'm..." Finn reached for the first excuse to hand. "Swimming. Barbecuing. Beach barbecue and a swim. Yep."

"Sounds epic." Justin flashed him a grin, and Finn swallowed his relief. Justin wasn't really the type to hold rejection close, anyway. Justin was already off and talking about his team's season record.

Finn was good at throwing in his standard phrases—"that was a great, clean goal," "their defense got crushed," and his favorite, "the ref needs an eye test" to pretend to participate in whatever the sports conversation was. Luckily, he didn't even need that much. Justin was practically entertaining himself talking about sports over the twenty-minute drive. All Finn had to say was "uh-huh" now and then.

When they arrived at the site, Finn was a bit startled to see the boss's truck there. Mike usually trusted Finn to manage the day's work, and it was pretty rare he came to oversee anything. He was a laid-back West Coaster himself.

That meant there was news.

But before he ever got around to finding where Mike was hiding out, the news stood out to him. Or rather, stood by the table saw, swinging a hammer idly, talking with one of the more experienced guys on the crew.

It was Rainier Hart.

It had been years since Finn had laid eyes on his dark-haired cousin, but he'd recognize him in a heartbeat. He had their grandfather's crooked smile and his whole family's way of standing like they were better than anyone else.

Few things got under Finn's skin more than them flashing that attitude all around Hart's Bay. And unfortunately, he couldn't even fume that they didn't own the place, because they did.

Damn it, why was Rain here?

Before he could ask, Mike showed up and swept him off to the side of the jobsite. "Hey, so..."

"You hired Rain." Finn arched his eyebrow and waited for an explanation.

Mike had been born and raised in Hart's Bay. He had to know it was an insane move to hire Finn's cousin. For God's sake, Mike's boss was Roy, the third of the three Hart brothers. Uncle Roy was on the good side along with Finn's dad. Had he approved the new hire?

Even crazier to ask Rain to take supervision from Finn. And Finn wasn't going to let him get away with shit because he was afraid of telling one of the bad branch of the Harts what to do.

"I don't think he'll give you trouble."

Finn nearly snorted with laughter, shooting another look at Rain. He was leaning on the saw now, arms folded, talking away like he was getting along fine with the other guys.

It made him grit his teeth. The Harts might be sitting on a dwindling fortune, but he was sure there was still enough money stashed away to ensure the youngest of Monty Hart's kids didn't have to work a job in his life.

Finding Finn here, supervising the crew at Hart & Hart Construction, shouldn't surprise Rain. Finn had been supervising this crew for months. Plenty of other construction jobs going if Rain wanted to play real-life K'Nex for fun. So why was he here, if not to cause trouble? Maybe this was the latest round of family politics. It had been a few years since the last big clash.

"I know," Mike said and clapped Finn's shoulder. "But we

had a good talk. He's earnest and willing to work hard. Give him a chance to surprise you. I needed a man with his talents."

"Which are?" Finn couldn't resist snarking. He cast a glare across the site to the slender guy. "Can he even lift a two-by-four?"

God, he hated being such a dick, but he'd never had a positive experience with any of his relatives. The few remaining Harts still in town stayed out of each other's way, and that was the best they could hope for. It helped that every other kid besides Finn in their generation had left town. Just Finn, his parents, and Uncle Roy left on their side right now. On the other side were Grandpa and Rain's parents.

"He's quick up and down a ladder. Like a goddamn mountain goat. He can fit into tight spaces. Takes a village to build a house." Mike eyed him. "But you know that. He's also been picking up a lot of general construction skills in the last year or two. I think he'd be good on roofing."

Of course. That had been Finn's specialty before he'd moved up in the world. Now, he supervised the rest of the crew, liaising with the bosses.

They handled framing, making sure buildings had solid exterior and interior walls, roofs, and windows and doors. In short, they took a site from a bare concrete slab to a real building, and Finn loved it. It was early enough in the process that the real time crunches rarely hit, and it was satisfying work.

Everybody on site worked, though. That included Finn. He'd never had much time for supervisors who used their role to stand around giving orders, an excuse not to get their hands dirty. So Finn still spent a lot of time scrambling around roofs, making them good and watertight. Nothing more important in the Pacific Northwest.

"Fine," Finn said tightly. As long as Rain didn't mess around, Finn could be civil to him. No doubt he'd soon get bored of playing contractor and quit, anyway.

"Thattaboy." Mike clapped his arm again and strode toward the half-built structure with him. "So, how's it coming? You keeping up?"

"We're hoping to get the roof on before the end of today. Speaking of Rain... it's supposed to rain this evening," Finn told Mike. They didn't have any time to waste. Perfect time to test his cousin's work ethic. "If we don't, it'll be first thing tomorrow if we get the break in the rain it calls for." *If only I could get a break from Rain, too.*

They lived and worked by the weather forecast sometimes; interior work could progress no matter the weather, but you couldn't let water get under the roof.

"Cool, great." Mike gave him a thumbs-up. "Call if you need anything."

He left Finn to his work, so Finn called the guys over for a morning huddle.

Finn could feel Rain's gaze boring into him as he gave them a status update on the roofing tiles getting delivered today, the load of lumber that had been delayed yesterday, all the details he had to keep straight.

Finally, he addressed the elephant on the site. "And we've got another new guy. Justin's not the baby anymore. Rain, welcome to the crew." No word about his relationship to the company owners, which was as it should be. Finn had never leaned on that, and neither should Rain.

"Thanks." Rain's voice was strong and sharp as he nodded around to those welcoming him. "Can't wait to get started."

Finn could see the bluster and posing that came with any

new guy—not wanting to be hazed, and showing that he was gonna work hard. Well, they'd just wait and see about that.

"Then what are we waiting for? We've got no time to waste today," Finn told him—and all of them. "Get going."

It turned out Mike was right. Whatever the hell had brought Rain home, he was at least working his ass off whenever he was given a job.

Grudgingly, Finn let down his suspicion but not his guard. Until he knew Rain's deal, he wasn't gonna trust him, but he could work with him if he had to.

Of course, it wasn't gonna be a walk in the park. The lumber load had been delayed yet again, leaving half their crew with nothing to do. That meant he could pull a couple guys onto the roof with him who *weren't* Rain, and they worked better together.

Finn knew he should be letting the new guy get experience, but as the rainstorm closed in, he worked faster and better with guys he knew at his elbow.

Until Tim got a call from the school to pick up his daughter early, and Finn spotted Rain standing at the bottom of the ladder waiting for a job.

Finn didn't like that one bit. Best to keep your friends close and your enemies closer, he figured.

He jerked his chin. "You swap places with him, Rain. See you tomorrow, Tim."

"Thanks a bunch, man." Tim was grateful for the early out, but honestly, it was only an hour's work he was losing, and for a guy with the experience and skill Tim had, Finn was willing to bend the rules.

"Hey." Once he was suited up in Tim's harness, Rain climbed the ladder like it was nothing and joined him on the roof. "What can I do?"

No bullshit snide comments or sideways glances. Finn's respect for him grew another notch.

"Pass me those tiles," he told him as he stapled them in place one at a time. Working in silence, they found a rhythm together a lot quicker than Finn had expected. By the time the first droplets of rain splattered on their faces, they were just finishing the last row.

He was aching all over and ready to get home. With the rest of the house weatherproofed, he could finally let the guys take off.

"Thanks for your work today," Finn told Rain, his voice almost cracking from disuse. That whole day, he'd been watching more than talking, seeing how the guys all worked together. He wasn't about to strike up a friendly conversation for the last hour, and it seemed safer to just pretend to be anti-social for an afternoon.

"Welcome. Thanks for having me up here." Rain headed for the ladder, leaving Finn shaking his head.

Whoever the hell had served Rain a slice of humble pie, Finn wished the rest of his family could get a serving of their own.

Maybe this wasn't the worst thing ever.

After the site was cleaned up for the night, Finn dropped off Justin at Hart Square. Sitting here, outside the grocery store, reminded him that he needed groceries.

"Ah, shit." Finn couldn't put it off. He was out of bread to make sandwiches for his lunch tomorrow. At least he was already here. He just had to park and drag his ass inside.

He still groaned as he eased out of his seat and headed for the store.

Balancing a basket on one aching arm felt strangely good. It helped stretch out the muscles after a long day of physical labor. Definitely better than going straight home and to bed—Finn had done that in the early days of his career, and he'd woken up in the mornings stiff as a board.

As he grabbed bread, his phone went off, so he shifted his basket to the other arm, dropped the bread in, and answered without really looking at the screen.

"Hey, Finn here."

"Hey!" He'd recognize Dash's voice anywhere. His little brother called for a chat at least once a week. The second oldest of the four boys, though only older than his twin by minutes, Dash had moved out to Connecticut years ago for college. Among other reasons, he'd wanted a good job without having to commute to Portland. Hart's Bay didn't hold that for Dash—or much else. Connecticut had given him the freedom to reinvent himself.

"Hey, Dash. What's up?"

"You'll never guess."

"You're running away to join the circus?" Finn headed over to the dairy aisle for milk. "About time, clown."

"Asshole," Dash laughed. "No, I'm thinking of coming home."

"Home?" As far as he was aware, Dash wasn't on vacation or anything right now. "You mean..."

"To Hart's Bay."

"You're kidding," Finn said. Dash was right. He never would have guessed that. "Why?"

"No need to roll out the welcome mat," Dash snorted, sounding a little peeved.

"No, no, it'd be nice to have you here." Finn didn't want Dash to feel like he couldn't come back. It wasn't like this town was only big enough for one Hart boy. And he'd missed his brothers since all of them moved out. It felt like he was the last one standing.

Dash laughed. "Just kidding, man. I'll come bug you whether you want me to or not."

"Just like old times." Finn grinned. "So, what brings you back? Can't be work." He was a teacher out there, and as far as Finn knew, he liked it.

"Connecticut just doesn't feel like home anymore."

Was that a veiled reference to Dash's love life? Were his friends being dicks? A familiar protectiveness rose in Finn's chest. He'd looked after all his brothers in school. "Yeah?"

"It's not solid yet. Anyway, how are you?"

Finn didn't have much to say, but he recounted the day—leaving out the fact that a certain sexy twink had been haunting his thoughts—as he finished up his shopping run.

Especially the part where Rain was working on the crew and acting cool about it.

"Huh. You're right. I bet he's up to something. Keep me posted," Dash said as Finn headed for the checkout. One was empty right now, so he steered that way.

"Will do. Gotta check out now. Catch you later, man." Finn pocketed his phone, shaking his head at how weird today was.

When his basket was unloaded, he looked up—and froze.

It was a group of five guys in their twenties, all chattering away.

He didn't recognize them... except for one. One who was impossible not to notice, and who had also frozen on the spot, staring across at him.

Jesse.

"We should get Cheetos." A peppy redhead was grinning at all of them, bouncing as he loaded up the cart at the end of the checkout.

"Dude, you would live on Cheetos if we let you." That was a guy with black hair and nails, rolling his eyes.

Don't act weird, Finn told himself and nodded once at Jesse, breaking the gaze as much as it pained him to do so. His heart was suddenly doing weird somersaults, and his thoughts —so neat and orderly normally—were racing all over the place.

Jesse looked no less gorgeous here in the harsh light of the little grocery store, supervising a cart filled with groceries while one of his buddies paid.

"That's ten sixty-five," the cashier told Finn, and he wordlessly pulled out his credit card to swipe. When he looked up again, Jesse and the cart were at the door.

His friends tagged along after him, looking over their shoulders at Finn. Two of them were having a whisper-conference with Jesse, trying to stop him, but Jesse was walking like he had a fire lit under his ass.

The whole world had probably noticed them staring at each other. So much for playing it cool, then. Finn blushed and pocketed his card, trying not to stare after Jesse. "Thanks," he told the cashier and grabbed his bags, trying to walk slowly to the doors to give Jesse a chance to get away.

But they had more groceries to unload, so by the time he made it out to his truck, he was hard-pressed to pretend not to notice the other four guys piling into a little scuffed-up hatchback next to his truck while Jesse sat in the driver's seat. All of them were conspicuously not talking or looking at him.

When Finn pulled out of the parking space, he risked a

sideways glance and nodded again at Jesse, who was waiting in the driver's seat to drive off.

It made him stupidly happy that Jesse nodded back, giving him a hint of that gorgeous smile he'd seen last night. He'd fled, but he obviously didn't hate Finn or anything. Maybe he just didn't want to admit that they'd been together. Only fair, really.

As Finn drove the couple of minutes to his house, he watched in his rearview mirror as the guys' heads bobbed and hands waved. It was a good old gossip session, it looked like.

God, he hoped Jesse hadn't told them everything. But at the store, judging by their body language, they'd been encouraging him to go talk to Finn. It hadn't sounded like giggling over what a good—or bad—lay he'd been.

Jesse was living here, then. A handful of people had been at the bar last night, and they'd known he took Jesse home—or to the cliffs; nobody had to know that part. As soon as Jesse met the neighbors, their one-night stand wasn't exactly going to be a secret.

He turned the corner, and so did they. He drove along the road that gently looped around behind the square, and so did they. He turned onto the street where he lived, and so did they.

The hatchback kept going—but before he could breathe even a sigh of relief, the guys' car pulled into the driveway next to his.

After his exhausting day at work yesterday, he hadn't really noticed anyone in the long-empty rental house next door. He'd just headed straight to the bar.

Aw, hell. That house was no longer empty.

Jesse slowly climbed out of the car and avoided Finn's sideways glances. Instead, he strode to the back hatch of the car and yanked it open like it had offended him.

Then, he peeked sideways and made eye contact with Finn—and turned bright red. Finn quickly scooped up his bags and kept his face straight, doing his best not to laugh at the mortification on Jesse's face.

This town was too small in a whole new way.

3

JESSE

It was incredible how quickly a day could pass. Cleaning and unpacking, dividing up housework, and debating meal logistics made time fly. Then they'd realized that despite planning meals, they hadn't yet had time to actually pick up ingredients.

A trip to the grocery store had sounded like a good idea, but most ideas did until they were executed.

Jesse had half expected to bump into Finn again sometime —but not right away over cans of peas and asparagus. It had been the hardest thing in the world to ignore his friends urging him to go talk to the hot guy who was staring at him. Not when every fiber in his being wanted to see Finn again—but not under prying eyes.

And then he'd pulled up in the driveway next to Finn's.

Now he just wanted a trip to the bar and several pints of beer to drown his mortification. Of *course* his wild fling lived right next door to him, and of *course* all his friends had seen the looks they'd exchanged.

Thank God he'd been driving today. He shared his beat-up

old car with the other guys to make two cars work between the five of them.

"He's so into you." Ezra grabbed a bag from his hands. "Go talk to him."

Jesse shook his head and grabbed another one from the back of the car instead. "Nope."

"Come on." Aaron winked. "You should get over Dominic sometime or another. How better than fucking a hot neighbor? That's not dating."

"Don't push him," Beau chimed in. "It's been a stressful week."

"All the better to burn the stress off," Aaron disagreed. He snuck a glance over his shoulder and then leaned on the car, suddenly dialing up his casual sexiness several notches. "Oh my God, he's cute. If you don't take him, I will."

Jealousy flared in Jesse's chest, and he glared at Aaron. "No. Didn't we agree when we moved here—no boys to break our hearts?"

Aaron sighed and wilted, taking a bag instead and shoving another into Ross's hands. "Fiiiinne," Aaron groaned. "You're no fun."

"I'm plenty of fun," Jesse muttered. He had to hold back a grin. Finn, of all people, knew that.

God, that beach sex had been fucking incredible. Totally worth swinging by Cher's End Table, the dim little dive bar opposite the grocery store. The cashier at the grocery store had warned him that it was only open when Cheryl, the owner, felt like it.

Living in a small town was going to be an adjustment and a half.

Jesse wasn't complaining that he'd bumped into this gorgeous stranger after just half an hour of sitting at the bar, people-watching. The locals all seemed to know each other. Jesse couldn't figure out if it was because it was such a small town, or if they were all the local drunks.

Maybe there really was nothing here to do except—well, each other. Visiting to find a house to rent was one thing. It was very different actually *moving* here.

Especially now that he knew he was living next door to his one-night stand from last night.

Jesse blushed and headed straight inside to unpack groceries into the fridge.

It wasn't like the sex had sucked. God, no. The complete opposite. He was so glad Finn had come straight over to talk to him, and that his friends had decided not to come out for a drink last night. Jesse had started off a little anxious about going out by himself, gay as fuck and unapologetic.

But this was their future, his new life. He was determined to seize the day, especially without romance to distract him.

Sex, though? He could do that.

"Oh my God, Jesse's so into him." Thankfully, Aaron waited until the door was closed to announce that at the top of his lungs.

"Fuck off." Jesse flipped him off. "I told you: no boys."

"I'm not saying take him home." Aaron dropped his bag on the counter next to Jesse's and then melted against the cabinet, spreading his legs and rolling his head back as he moaned, "Not for more than one night."

"Boo. Get up, you slut." Jesse tossed a bag of frozen peas at Aaron's crotch.

Aaron caught it and pouted, straightening up again. "Fine. Don't blame me for trying to get you laid."

"But it *would* be good for you to get past that asshole." Ezra announced his presence.

"The first inch is the tightest." Aaron coughed behind his fist, but it was unmistakably his voice.

Looked like Ezra and Beau had joined the kitchen debate now. Thank goodness Beau was on his side, at least.

"I'm over him. Honestly." Sure, Jesse had to grit his teeth as he said it, but he was determined to mean it. If not yet, soon.

Ross, Aaron, Ezra, and Beau all stared back at him with expressions that meant they didn't believe him.

"What?" Jesse resisted the urge to snap. That would only confirm their suspicions, and he didn't want to be wrapped up in their sympathetic hugs. He wanted to key his bastard ex-boyfriend's car and pour glitter into an open window. "Just because he's a cheating McCheaterFace... doesn't mean I have to pine over him."

"Dick," Ezra scoffed. The redhead's eyes glinted fiercely. He slammed the butter into the fridge. "And dumping you in public! I'll never not be mad about that. You deserve better, baby."

Jesse sighed and took the bottles of juice the guys passed him. "I know." It had sucked to realize that not only was Dominic unfaithful, but his sex drive was a lot higher than he'd pretended. He'd just been satisfying it elsewhere.

That had been a hell of a public breakup. Afterward, the poor steakhouse waiter had hardly known where to look as he handed the bill over. Which Jesse had left with Dominic.

"It's okay." Jesse closed the fridge and stepped out of the way as Beau barreled over with the ice cream. "This just leaves me open for more opportunities."

"Open for opportunities," snickered Aaron. "Like my ass is open for Mr. Sexy Neighbor's cock."

The guys cracked up and groaned, which at least filled the moment.

"Well, maybe you should have come out to the bar last night with me, then," Jesse told them with a grin. "You might meet a cute one-night thing here."

"Here?" Beau sounded doubtful.

Ross clicked his tongue as he adjusted the buckle on one black glove. His kinda emo style didn't fit into the laidback crowd here. True to his cynical nature, his first comment was, "Like there's more than one hottie in this town. I think we've already found him."

"And someone doesn't want to share him," Aaron cut in with a sly smile at Jesse.

Jesse stuck out his tongue. "He *was* checking me out." God, why was he so possessive? He latched onto the first explanation: it was just weird for one of his friends to sleep with Finn, too. That was all it was. He was saving them from an awkward moment. Plus, he didn't want them all thinking that Finn was just a rebound. Lots of good reasons not to talk about their encounter.

"And you looked like you got caught with your hand in the cookie jar." Aaron pinched four fingers together and curled his thumb in. "Or in the..."

"Aaron!" Jesse elbowed his friend before he could finish the joke. "Dude."

Aaron gave him an unapologetic grin and yanked a chair from the dining room table, turning it around to sit backward on it. "I'm just saying. Burn off a little stress."

"Or at least don't be totally weird to our new neighbors." That was Beau, bringing some sense to this conversation at last.

Jesse nodded. There was nothing they could do now about them being neighbors except get along and pretend none of that had happened. "Right. I'll talk to him when I see him next. Just... be normal. But first, we should talk while we're all together."

"Oh, this sounds serious." Ezra closed the fridge and stuffed their bags all into one bag, then hung it on the back doorknob. "What's up? Is it wine-serious?"

"Probably."

He poured a glass for each of them, and they settled around the table.

Jesse took a long sip and sighed with contentment at the sweetness rolling over his tongue. "Right," he said, glad for the change in subject. "So it was my first day trying to work back there." He nodded at the big, mostly empty room off the kitchen.

They'd envisioned it as a workspace for all of them to share while they started producing art for their co-op, before they could get a storefront up and running. But pottery took up a lot of room. With just his supplies and drying pots, he told them, the room already felt too small.

"It's just not gonna work," Jesse finished explaining. "When you guys get unpacked and set up, too?"

"Ah, shit." Beau rested his chin on his fist. "So how about we rent a place? Property's cheap as dirt here."

Jesse nodded. "That's what I was thinking. A place with an actual storefront built in, downtown?"

"Probably as cheap as anywhere else," Beau agreed. "Ezra needs space for his canvases to dry. At least my jewelry doesn't take much room; I just need good lighting."

"I win the contest if we're talking minimal workspace," Ross pointed out. His photography brought in quick income. Since he didn't develop photos like an old-school photographer, it took up almost no room. But he could bring in better money with headshots and family portraits from an actual studio space.

"No, I do," Aaron interjected. He was right now working in a coffee shop farther down the coast, a surfing hotspot. He was a damn good barista, and they'd agreed that it was smart to have at least one of them working a more traditional job until their sales took off.

"Okay, we'll look for a place in the morning," Jesse decided. "Now, let's go to the bar. There might be hot men." *Again.* He wouldn't admit it, but he kind of hoped to run into Finn. They had a lot to clear up, and if he just went next door to talk to his neighbor, all his housemates would know something was up.

"Hot men for all!" Aaron leapt to his feet. "I'm ready literally anytime."

Luckily for them, Cher's End Table was open.

Unluckily, there were no hot men.

On the bright side, the locals had noticed that it was Jesse's second night here. The bartender greeted him with a bigger smile this time. "Back so soon?"

"It's too much fun to stay away," Jesse responded without missing a beat, winking.

The pool tables in the corner and the rusty jukebox were about the most exciting part of the bar, but it worked. She laughed and moved for the fridge. "Cocktail again?"

"Hit me with your best one. Same for my friends here, please."

A mojito seemed like the most creative she could do here,

but Jesse wasn't complaining. He leaned on the edge of the bar and glanced around.

"Look who knows his way around town already," Ross leaned in to murmur. Ezra nodded in agreement.

"He'll be on a first-name basis with the postman before we know it." Beau grinned. "Get his number for me."

"I keep telling you: steady employment is boring. No spontaneous holidays," Aaron said, shaking his head. "Find some cute thing in media or digital design or something."

"You're the only one of us who does spontaneous holidays," Jesse said with a laugh. Aaron seemed to have a knack for attracting random guys on Grindr who wanted hot arm candy.

"Here you go. Five mojitos."

"Thanks...?"

"Cher," the woman behind the bar answered and grinned. "Like the icon."

"Great to meet you, Cher. I think we'll all be good friends," Beau said. "Especially if you save the hot guys for us."

Cher glanced at Jesse, and Jesse shot her a pleading look. No doubt everyone had noticed him leaving with Finn last night after ten minutes of conversation at the bar. He didn't want to explain to his friends that he'd already been there and done that.

She winked at Jesse and said, "Oh, I think the best-looking men are already taken."

"Or straight!" Aaron leaned in to complain.

Cher shook her head. "Or gay, I was going to say."

Ross cracked his idea of a joke. "If the grass is always greener on the other side, why do we bother fencing it off?" They all blinked at him, and he sighed. "The moment's gone."

"Anyway, thanks," Jesse said, and he meant for more than the drinks. Thanks for her silence on his new man.

Wait. No. *Not* that Finn was his new man, however strong their connection had been. *Jesus, Jesse. Put a lid on it,* he thought. *Next thing you know you'll be walking down the aisle with him in your daydreams.*

"Here's to Hart's Bay, and our new future!" Beau clinked glasses with them all, and they drank.

The breeze of the door opening caught Jesse's attention, as did the man walking through it.

Crap.

"Two nights in a row?" Cher greeted Finn, who looked even hunkier in this tight T-shirt. It hugged his biceps. The goddamn fabric even emphasized each little groove between his abs, and best of all, the cum-gutters framing his hips.

This was just goddamn unfair.

"You know how it is." Finn's eyes landed on Jesse, and for a long second, he didn't break the gaze. The heat crackling between them made Jesse's cheeks burn. "I just can't seem to stay away."

The corner of his lip curved up in a sinfully delicious half-smile, and his eyes were half-lidded like that had been an invitation. Straight into his bed.

"Well, no complaints from me. Beer?" Cher offered.

An elbow landing square between ribs made Jesse gasp, tears springing to his eyes. He whirled around and glared at Aaron. "What?"

"That's that guy from earlier," Aaron hissed as the others put their heads together. It looked like they were trying to pull him in for a huddle.

Annoyance flared in Jesse's chest. Of course they were into him, too. And Finn had been clear that it was only an offer valid for one night. With someone as hot as any of his friends, no way would he turn them down. Only a matter of time before it happened.

"Yeah. You fight it out over him," Jesse said coolly instead, hoping his blush had faded into the ice of his tone. "Since 'no chasing guys' is too hard to keep up for two days, apparently."

He grabbed his glass and headed for the door. He'd spotted a couple of plastic lawn chairs and a patio table out front of the bar. It wasn't like the liquor laws of Portland applied here.

Sure enough, nobody stopped him—the others were too busy whispering to each other, probably planning their attack.

Jesse breathed in deeply once he stepped outside, closing his eyes to enjoy the breeze. This close to the water, he could still smell the sea.

And he could reflect on how damn good that hookup had felt, even if he hadn't really meant to get involved with the town *that* way quite so soon.

But no way was he able to commit to anything more permanent than the next ten minutes. Not until he had a stable studio running and sales to cover the bills, at least. He didn't want to be famous—just make a living.

"Cooler out here."

The voice made him jump. He turned and spotted Finn standing by the door, a pint glass in his hand.

"You like following me around," Jesse told Finn, but despite his disapproving tone, he couldn't resist a smile. Who could, faced with those eyes?

"I think you followed *me* last night," Finn countered, pointing his glass at Jesse. "But I'll admit: I was curious what brought you back here. Usually tourists are gone the next day. And then I saw where you're living."

"Bad news. Or is it?" Jesse bit his lip and looked up at

Finn, trying his damnedest not to flirt. It wasn't working. "I've had worse neighbors."

"Another argument for you following me." Finn winked and sauntered closer. And even though Jesse knew he should keep his distance, he couldn't account for the way the stress melted from his body.

His body had made quite a different decision on Finn than his brain. So when Finn nodded toward the rickety bench in the middle of the dead square, he nodded.

"Is it safe to walk through?" He lingered on the corner, eyeing the tufts of unruly grass.

Finn looked offended. "It's safe around here. Just... down on its luck."

"So I heard. That's why I moved here."

"Not a sentiment I usually hear," Finn said, his lip quirking up in that damned attractive half-smile again. "What's up with that?"

"Property's cheap, workshop and studio space is cheap."

"Studio? You an artist or a painter? Oooh." Finn leaned in, his eyes gleaming with intention. There was no way he could mistake that as anything but flirtation. "Can I ask you to paint me like one of your French boys?"

"No, you want Ezra for that. The redhead who was with me. He's the painter. I just do pottery." Jesse resisted the knife-twist of jealousy in his belly.

"But I *don't* want him." The emphasis on *don't* was slight but definitely there. Finn wanted him to hear it.

Jesse licked his lips and downed a few more gulps of mojito. "What's your deal, then? Why are you here if you think the town is falling down?"

"I'm kinda stuck here. Oldest kid. Feel like I owe it to the town to stay around."

"Why's that?"

Finn hesitated and then stared around the square like the shabby buildings held the answer. "I'll get back to you on that."

They sat in companionable silence for a few minutes. Jesse might have expected it to be awkward, but it wasn't. It actually felt kind of good not to feel the pressure of making conversation and connections, like it was a speed date in the big city.

A lifetime of getting to know everyone here, if all went well. Or at least a few decades. It was hard to think even that far ahead. A few years?

Finn's voice interrupted Jesse's thoughts at last. "So, when are you gonna tell your friends we fucked?"

That was a good question. A really good question. And Jesse had no fucking idea what the answer was. Before long, people would see them together and make assumptions anyway.

What the hell were they going to do now?

4

FINN

"Pfffthhh."

The exhalation came with a raspberry and an elaborate shrug as Jesse flourished his hands to finish it. *Who knows,* he might as well have said.

He really shouldn't have looked so cute blowing his tongue at Finn, but those sinful lips were a focal point for everything Jesse did. Every little expression made Finn stare at them like he was a dying man and Jesse was a shimmering mirage on the sand.

With great difficulty, Finn dragged his attention back to the question. Right. He'd asked when Jesse was going to tell friends, and it sounded like Jesse had no idea. Fair enough. Finn hadn't expected it to last more than a night, so Jesse probably hadn't thought it through, either.

"Are we going to give them something to gossip over?" Finn winked, dropping his voice just a shade.

He'd be a damn fool *not* to flirt with the gorgeous guy sitting next to him, brightening the whole square with his smile. That smile only brightened at his words.

"I don't want to date." The words that spilled out of Jesse's lips stood in direct opposition to the way his foot slid steadily closer to Finn's.

"Well, that's good." Finn's lips twitched into a smile. "Glad we cleared that up." How much clearer could he make his intentions? He leaned in. "But I didn't say anything about dating."

The air crackled to life between them. In truth, it had never really stopped. Finn found himself constantly aware of how much space there was between them—or how little.

Leaning in and down, shadowing the slender man in his perfectly fitted crisp shirt and jeans only underscored the difference in their sizes. And like a jolt to the senses, it made him acutely remember pressing Jesse against the rock face while he fucked him.

Jesus, was this what addiction felt like? The irresistible pull toward what he logically knew was a terrible idea?

"Hey, it's a Hart in Hart Square. Is that the square root of a Hart? Ha ha!"

Annoyance flared in Finn's stomach. He stiffened and pulled back, whipping his head around until he spotted Gregory.

The guy was harmless enough, spending most of his evenings at Cher's. His thick Irish brogue was a familiar cadence in the background hum of the bar.

Come to think of it, when it wasn't open, he wasn't sure Gregory existed anywhere else. He'd never seen him at the store or wandering the waterfront. Maybe he was a collective figment of everyone's imagination.

"Very funny." Finn flipped Gregory off, his stomach dropping. Well, the cat was out of the bag now. Jesse was about to find out who he was.

"Yeah, yeah, whatever." Gregory gave him an unrepentant grin and strode toward his Guinness, and Finn turned back to Jesse.

This was it—the moment he'd been dreading. The reason he drove to Portland to hook up with guys and felt like he was living two separate lives. Because both times he'd tried dating someone living close by who knew who he was... well, it hadn't ended prettily.

Last time, a couple of years ago, he'd ended up with a clinger who'd stuck around like a bad penny. Blake had kept dropping Finn's name long past the end of the relationship. For everything from opening a tab at Cher's to getting a job at Millie's, Blake had leaned on Finn's name. And Finn had only ever heard about it later—when someone gently nudged him that "his boyfriend" hadn't paid his tab or hadn't followed through on a promise.

Ugh, it had taken months to clear that mess up. Hopefully specifically not-dating would go better for him.

"A Hart?" Jesse questioned him.

Finn's cheeks burned as he settled back against the bench, the moment between them well and truly gone. "Yep. That's why I feel like I can't skip town."

"Hart, like... Hart's Bay?"

Finn couldn't keep the sigh inside. He nodded, watching Jesse's reaction. He expected the usual awe, or comments meant to put distance between them, or worse, the opportunity that his name meant to some people with outsized ambition. Like his name meant anything these days or came with deep pockets.

Not on this side of the family, it didn't.

Worse yet, he feared that Jesse might think badly of his

family for letting the town—hell, the very square they were sitting in—fall into disrepair.

Jesse couldn't possibly understand how humiliating it was to watch distant relatives you only remembered from childhood Christmas suppers buy up the town and let it fall to shit.

But as much as Finn braced himself, Jesse's reaction was... underwhelming. "Oh. Cool."

It took a moment for Finn to realize that was it. "Cool?" He'd found himself staring intently at the boarded-up building across the square.

Jesse was staring at it, too. "I wonder who owns that."

A harsh laugh escaped Finn. He tried his best not to talk shit about the other relatives, and he could only assume they did the same. Those had been the terms of the truce a decade ago, when they last clashed. "I'll give you one guess."

Jesse's puzzled look turned knowing. "Oh. So is everything named after you because—"

"Not *me*. I'm named after it, at best."

Finn's throat felt strangely raw, his heart bare. Emotions were escaping that he'd kept locked away for years, maybe fucking decades. Only because a sweet man with kind eyes asked innocent questions. What the hell was going on?

But Jesse's hand, warm and firm, pressed against his knee, and Finn couldn't help but believe that he was sincere. And it felt good to talk, to explain all this before Jesse could get the wrong idea.

"I mean, some of my so-called relatives. They own most of everything 'round here. But they don't do shit with it." Just so they could have their name on a building, they'd bought it. They'd gotten greedy, and now they either couldn't afford the upkeep or they didn't give a shit about it.

They should have. Money was all they cared about, and

property depreciation was real. But what did Finn know? He was one of *those* Harts, and he was sure as hell never invited to the *other* Harts' casual jaunts around the world or set up with savings accounts for grad school at birth.

"I heard about the Hart fishery collapsing. I assumed it was named after the town..."

Finn sighed. The spiel came to his lips almost automatically. "My great-great-great-grandfather Floyd Hart came here not long after the Klondike gold rush ended. It was a tiny town then, back when Seattle was a hub of commerce."

Looking at the wooden building frames around them, he could almost see it: the general store, the hotel, the stagecoach station. Now, it felt like he was a museum curator staring at dingy, broken ruins and trying to pull meaning out of them.

"It developed into a fishing town and thrived for generations, until just before the fishery collapsed. With no idea what was coming, my family split the business into two. When the ground fish populations collapsed, so did the town."

There was a lot packed into that last sentence, and Finn pressed his lips together tightly to resist the urge to add more detail.

It had seemed like such a good plan to divide the fishery into the catching, processing, and shipping components, allowing the siblings to work together yet separately after the big argument. Dad and Roy had fallen on one side of the split, and processing and shipping were about half the business, so they were happy to take that over.

On the other side of whatever the hell that fight had been were Uncle Monty and his grandfather, named Floyd after the town's founder. Monty—Rain's dad—had been supposed to take control of the other half. But he'd been young and uncertain in how to run a business, so Floyd had held on to his part of the company to look after it for him.

And then shut down his half as soon as he could to save as much money as he could for himself, Finn thought, biting back the low simmer of anger about that selfish choice.

Finn's dad and uncle, though, had kept the processing plant running as long as possible rather than letting good men and women hit hard times. Eventually, despite their best efforts, it had all folded.

Leaving Finn working as a construction foreman these days in Uncle Roy's new business—the only line of work they could get into with a credit history like that.

It was good, honest work. Finn couldn't complain. He liked being outdoors, working with his hands, and making miracles happen on a budget and strict timeline.

But the wounds chafed when he had to poke at them. Growing up with whispers and mutters about your own parents and uncles was harsh, and while guys his age might not care so much, their parents usually did. They'd been the ones laid off and scrambling for work when Grandpa got greedy.

Better just to stick to cheap sex—hookups where his past didn't matter and nobody expected anything from him that he couldn't deliver.

"Sounds like you're used to telling the story." Jesse's words cut through Finn's thoughts, bringing him back to the moment. His hand was still a solid, warm comfort on Finn's knee.

Finn rested his hand over Jesse's and gently ran his thumb across the smooth skin up to his wrist. "Yeah. Anyone who's not from around here asks as soon as they find out I'm a Hart."

"Sorry to be predictable, then." Jesse's eyes sparkled. "I'll ignore you in the street if that helps counterbalance the effects of all this fame."

Finn grinned back at Jesse. This one was a little trouble-maker, wasn't he? Damn, he liked it. "You were doing me a favor with your friends, then. Keeping my ego in check. Thanks."

"Don't mention it and I won't." Jesse winked. "Which is probably the best approach for us, huh?"

Us?

The word did strange things to Finn's blood. It heated his cheeks and made his toes tingle. It made Finn want to press closer and ask exactly what he meant by it.

Made him want to explore every inch of Jesse's body across every inch of the town he knew so well. Take him to every secret nook and cranny. Sneak him in the back door—or in his back door. Pun totally intended.

Finn licked his lips, his mouth suddenly dry. "Oh?"

"Not tell everyone about what we did on the beach." Jesse's voice was surprisingly firm and polite, like he was trying to keep him at arm's length. He even pulled his hand back from Finn's knee.

The sudden absence of touch made Finn want to test the limit. He needed to see what Jesse *really* wanted, not just what he said he wanted.

Finn silently leaned closer, sliding his arm along the back of the ragged wooden bench behind Jesse. As he turned toward Jesse, their knees knocked, and then suddenly their thighs were pressed together.

His mouth was inches from Jesse's, their breath warm and quick as Jesse's gaze flickered between his eyes. He wasn't leaning backward or standing up to escape. No, he was standing his ground. Even defiantly staring back into Finn's eyes.

But even when Finn licked his lips, Jesse didn't move in for the kiss.

Finn could feel that he wanted to. He could feel the subtle vibrations of Jesse's body and the air between them. The way Jesse's eyes flickered across his face, studying every detail.

What was stopping him?

"You said earlier you weren't talking about dating." Jesse's words were low, almost a whisper that reached Finn's ears only. "So I can only assume you're after one thing." Even here, in the middle of town, it felt like they were totally alone.

And for the first time, Finn was glad to see the town center deserted. It was just the two of them, and the low mumble of noise that spilled from the bar close by, and the whisper of the ocean beyond the buildings.

What did Jesse want, if not to kiss Finn? To fall into his arms again and lose himself in ecstasy for a few minutes that felt like a lifetime?

"Tempted?" Finn breathed the word against Jesse's lips, closing the distance until their noses almost brushed. He waited there for some sign—a yes or no, spoken or not.

"Beyond. But I've made promises I have to keep." Jesse's voice wavered at last.

Finn knew that feeling all too well. "To others, or yourself?"

"Both."

"Why do they have to be incompatible?" Finn asked, his hand sliding across his thigh to Jesse's. He let it wander up just a little, listening to the catch of Jesse's breathing. If he made a sound now, it would be a low whine of pleasure cutting through the cool night air.

And Finn's self-control would be swept away like surf on the jagged rocks not even ten minutes away.

Jesse gulped once, then again. His hand rested on Finn's,

stopping its movement, and then his fingers wiggled under his, peeling them away from his leg. He held hands loosely, not quite a handshake but not a romantic gesture, either.

"I have to go," Jesse finally said, and he pulled away, rising to his feet. "My friends are in there."

That makes one of us.

Finn tried to brush away the prick of jealousy, but like any burst of clarity, it was hard to let go of now that it had struck.

It was ridiculous. He knew everyone in that bar. Most of them had watched him grow up—helped him along the way, even. They all greeted him on sight, and he knew some of their kids. In the last few years, he had even worked on their houses when their families grew and they needed more space. That was more than anyone could say for the *other* Harts.

It was stupid to be upset that he got so much attention from friendly neighbors. Made him sound like a self-absorbed asshole.

"Yeah," Finn murmured. He gazed up at Jesse, taking in every inch of his lithe body. Especially the bump in the front of his pants, telling Finn that he wasn't the only one barely clinging to self-control.

Finn stayed seated on the bench. If he stood, he didn't trust himself not to sweep Jesse off his feet again and cradle him into his chest, kiss him until they couldn't think straight.

Take him home this time, not to the beach. Give him some sugar like the very best kind of neighbor.

"I think I'll stay out here for a while." Finn hoped his voice sounded less choked to Jesse than it felt. His hard-on was painful, and so was prying himself away from the gorgeous man with the sad eyes and bright smile and insatiable moans.

"See you," Jesse breathed out, and then he was gone.

Fuck finishing that beer. Finn left the bottle on the bench and strode for home, his gait awkward but destination fixed.

Not even twenty minutes later, his load splattered across the shower wall and his body sagging against the tiles, Finn closed his eyes and rested his forehead on the cool surface.

The tension drained from him, but that ache in his chest didn't leave. If anything, it grew worse. What the hell was that about? Just unfair. Busting a good nut was supposed to fix things, not make him even more desperate.

Even the thought of driving to Portland next weekend to find some other cute twink to screw into the mattress didn't do a thing for him.

It was like he'd found someone who fit perfectly against him, and shoving anyone else into that space just felt wrong. He was keyed to Jesse now. It had to be a crush, which was even more unfair since they'd hardly even talked. All he could do was hope that Jesse had some huge, glaring personality flaw that would loosen the grip his imagination had on the man.

The kind of desperation that had gripped Finn tonight... it had been years since he'd felt that. What the hell had Jesse done to him?

And, perhaps more importantly, was there any way of getting him to do it again?

5

JESSE

"So, it doesn't say who's the owner. But can you help hook me up with a viewing or something?" Jesse shaded his eyes and stretched on tiptoe, trying to see through a rip in the bleached newspapers covering the windows of the place.

Jesse had walked all around town and only seen one phone number on all the commercial storefronts that even bothered to have signs. But the real estate agent on the other end of the phone line wasn't budging. "You said around Hart Square?"

"Or the waterfront." Jesse had already spotted the warehouses by the harbor. There were gorgeous old buildings—too much building, maybe, but he could fix them up.

"Oh, no, no. Nothing in the downtown core."

Calling this street a *downtown core* was a stretch even for a real estate agent, but Jesse let it go. "Oh yeah? Who does?"

"I'm not completely sure. Sorry I couldn't help you."

The sound of his voice was like a door slam in his face. "Okay... thanks?"

The least helpful agent ever hung up and Jesse stared at

his phone, then back at the storefront. It looked like it had been unused for months, at least. Maybe years.

There wasn't even a local library he could walk in for research help: who had owned the buildings, the property history. He'd probably have to go back to Portland for those kinds of records. Or town hall, which appeared to be run out of the same building that housed the police station.

Jesse sighed. That had definitely been an excuse on the agent's part. What he really needed was someone who knew everyone in the area. Maybe Cher? But who knew whether she'd open today, and if so, when. The bar was firmly shut right now.

He'd talked to everyone he could think of: the agent back in Portland who'd handled their house rental, the local bank manager, and even the owner of the surf shop by the water.

Everyone had been warm and welcoming, but had made it clear through their words that they didn't know who to talk to about the buildings—even if their faces said something else.

Jesse set off on another wander around the town. If he couldn't get a studio and workshop in the square or the waterfront, he wasn't sure what he'd do. With all the vacant storefronts, it had seemed like an easy proposition before they'd moved here. And with the town on the coastal highway, plenty of tourists passed through every year—it was just a case of throwing up a few signs promising nice art to get them to stop.

There was always something he could do, though. He could line up sales at shops in more touristy towns, but he and his friends would have to work separately, each of them hustling harder to sell their own work. Combining forces so they all had room to work and attracted sales of each other's finished crafts just made sense.

As he looked around the square, Jesse's gaze settled on the

bench. Just a few nights ago, he'd found himself creeping closer to the fire, heedless of whether it might burn. He'd gone within a hair's width of it, only to remember his promise to his friends.

No men. A better life built together. Cooperation, not competition.

While they were making the large room at the back of the house work for them all for now, it wasn't sustainable. Only one or two of them could work at a time, and Jesse's pottery wheel and clay were heavy to move around when Ezra needed room to dry canvases. They couldn't afford to keep that up much longer.

The harbor was gorgeous, too, but clearly past its prime. The warehouses on the edge still read *Hart Fisheries* and *Hart Packing*. With the distinction pointed out to him now, he could see the division in buildings, but all of them looked as shabby as each other.

The building exteriors in Hart Square were gorgeous. They looked like pieces of Americana in their own right. But the peeling paint on the wood shutters, the dark windows covered in newspaper... it made them almost an eyesore. And looking past them to the coast, the short road that led down to the harbor was tragically underdeveloped. A seafront view like that could go for millions in other cities.

So many tourists passed by on the coastal highway. It wouldn't take much to lure them in here—a decent restaurant or two, some scenic views, a few art galleries or kitsch shops. And less tufts of dead grass, more bright paint.

Even if they didn't get along with Finn's part of the family, surely the Harts who owned the buildings here were business-minded. Who would turn down an offer that would increase their property value and bring people to town?

Whether they wanted to rent out property or sell it, Jesse was flexible.

Anything to make this work and avoid the awful happy hour mixers, rubbing shoulders with the right people under the guise of networking, updating his LinkedIn profile every time someone gave him a gold star at work...

Ugh, his blood pressure rose just thinking about it.

It would take a different kind of networking to make his plan come to fruition. Patience, hard work, and a friendly smile—those opened doors sooner or later.

Maybe he needed to stop looking past the obvious. There was one person who clearly knew who to talk to in the area. Finn might not talk to them himself, but he could at least point Jesse in the right direction.

Finally, Jesse had an excuse to rub elbows—and shoulders, and anything else that might be required—with Finn.

Not an excuse, he tried to tell himself as he walked back up from the harbor to the grocery store. *A reason.*

Because that word choice *totally* made a difference. Right?

It turned out the grocery store here only had one kind of veggie burger and no vegetarian sausages at all. Ross was going to be even gloomier than usual when he found that out.

Jesse hoped the halloumi and tofu he'd found would make up for it. And, of course, he'd loaded up with real meats, charcoal, and a lighter before heading for the beer and wine. They'd found the barbecue in the back yard on the night they'd moved in, but they hadn't yet used it.

Time to fix that.

By the time Jesse drove back home, his spirits were lifting.

Sure, the end of the day had been another fruitless search, but he was about to make leeway—he was sure of it.

And he was about to see Finn again.

He couldn't stop thinking about him. The taste of his lips, the heat of his body, the way his ass flexed under Jesse's palms when he drove forward into him, picking him up off the ground, crushing him into the rocks, nails biting into skin...

Fuck. He shifted under the steering wheel and pressed against the hard line of his cock with his palm to get it to lie flat as he shut off the car. Just the thought of Finn's hot breath on his lips, daring him to lean in and kiss him...

Everything in him wanted to say yes. Their first hookup had been amazing—the kind of sex Jesse hadn't even remembered existed. Surely the second one would be even better. How much more could Finn blow his mind, if he let him?

How much distraction would he be? Jesse reminded himself in a futile effort to rein in the horniness. He clambered out of the car and grabbed the bags, trying his best to keep his mood up.

If Finn helped him out with this, he'd owe him one. And oh boy was that thought exciting. It made little prickles of pleasure dance down his spine, which only reminded him of the sensation of Finn's rough fingertips running down his spine and across his ass.

Finn's fingers in his ass, his lips hot on his neck. His cock buried deep inside him while Jesse clung to the rock face and whimpered. The way the breeze swept away each moan and gasp. The burning heat that slammed through Jesse's body with every rolling thrust of Finn's hips.

Fuck, Jesse. Keep it together.

Jesse shouldered his way through the door and left the bags on the floor, heading back out to the car to grab the beer and wine. He needed another thirty seconds to drag his brain to something that wouldn't give him a tent the size of a yurt in his pants.

"Oh, hey! Look who's here!" Aaron yanked the door the rest of the way open as Jesse shifted the box lower in his arms to cover that area, just in case.

"I come bearing alcohol."

Aaron grinned and picked up the bags from the floor. "You're my best friend. Fuck those other guys."

"Hey!" Ezra called indignantly from nearby. He joined them a moment later. "Whoa, are we doing a barbecue?"

"We are. Grab the charcoal from the car." The distraction of his friends helped Jesse get his mind off... well, getting off.

"Sweet!"

Even Ross seemed happy, though he rolled his eyes when they unpacked the bags and Jesse had to explain his food options tonight.

"Small towns," Ross sighed. "God forbid you don't feel like slaughtering an animal."

"I'll take your share. I feel like beating meat all the time," Aaron said cheerily.

Jesse laughed and elbowed Aaron as he unpacked the wine. "I got the cheap stuff. Red, white, rose. And beer."

Beau tilted his head. "Beer? Who here drinks beer?"

Jesse braced himself. *Here I go*, he thought. He'd never live to hear the end of this, but the end goal was most important. "I thought we'd invite Finn over."

"Oooooh." The other four guys chimed in almost simultaneously, stopping what they were doing to look at him.

"Look who's on a first-name basis now," Ross said.

Beau snorted. "And still won't tell us what went down outside Cher's..."

The blush that followed heated Jesse from head to toe, and he cursed his nerves. He'd always been an easy blusher and easy to read as a result. "Because nothing went down, dumbasses. He knows the town, and I *still* can't find anyone who'll tell me who we have to talk to about a studio downtown."

"Wait, seriously?" That distracted Beau, at least, although Aaron was still giving him an obnoxious grin.

Jesse bit his lip and leaned against the counter, hitching his thumbs in his pockets. "Yeah. I walked around, couldn't find any signs. Nobody knew, or they're not saying."

"Maybe it's a Mafia thing. Like a money-laundering conspiracy. Buy up unused real estate, and…" Aaron narrowed his eyes and scrunched up his face while they all looked at him.

"And?" Jesse asked, grinning. "How do you launder money that way?"

"I don't know!" Aaron exclaimed. "If I did, I'd have a profitable Mafia career instead of hanging out with you losers. Jeez."

Jesse snorted with laughter as they grabbed wineglasses and utensils. "Someone go light the barbecue. I'm gonna see if Finn's home from work."

Damn it, that sent another round of *oohs* and *go get him, girls* through their group. As he left, he heard Aaron wondering aloud, "Is anyone here masc enough to barbecue? If we put our heads together, maybe we can manage it…"

They were gonna make fun of him every time he so much as looked at Finn, but it was worth it.

Climbing the steps of the porch, Jesse took a moment to admire the house. It was well-kept—even better than the rental place they were sharing next door. The porch looked shiny and new, the rails painted bright purple and white. A pot spilling over with flowers sat on the steps, along with a metal sculpture and a piece of driftwood.

The window shutters were freshly painted and the curtains inside were bright and airy, too.

Jesse found himself all the more curious about Finn. What was he like when he wasn't cornering him, all sexual tension and broodiness? Did he like beer and a game, or wine and a show? Did he go fishing, or was that too close to home? What did a guy like him do for work? Did he work?

A hundred questions hit him at once, and it occurred to Jesse that he might even have the chance to ask some of them tonight. Over beer and a barbecue, like a normal neighbor.

Not one who desperately wanted into his pants.

Jesse licked his lips and rang the bell, listening for any sound of movement. Steps and a voice calling out something were quickly followed by the door opening.

Oh, holy fuck.

Jesse's brain short-circuited for several long seconds. All he could do was take in the glorious sight while his cheeks no doubt turned tomato red.

Finn stood there wrapped in a towel, water droplets trickling down every groove between perfectly formed muscles. His nipples stood as little hard points, his biceps distractingly close as his hand rested on the edge of the door by Jesse's face.

And down the flat plane of his stomach, a trail of dark blond hairs disappeared under the towel—but more of them were appearing. That didn't make sense. Were they growing in front of his eyes?

No, the towel was slipping.

The sound Jesse made was supposed to be "hi," but it came out as more of a whimper than anything else.

One broad hand interrupted the stunning view as Finn

caught the towel. His teeth flashed in a grin. "Hi, yourself." He didn't move to pull it back up, just let Jesse glimpse the dark fur of his pubes, and even—if Jesse squinted, which he definitely wasn't doing right now—the distinctive lines that were absolutely the base of his cock.

Oh, fuck, Jesse *was* staring. And the towel twitched. Which made Jesse's heart flip-flop and his toes curl.

Fuck. Get your eyes on his face!

But he could feel Finn's smile growing, and Jesse was already shuffling backward to try to escape as soon as possible. Before this blush actually killed him as he lost the blood from everywhere else in his body as it pooled in his face—and his dick.

All he had to do was say "come over to ours, barbecue tonight." A few little words. Maybe a few more to be polite.

Then the world tilted and his adrenaline peaked as he slipped on the edge of the porch, a foot flying backward. He grabbed for the rail but only found thin air.

Until a hand closed around his shirt, hauling him forward. The thin fabric wasn't made to hold his weight. It ripped, but enough of it held that he flew forward instead.

Into Finn's arms.

His body crashed into Finn's, and he knew without even looking down that the towel was well and truly gone now. Both of Finn's hands were on him now, one around his back as he let go of his shirt with the other and grabbed his hip, steadying them both.

Even having Jesse's whole weight slam into him didn't knock Finn off balance. He just plucked Jesse from thin air and set him on his feet like it was nothing.

And Jesse's knees were weak for so many reasons right now. The adrenaline running through him felt a lot like an incitement to something else. Something hotter, and more tempting, and only ever half a second out of his thoughts these days.

His cock hardened in about that time when bare skin on his stomach pressed against Finn's. The rip in his shirt left it hanging open, and the dampness only made his skin hotter against Jesse's.

Jesse became acutely aware that his face was pressed into Finn's shoulder, his hands scrabbling at his chest.

"Fuck," Jesse panted. "Sorry." He let go of Finn and stumbled upright again, clinging to the doorframe.

Logically, he tried to stop himself. *Don't look at him—he just sacrificed his dignity to save your ass.*

But he couldn't help it. Even as he thought it, his eyes flickered south.

To the semi that Finn was now sporting. And fuck, he was big even at half-mast. Jesse still remembered the weight of it in his hand—and buried deep inside him.

"No, my bad." Finn said, his voice a low, warm growl. "Maybe I need another rail."

Rail me. The words nearly burst from Jesse's mouth, but he took a deep breath in and tried to shake it off. The heat between them was no less intense even with a few inches of separation. *Fewer inches of separation at belt level,* Jesse's treacherous brain reminded him.

Finn stooped to grab his towel and then straightened up, tossing it over his shoulder. He turned to head inside but left the door ajar. "I should step inside before I get arrested, but come on in."

Inside? Jesse caught his breath. If he walked in there, he was certain he would just drop to his knees and swallow that beautiful erection whole. Jesse would suck Finn off until he was panting for breath, his hand tangled in Jesse's hair to hold his head in place and fuck his mouth.

"Oh, I..." Jesse didn't dare peek around the door. Words suddenly returned to his mind. Maybe not graceful words, but it was something. "I just wanted to say we're having a barbecue come on over we're lighting it right now and we have lots of meat and veggie options and beer and wine. Bye!"

He didn't stick around to see if Finn replied. In fact, Jesse didn't even draw breath until he was at the bottom of the porch steps, striding briskly across the strip of lawn that separated their driveways.

He spent so much time focusing on unsexy thoughts that it wasn't until he reached his own yard that reality hit again.

Ross was the first to speak. "What the...?"

His friends were clustered around the barbecue with lighters and fuel, but all of them stopped and stared at him. Even Aaron was speechless. For a moment, Jesse wondered if he was *still* blushing, if it was that obvious.

Then the breeze caught the ripped edges of his shirt, and Jesse gasped and clutched them shut. Oh, fuck. He would *definitely* never live this down.

Ever, ever, ever.

6

FINN

God only knew what Jesse said to his friends, but it seemed to have worked.

In fifteen minutes, Finn had somehow crammed in a fast and furious jerk-off session, grabbed clothes, and thrown together a salad to bring as his contribution. He hadn't wanted to leave Jesse to explain this all by himself, if need be.

Finn had expected a lot more giggling and sideways glances when he showed up on the front doorstep.

But Jesse's friends welcomed him inside and introduced themselves one by one like he hadn't just sent their friend back to them disheveled, bare-chested, and blushing like a deflowered virgin.

Even Jesse played it cool. He'd changed his shirt, leaving Finn to wonder if it had all been an elaborate shower fantasy. No, that had come *before* the knock on the door. And after. And, no doubt, tonight—like every night this week.

"Thanks for supper," Finn told Jesse with a grin when he finally caught him alone for the first time. They were both sitting on plastic lawn chairs on the concrete back patio over-looking a grassy yard.

The other four guys had piled inside to watch a YouTube video about grilling marshmallows for dessert. Their voices were loud enough to be heard out here, so Finn kept his own down.

"No sweat. Nice to be neighborly," Jesse said. "Besides, I wanted to exploit you." His cute, mischievous little grin did nothing to dissuade Finn's interest.

Quite the opposite. Finn would happily let Jesse exploit him six ways from Sunday. "How so?" He leaned in, as much as he could without tipping over the chair. Scooting it closer wouldn't be very dignified or sexy.

"Well... I was wondering if you knew exactly who to call about renting one of those storefronts."

Finn's stomach dropped. Of all the things Jesse could ask from him, it had to be that.

Meddling with the other Harts would start another years-long war of tampering with city planning approvals, voting each other's proposals down at school board meetings, or—as it had nearly escalated to last time—hiring a ghostwriter to produce a slanted "historical" account that made them out to be the good guys here.

The smile vanished from Jesse's face, and he leaned forward and put a hand on Finn's thigh. "Sorry. Are you okay? We don't have to talk about that. There's other people I can talk to..."

No, there weren't. As soon as Grandpa found out Finn was interested in Jesse, doors would close that Jesse didn't even know were open right now.

Including the rental of this very house. They'd bought it

not long after Finn had gotten his, right before the ceasefire was called between the families.

"Anyone can tell you how to contact him. Floyd Hart. Named after his grandfather, of course. Question is... do you really want to?"

Finn still remembered the ugly glare Floyd had shot him last time they caught sight of one another—at the hardware store on the edge of town. If he could treat his own grandson like that...

There's bad blood, though, he reminded himself. Jesse might get fair treatment.

"Thank you." Jesse squeezed Finn's knee. "I didn't mean to bring your mood down. I guess this is all pretty heavy stuff for you."

Finn managed a smile at him. "You can say that again."

"We don't have to discuss it." Jesse brightly smiled at him. "You're just Finn to me. A friend. I don't care about any of that family background."

Finn's spirits lifted. "A friend?" he echoed. That was more than Jesse had given him a few nights ago outside Cher's.

Jesse's eyes were dark suddenly, like someone had cranked up the heat between them. "Yeah."

"Does that friendship include benefits?" Finn tried to summon up the cool, casual courage he might show if this were just any city boy he didn't know. *Don't ask, don't get.*

But he was anxious about the answer. He wanted—needed —a yes from Jesse, and he didn't fully understand why.

Jesse's breathing was quick and harsh now. It was impossible not to notice the blush creeping along his cheeks, even up to the tips of his ears. He didn't say anything, but he licked his lips, his gaze wandering up and down Finn again. He didn't move his hand, which was resting on Finn's knee. A little too low for Finn's liking.

And Finn sure hadn't been imagining his reactions earlier, when he'd been unable to keep his eyes off Finn's naked body. Or the semi that he'd given Finn by crashing into him, his hot body pressed against him while groping at Finn's chest.

"Because it sure seems like we're into each other," Finn murmured, covering Jesse's hand and dragging it up his thigh, a fraction of an inch at a time. "And I know you said you're not up for dating right now. But it doesn't have to be dating."

"It can just be fun?" Jesse's answer was quick and eager, and so was his gaze. His tone was barely a whisper, forcing Finn to lean in to hear him. Jesse's breath was hot on his cheek.

Finn grinned. "Always," he promised, pulling back to look him in the eye. He might not have many talents in the world, but sex was one of them. He'd had more than enough experience there.

Relationships were a different matter—but they were off the table, so he was back in his area of expertise.

"So, since I dragged you down... can I make it up to you?" Jesse dropped his gaze, letting it wander down Finn's body, and then looked back up, licking his lips slightly.

"Down?" Finn gave in to temptation. Damn it, this guy was too hot to handle, and he was going to flirt like his life depended on it. "You only ever seem to get me up."

"Your towel disagreed earlier." Despite his earlier blushing, Jesse didn't look away.

Finn swallowed hard. Jesse wasn't going to be some boring-and-bored guy glued to his phone. He gave as good as he got, and he stood his ground.

It pulled Finn to him, irresistibly. It made him want to

break down whatever walls Jesse flung up. He wanted to test and tease and torment Jesse with ecstatic bliss.

He silently nodded toward the gate in the yard. It led to the alley between their houses, and they could slip from one yard to the other in just moments.

Jesse almost launched himself out of the chair to lead the way there. When Finn glanced over his shoulder, nobody had noticed. They were still clustered around the laptop in the living room, all gesturing wildly to each other.

Finn grinned and followed Jesse, hot on his heels. When they got out of one yard, he pressed himself up against Jesse's back as he opened the gate to his own yard and pushed him through it.

Before it was even closed, they were making out—hot and hard and silent this time. Just one thin wooden fence lay between them and Jesse's friends, and that wasn't going to do.

Not with the sounds of pleasure Finn planned to wring from Jesse's lips.

But his mouth was hot and insistent, and he barely yielded as Finn tried to push him toward the house.

Fine. He could lead a horse to water another way.

Finn slid his hand down Jesse's chest to his crotch and then, as soon as he felt the line of Jesse's cock against his palm, squeezed it.

Jesse jolted and gasped, his nails digging into Finn's skin as his eyes went wide. Then he grinned, looping his arms firmly around Finn's shoulders as he pushed forward into the touch.

"Inside," Finn hissed. He could see from the look in Jesse's eyes that he was still considering resisting, making Finn work for it. Finn sweetened the deal. "I'll let you suck me off first. I saw how much you wanted to earlier."

That did the trick—Jesse went all red and flustered as he

stumbled up the steps to the back porch. Finn let them in, and in moments they were in his dark living room, kicking off their shoes.

He knew the way by heart, so he wrapped his arms around Jesse, pressing himself up against Jesse's back again. Not only could he steer him through the living room to the kitchen counter, but he could feel his hard cock pressing against his ass.

The kitchen was a little lighter thanks to the window that looked out toward the guys' rental house. As they reached it, Finn pushed Jesse up against the counter and kissed his neck.

"Light?" Jesse murmured, looking around.

Finn chuckled. "I'm not sure you want your friends to get a view of this. Or maybe you do. You could be kinky like that. Are you into any of them?"

Jesse caught his breath and then shook his head. His whole body seemed to thrum in Finn's hold, melting against him. "Fuck, no. They're all just friends." Then his voice dropped. "Are you?"

Oh, that jealous note in his voice was hot as hell. Finn debated dragging it out and making him squirm, but it might just be too mean. "No. I'm not planning on sleeping with any of them, don't worry."

Not when he had this gorgeous guy pressed up against the counter, squirming to turn around in his hold. Finn loosened his grip enough to let him do it and then ran his hands down Jesse's sides when their fronts were pressed together.

"Hold up," Jesse whispered. He ran a finger down Finn's spine. "I got tested before I moved out here, so I know I'm negative. What about you?"

Finn grinned. It had been way too long since his last hookup before Jesse. Looked like there was a silver lining at last. "Oh yeah. Me too. I've got condoms, though." He didn't want Jesse to regret it later.

Jesse shook his head. "I wanna taste you."

Well, fuck. How could Finn resist those words? He braced himself on the counter as Jesse's hands wandered up his back, exploring every plane of muscle and igniting an unquenchable thirst in every fucking cell of his body.

By the time those hands made their way to his belt, Finn was nearly panting for breath. Even if he'd only come an hour ago, he was rock-hard and even needier now. For once, his own hand felt inadequate compared to another guy's touch.

When his pants were down to his ankles, he kicked them off as Jesse's fingers grazed his bulge through his underwear.

"You looked so hot earlier," Jesse whispered, and then he did something that made Finn want to blow his load on the spot. He slowly dropped, shimmying down between Finn's body and the counter until he was crouching on the kitchen floor, his head barely higher than the cabinet tops.

His mouth at crotch level.

"So did you. I want to rip your clothes off more often," Finn breathed out, pulling Jesse's shirt up. Jesse let him pull it off and toss it aside so he could run his hands along bare shoulders before bracing himself against the counter again.

Finn could see into the guys' yard. No sign of Jesse's friends yet, so either they'd noticed him going missing and were pretending not to, or they were engrossed in their marshmallow argument.

Jesse's mouth was hot and firm against his cock, even with a layer of underwear in the way, but it was a fucking tease.

"Now," Finn growled.

"So impatient." Jesse's giggle made Finn want to slam him on the ground and pin him down, suck his nipples, graze his hands over his thighs... just tease him for hours, until he was begging for mercy.

Finn ran his hand over Jesse's hair until he had enough of the short, straight locks between his fingers and then slightly tightened his grip. "For you, I am."

Jesse moaned sharply. "Yes," he whispered. Down came Finn's underwear, and then a hot, wet mouth closed around the tip of Finn's shaft.

Finn closed his eyes for a moment and steadied himself. It took all he had not to thrust forward into the tight, sucking heat that enveloped him from tip to base in one slow swallow.

"Fucking fuck, you're good!" Finn gasped, transfixed by the sight of those pretty lips stretched around his thick, hard shaft. The feeling of himself bumping the back of Jesse's throat was even better.

The answering strangled moan vibrated its way through the very core of his body.

Jesse started bobbing his head, his tongue swirling around the head every time he pulled up for a breath. Finn's thighs shook and his nails curled into the countertop.

Time slid by with barely a whisper, and soon Finn realized how close he was to the quivering, shaking edge of bliss. He was coming apart at Jesse's hands, and very soon, into his mouth.

Oh, fuck. Even his voice was strained as he warned Jesse, "I'm close."

But when he lost control and counted down the last few frantic seconds to relief, Jesse just took him into his mouth. He was going to swallow.

"Fuck! Yes! Jesse!" Finn caught himself with a forearm on the counter as he buckled, his hips slamming forward into Jesse's mouth as Jesse eagerly swallowed every drop.

He was never going to forget the sight of those wide, hungry eyes as Jesse's throat bobbed and tongue lapped at the head of his cock.

Finn almost whimpered as the thrusts slowed and stopped, and Jesse kept him in his mouth for another minute. Only when he was halfway to soft did Jesse let him slide out, the sudden burst of cool air on wet, hot skin making him shiver.

"That good?" Jesse murmured with a wicked grin up at him. Both of them knew that he knew exactly how good it was.

"Come here and let me show you how good," Finn breathed out.

He hauled Jesse to his feet and kissed him hard, not caring that he could taste the salty musk of himself. All he wanted was to consume Jesse's mouth and stoke the fire in him again. Tongues clashed as Jesse gasped and grabbed the counter behind himself, leaning back.

Perfect chance. Finn kissed the base of Jesse's throat and then his chest. He flicked his tongue around one nipple and then the other until Jesse was whimpering his name, and then worked his way down the center of his body.

It took him just seconds to get his jeans open. In one abrupt movement, he hauled down Jesse's jeans and under-wear to his ankles, letting his cock spring free. Swollen, pink, and beautifully hard.

Finn knelt in front of Jesse, running his hands slowly up his thighs to part them. The closer his hands got to Jesse's cock, the more Jesse trembled under the touch.

"Please," Jesse finally panted as Finn's thumbs grazed the base of the shaft and then kept traveling up over his stomach. "Fuck. Don't tease me like that."

"You that turned on already?" If he got that happy from sucking Finn's dick, they could have some great benefits together. Already, Finn was itching with warmth. If Jesse didn't come quickly, round two was on the table.

Jesse growled under his breath, which was the hottest noise Finn had gotten out of him yet. "Now."

As you wish. Finn grinned up at Jesse and then lapped from base to tip, enjoying the taste of him for the first time. The velvety weight felt perfect against his tongue, and the more it twitched, the more Finn wanted to tease.

But he was being nice tonight, he reminded himself. They had plenty of time later to explore the things that would make them lose their minds. No strings attached—just pleasure, as much of it as possible. How had Finn gotten this lucky?

"Please," Jesse whimpered again, his voice echoing in the kitchen. "I'm so close to coming already."

If he wasn't going to have long, Finn didn't want to waste a second. He instantly wrapped his lips around the swollen, mushroom-shaped head and let the weight of him slide over his tongue. With each bob of his head, he took a little more of Jesse in.

"Yes!" Jesse gasped.

The whimpers and moans that Jesse made when he was giving in to pleasure were utterly breathtaking. Just like on the beach, Finn found himself wanting to prolong this for hours just so he could hear every vocalization in Jesse's repertoire.

Finn took measured breaths around each bob of his head, swallowing Jesse over and over until Jesse clutched at his shoulders and begged him to keep going.

To never stop.

Jesse's sticky, hot load shot down his throat moments later, and Finn swallowed every drop like it was made of ambrosia.

When he finally rose to his feet, Jesse clung to him. It was easy to tell he was still weak at the knees, so Finn held him tightly. Jesse buried his nose in Finn's neck and pressed close as he caught his breath.

"Fuck," Jesse finally mumbled through the half-dark stillness of the kitchen.

Finn nodded, slowly pulling away when he was sure Jesse had his footing. "I know, huh? I like these benefits."

Jesse twisted and stretched onto tiptoe to look out the window, and Finn followed his gaze. The guys were outside again, and there seemed to be a lot of waving around flaming things.

"Oh, God," Jesse moaned as he scrambled for his clothes. "I can't let them burn down the house."

"No," Finn agreed with a laugh. At the last minute, he thought to grab another bottle of wine and a six-pack of beer to bring over. Together with some hasty finger-combing of hair and tucking-in of clothes, the excuse worked.

And, as Finn leaned back in the deck chair and watched the guys set fire to marshmallows on skewers, his last bit of resistance gave way.

He wasn't being used. If anything, he was being useful—and he missed feeling useful. If he couldn't help them find a place to rent with his family connections, he could perhaps help them buy land and build. They could work something out.

But a group of young, enthusiastic guys like this? With kind hearts and playful natures? They deserved to succeed, and if they did, they'd be lifting the whole town up.

Finn wasn't going to let the Hart's Bay cynicism scupper them. Not if he could help it.

"Okay," he told Jesse abruptly as he accepted his own marshmallow skewer and joined the circle.

Jesse just looked confused, and the other guys stared at him, too. "Okay what?" Jesse asked.

"I'll help you get in touch with Floyd."

Jesse flung himself at Finn for a hug, and Finn only reminded himself at the last second not to kiss him in front of his friends.

"Don't skewer yourself!" he joked instead as everyone laughed.

But a tiny part of him wished that Jesse *had* kissed him. Even though it was weird, and sudden, and... almost certainly romantic.

What the hell was going on?

7

JESSE

"If the sales volume is right, I can work with you to develop and reserve a design exclusively for your store."

Jesse hit with the clincher as he perched on the rickety metal table outside a kitschy boutique in Cannon Beach. So far, every boutique he'd approached with his portfolio had shown interest in that idea.

He understood why, from their side. It was easy to get any old ceramic artist or potter to produce for them, but something custom-made for them? That no other shop had? That was a tasty proposition.

Within twenty minutes, he had a handshake promise and a spring in his step as he carefully carried the heavy box back to his car.

A sale here and there added up. By now he'd driven from Cannon Beach to Port Orford three times—first to scout out boutiques and art galleries that might show an interest, then to find out the best times to catch the owners at each of them, and now to start hitting them up.

The day was wearing on, though, the sun dipping toward the ocean as he stopped for a breather.

Jesse didn't mind hustling—in fact, he was finding it strangely enjoyable. But all the time spent on sales pitches took away from the time he had to produce new pieces, and not for the first time he found himself frustrated.

After a few lungfuls of salt air, he decided to head home. He'd made three deals today, and he couldn't guarantee any more supply until he saw their sales volume. So it was time to shift the balance back to doing what he loved most—making new pieces.

But to do that efficiently, he was going to need the larger space they'd been working on getting, and they were still waiting for a call back from Floyd Hart's office about the downtown properties.

If he could figure out where that office was, and if he could rob a bank on the way, Jesse would march in there and offer him cash on the spot just to fix this headache. He'd already told them he was interested in either buying or leasing—whichever they preferred. Even that wasn't enough.

The drive back along the coast was pretty, at least. The view of the sea never failed to amaze a boy who'd grown up in the city, even though he'd had trips out to the coast with his grandparents every summer.

Summers had been Jesse's escape from the real world. But he didn't like thinking about those days, back in school.

Instead, Jesse smiled as his phone went off. His car sure as hell didn't read out texts, so he had to pull over to read it.

I'm going to cum all over my shower wall tonight thinking about you.

Well, fuck. Jesse's jaw dropped open, heat bursting in his

cheeks. He squirmed in his seat, his breath suddenly hard to catch, and tapped out a response to Finn.

Sounds like a waste... unless you share some. ;) Driving home now. The guys are making pasta tonight. It might even be edible. Come over for supper?

You can count on it. If supper doesn't work out, I have dessert for you.

Jesse whimpered and rested a hand on his crotch, trying to resist the urge to let his thoughts run away with him.

In the last couple of days, their texts had been escalating. They'd started with light innuendo and flirting. Now, apparently, they were nearly at the bursting point.

Hopefully tonight, he could entice Finn into his bed again. This whole friends-with-benefits thing was fucking fantastic.

Who said he couldn't have it all?

All he had to do was ignore the hot tendril of jealousy that coiled its way around his innards whenever he thought about Finn hanging out around his friends.

He didn't want to share Finn with anyone, and even if Finn said he wasn't interested... well...

Something had made Dominic stray, and Jesse had never been able to shake off the feeling that it was him. He'd never been able to devote enough attention to Dominic, so of course he'd strayed. He'd spent too much time with hands on clay and not enough time with hands on Dominic.

It had to be his fault somehow. And if he wasn't careful, he'd end up falling into the same pattern again. Round and round the wheel spun, the patterns of his life deepening and hardening.

Jesse rolled down the window as he pulled back onto the road. The fresh air ruffling his hair left a faint salty taste on his tongue, and that only reminded him of their last encounter.

Hot sex. That was all it was between them. With Jesse's issues and priorities and Finn's focus on what was best for his family, what else could it be?

But that was enough for Jesse. It scratched the itch and filled his evenings—and shower times—with far more interesting specifics than the generic fantasies he'd contented himself with in the month since the breakup. Or even before the breakup, since Dominic had claimed a low sex drive while fulfilling it elsewhere.

Hot thoughts, Jesse scolded himself. He didn't want to bring down the mood at supper tonight. The past was in the past, where it belonged. He had a hot guy next door who gave him exactly what he needed. What did he have to complain about?

"Where the fuck are my boxes?"

Jesse hadn't meant his tone to be so sharp, but apparently it was enough to bring Ezra into the room instantly.

The large room at the back of the house stretched farther back than any other part of the house. It looked like it had been added as an extension after the place was built and used as a playroom or extra living room. Now it served as their workroom, and it was too cramped for all their gear.

"I moved them all to the back of the room." Ezra's tone was guilty, and the redhead twisted his fingers together as they both looked at the wet canvases that stood between them and the boxes. "I'd like to wait for those ones to dry a bit more, but if you need, I can get to them tonight."

Jesse drew a breath and let his stress out along with the air in his lungs. So far, nobody had chipped or damaged any of his pieces. He really needed to relax.

Neither of them had disturbed Beau much. He'd found a spot in the corner for a little desk with a bright lamp, and his small plastic containers were all neatly stacked upon it.

But there was a constant struggle between Ezra spreading out his canvases in varying stages of completion and curing, and Jesse doing much the same with ceramic art.

It was only a matter of time before things grew explosive in here, and not just because of the paint fumes.

"I'm sorry," Ezra offered in the silence. "I didn't know you needed them today."

"I don't. I'm sorry I'm being a dick," Jesse admitted. He held his arms out for a brief hug with his friend.

They'd all anticipated it would take time to learn to live together. But goddamn, they hadn't accounted for the stress of suddenly relying financially on the exact same space for each of their sources of income.

"Everything good in here?" Beau stuck his head in. Ever the peacemaker, he wanted to make sure they all got along. At the slightest hint of an argument, he went into overdrive to defuse it.

Which was just as well, because Ross's reaction was to silently disappear into his own little rain cloud, and Aaron's dirty jokes didn't always crack the sour moods.

"Fine, fine." Jesse pulled away from the hug and wiped his forehead. Shifting boxes around looking for the mugs he'd promised Glenn—owner of the closest boutique to Hart's Bay, just half an hour's drive up the coast—was hard work.

Beau grinned at them both and gave them a thumbs-up. "Supper's nearly ready."

Oh, right. That reminded him. "Uh, is there extra?"

Beau looked at him like he was crazy. "Of course. We all agreed to make extras. Five guys? We could demolish a stockpot and then some."

Jesse grinned. "Enough for a sixth? Finn," he answered the question in Beau's eyes.

The delighted grin that spread across Beau's face made him roll his eyes, but at least he was pretty sure he'd avoided a blush. Nothing to be embarrassed about, inviting over the neighbor.

"Oh, really?" Beau stepped backward into the kitchen and craned his neck to the side to yell, "Jesse's boyfriend is coming over. Again."

"He's not—oh, fuck off." Jesse glared, his stomach going all tight and weird for a moment.

And not really in a good way.

Jesse shouldered past Beau to step into the kitchen and grab a drink. As he stood at the fridge, Ezra shadowed him inside and laid a hand on his arm.

"Jess, man. We're just kidding. Don't rush into anything."

They were right. It *had* only been a month since Jesse had walked out on that cheating bastard in the steakhouse and out of his old life. Thinking of dating anyone else was crazy, which was why he wasn't.

He didn't want Finn to just be a rebound. Maybe more importantly, he didn't want anyone else to think that was the case. Least of all Finn himself.

"Yeah. I know. Sorry, I'm just stressed about the new place."

That worked to change the topic, at least. "Still no word back?" Beau frowned as he grabbed bowls. "Jesus. They move like molasses around here."

"Coastal time." Aaron shrugged. "Can we turn up the pressure?"

Ezra was leaning against the counter with his arms folded. He chimed in, "Finn could."

Jesse bristled. The protective nature in him flared up. They had no idea what bad blood there was between Finn and the Harts who could actually control the sales and leases around here. "No. Don't ask him to."

"All right, all right." Ezra raised his hands. "I'm just saying..."

The doorbell went off, and Jesse nearly bowled over Ross to go answer it. Saved by the bell, quite literally.

"Hey," he greeted, pulling the door open.

And there was Finn in the doorway, but instead of the clean-cut man in a tight T-shirt and jeans, he wore paint-stained jeans, a clingy old T-shirt, and a baseball cap. Backward.

Oh, God. He was the boy next door after a day of hard, sweaty manual labor. A little piece of Jesse died and went to heaven. The only thing better would be if Finn were holding an all-American apple pie.

"Evening," Finn greeted with a smile. "I just made it home, and I wasn't sure what time supper's ready. I'll shower and change—"

"No need," said Beau from behind Jesse. When he glanced behind him, he saw Beau giving Finn a cheery wave. "Come on in while supper's hot. We don't care."

"That's kind of you," Finn told them as he stepped inside, his body suddenly way closer.

Close enough for the musk of sweat, lumber, and sap to wash over Jesse, making electrons fire in his brain that he hadn't even met before. He'd always figured a clean-cut, freshly showered guy was the hottest.

Hell, no. There was something way more primal at work now.

"Our pleasure," Beau said, since Jesse couldn't seem to make words come out of his mouth. "Come on, guys. Table's all set. Beer or wine?"

"Beer would be great, thanks," Finn told Beau.

Walking to the kitchen. Yeah. That would give Jesse something to do that wasn't staring at Finn's chest and the way his nipples poked through his shirt, and the rip in his jeans near his knee, and the belt that held up his jeans. This pair was baggier, unlike the ones he'd been wearing the first night at the bar. Even so, that magnificent ass filled them out.

How on earth was he going to pretend he wasn't a thirsty ho tonight?

They were alone in the front hall for a moment, and Finn's hand came to rest on Jesse's shoulder. "How was your day?" Heat prickled through him at the contact, but he'd come to his senses a little.

"Good. Real good. Made some deals with boutiques to sell my stuff. That'll help 'til we get our own gallery."

Finn lit up and gave him a mile-wide grin. "Great! That's good for you. You know, I don't think I've seen your stuff."

That reminded Jesse of the ongoing space conflict, and he rolled his eyes. "Most of it is... buried beneath a mountain of stuff right now." But he had his portfolio, at least.

Upstairs, in his bedroom.

Jesse fought back his grin at the naughty thoughts that produced. "Wait, I've got some. I'll show you after supper."

"I'd like that," Finn said, his voice just as polite as ever but his gaze dripping with suggestion. As he made for the kitchen, his hand ran down Jesse's arm, and then "accidentally" brushed over Jesse's crotch—and his aching, half-hard cock.

Fuck, Jesse shivered at the half second of contact. He smacked Finn's shoulder, but Finn just grinned at him and winked before heading into the kitchen.

Jesse took another moment to glance down at himself and make sure he was decent. Oh, crap. He strode through the kitchen and took a seat at the kitchen table, pulling his chair firmly up to the table.

Thankfully, nobody seemed to be paying attention. Everyone was greeting Finn.

And Jesse watched them like a hawk as they noticed the sexy working man in their midst.

"What do you do for work?" Ross asked right away.

Finn chose the seat next to Jesse, which made him relax. "Construction. I'm the site foreman. We were putting on a roof today."

"But it rained this morning," Aaron gasped. "That's gotta suck."

Finn's lips quirked into one of those gorgeous crooked grins. "Yes, it does." He glanced at Jesse. "But at least it keeps us cool. And it got sunny by the end of the day."

Jesse couldn't keep up with the conversation very well, but Beau in particular kept pulling him into it.

"Jesse's the one who found this house, didn't you—?"

"And Jesse makes ceramic art. He's really good!"

"Jesse's great at troubleshooting computer errors."

That last one was just outright false, and it was then he realized what was going on. They were trying to get him alone with Finn. Like they needed any help being set up.

Finn's gaze met his, also slightly wide. His lips were twitching. Just watching him try not to laugh made Jesse want to laugh, too.

If only they knew what was really going on here.

"I'll ask around here next time I download the wrong porn." Finn flashed a grin at them all.

"Sketchy porn sites are the worst. Such a betrayal of trust." Aaron covered his heart solemnly.

Ezra rolled his eyes at them both. "Anyway, I'll clear up the dishes."

"Are you sure?" Finn tried to gather his dishes, but Ezra lightly smacked his hand away.

"Yeah, yeah, it's my turn. You're the guest. You go... do whatever."

Well, there it was. The look Ezra exchanged with his other housemates made Jesse blush. At least he'd resisted for this long.

"I wanted to show you my ceramic art," he told Finn and then winced and cut a sideways glance at Ezra. That was going to sound like he had a bone to pick. *Dick move, Jesse. Great*, he thought.

But Ezra hadn't taken it to heart. He was whistling and clearing up dishes.

"Right. You said you have some around?"

"My portfolio." Jesse casually rose to his feet and led Finn up the creaky, twisting flight of stairs to the top landing. He dipped to the left, pausing just long enough to gesture at the rooms. "This one's mine. Ezra, Aaron, Ross, and Beau."

"You got the one facing me," Finn observed, his eyes dancing. "That's good to know."

Jesse cleared his throat as he showed Finn into his room. It wasn't much yet, but he was trying to cheer it up with some of his own work.

There were built-in shelves and a wardrobe that was firmly

closed. Luckily he was tidy by nature. Work clothes stayed in the top drawer of the chest tucked into the corner of the room.

He'd just set his box of fragile pieces on the bed before taking off downstairs to check on his inventory. He sat on the bed next to it, and the bed dipped as Finn sat next to him.

Instead of looking at the portfolio, though, Finn was looking at his bedside table. "This is pretty."

Jesse leaned around to see what he was looking at and then caught his breath. It was the sea glass he'd picked up after their first hookup. His smile was sheepish. "It's from... uh, that cove you showed me."

Finn's brows rose, and then he laughed. "Is it? Huh."

Jesse didn't want to admit how special it was to him, so he cleared his throat and opened up the box that held his pottery. Thank God Finn didn't ask any more questions.

The sexual tension was still there—it never seemed to sizzle out—but it was a low heat right now. It felt more important somehow to show him these pieces of who he was.

One piece at a time, he pulled them out of their foam casing. They'd been carefully selected to show the variety of what he could do, from folksy and rustic to slick and modern.

"These are amazing," Finn breathed out at last, carefully picking up a cup and turning it around in his hands. "Did you study for this?"

Jesse shook his head and cracked a smile. "Nah. It was a hobby at first."

He was surprised at how easily he spoke to Finn. Before long, he was sitting at the head of his bed, one knee by his chest and his arm loosely wrapped around it.

He told Finn about growing up gay—and out since middle school. It had been easier on him than many other guys. Living in a progressive paradise had its perks. But teens still said what they thought online, and he hadn't been able to escape.

The bullying had escalated between sixth and eighth grade, culminating in an anonymous Facebook group with an unoriginal title: *Jesse Stone sucks dick for free!!!*

"They were just jealous they weren't getting their dicks sucked," Finn told him with a firm nod, but he laid a hand on top of Jesse's hand on his knee. "Still, that's awful."

"Well, as soon as Mom found out, she tried to fight for me. But nobody wanted to catch them, or even identify them. It was easy to make fake accounts back then. So she banned me from Facebook."

"Oof. Bet you loved that," Finn winced.

Jesse laughed. "Yeah, I hated it at first. But I've grown to appreciate it. If you're not there to accept the gift of intimidation... well, they can't really give it to you, can they?"

Finn blinked at him a few times. "Yeah. Yeah, I guess so."

"So then she gave me a hobby." Jesse gestured at the materials. "She'd been doing this since *she* was my age, and I always thought it was dumb."

Until that first time he'd gotten his hands on clay, anyway. Then it had all clicked into place like it was meant to be.

He still remembered the afternoons around the newspaper-lined kitchen table with her and the foot-pumped pedal.

And he remembered her words when they'd fired his very first lumpy, pink-painted pot.

You don't need them. You have the power to create. They need you, because they're too afraid to try creating something new and magical themselves. They can only try to tear down others. That makes them the weak ones, Jesse.

Jesse swallowed hard. "She told me a few smart things about bullies back then. I learned to ignore them and *make* things instead of focusing on what they were tearing down, you know?"

Finn's thumb gently stroked the back of his own. It was a slow, steady, comforting rhythm.

"So then I worked at whatever jobs I could get without a degree—you know how it goes," Jesse mumbled with a shrug. He was embarrassed sometimes about not having a degree when everyone else his age seemed to. But no way could he have afforded college, and he'd been afraid of trade school. And an MFA was a waste when he had a mom who could teach him everything he needed to know about pottery.

"Yeah. I went straight into construction after trade school."

"Oh, I was afraid of trade school. They'd chew me up and spit me out," Jesse laughed.

Even here, sitting on the bed with his life's work between them, he was aware of how much bigger and stronger Finn was than him. He'd turned his delicate hands to his advantage in his newly full-time pottery career. A manly man's industry like construction was no place for a delicate twink like him.

"There's other trades out there," Finn said with a smile and squeezed his hand. "And I know all kinds of people—guys and gals—in construction. But you seem happy doing this."

"I am. Very." Jesse's smile grew until his cheeks hurt.

Now? He was free. He could create a whole new life for himself and soar to new heights. Meanwhile the bullies who'd hidden behind anonymous accounts had to make something of themselves.

"I admire the hell out of you," Finn murmured. He patted Jesse's hand before he slid his own hand away. The absence of touch always made something twinge in Jesse like a piece of him had just been removed.

Jesse shrugged. "It's not that much different from what you do, is it?"

Finn built houses. From the ground up. That was pretty cool.

And every time Jesse shaped clay between his palms, he could make anything he wanted. Cups, saucers, vases, bowls, sculptures, jewelry, candleholders—you name it, Jesse could make it come alive with color and texture.

He could brighten the world, one piece at a time. Just like he was going to do to Hart's Bay, however much the founding family resisted. If he could just get a foot in the door, he could start spreading a little magic.

Finn rose to his feet, his hands tucked in his pockets. "Look, uh... I promised to call my dad this evening. He'll get snippy if I wait much longer."

Yet despite his twinge of disappointment—entirely his blue balls talking—Jesse was happy that he'd talked with Finn. He saw him downstairs and outside, chatting with his friends for a few more minutes before Finn left.

The conversation kept turning over in his head as he tried to focus on hanging out with his friends in the living room.

For the first time, he'd let Finn see a glimpse of him, and Finn hadn't just ignored him in favor of a quick fuck. They totally could have squeezed one in if they'd wanted.

Wait, why am I happy not *to have the benefits?*

Because, Jesse's heart told him, he needed the friendship, too. It was too terrifying to give it any other name. And he still kept checking his phone... waiting for the good-night text.

The signs clicked together in his mind: his wanting to spend all the time he could around Finn, his jealousy when anyone so much as looked at him, and his enjoying sex way more than usual.

This wasn't just about Jesse working out his relationship issues.

He *wanted* Finn, in more ways than he wanted to want him.

Oh, fuck.

8

FINN

Finn had to get out of there before he did something he regretted. Or, more to the point, *said* something he regretted.

He admired the hell out of Jesse, that was for sure. As far as Finn could tell, he was five years older than Jesse, yet Jesse had started his own damn business and spent ten years honing his skills already.

The legacy Jesse had been handed would serve him well. But more than that, Jesse's drive and focus would land him exactly where he wanted to be.

But Finn found himself wishing that Jesse wanted to be by his side.

It was a crazy thought. Jesse had been clear from the very beginning that he didn't want a romantic entanglement. He'd dropped enough sideways hints that Finn figured he'd gotten out of a relationship not long ago, or something like that.

Asking him out anyway would be a dick move.

But even though he'd offered friends with benefits—no strings attached—Finn wasn't sure he could keep the strings off for much longer.

He wanted Jesse. Hearing him talk about the cyberbullying in his past had made him want to wrap him in his arms, find the little twerps who had taunted him, and teach them a lesson.

But Jesse was right. They'd made their own bed by spending years tearing people down instead of becoming whole, creative, proud people like Jesse now was. Whatever lay ahead for them in life, they'd always know deep down that *they'd* been the asshole making a queer kid feel like shit about himself... without even the guts to do it to his face.

God, bullies just made Finn's blood pressure rise like nothing else. Anyone with human decency who had made something of themselves ought to use that to help others. But instead, anyone with an ounce of power seemed to use it to beat others down, off the very ladder they'd climbed.

The only escape from the whirlwind of thoughts plaguing Finn was to grab a beer, settle on his couch, and call his dad.

Finn talked to all of his parents and siblings at least once a week, and tried to see them just as often. He talked with his uncle through the course of the average workweek, too. They might not have a huge family, but everything they'd been through together—mostly before Finn was old enough to remember—had knit them together tightly.

The phone barely rung before his dad answered, his tone clipped as usual. Finn never took it personally. He just came off as brusque to those who didn't know him because he preferred to keep his thoughts on the inside until he had something worth saying.

"Hey, Dad," Finn greeted. "How's it going?"

After the polite greetings and highlights of their days, his dad didn't seem to be saying whatever had made him need to talk to Finn. So instead, Finn brought up what had been bothering him.

"Do you know why Rain's working on our crew?"

"I don't know, son." His dad's voice was heavy with foreboding. "But it can't be good, whatever it is."

"That's what I thought."

"Why? Is he just hanging around keeping his nails clean?" His father sounded almost eager for an excuse to come down on him.

"Nah. He's actually putting a lot of elbow grease in. I'm impressed." Maybe that was a good thing, maybe not. "And he's hanging around Justin a lot. Learning a ton from him."

In fact, he'd asked for a ride home along with Justin tomorrow since his car was in the garage. Despite his better instinct, Finn had agreed. It was going to be beyond strange to have someone from *that* side of the family in his damn truck, but it was only twenty minutes.

"Well, still. Keep an eye on him. There's rumblings."

Finn sat up straighter. "Oh?"

"Don't poke the hornet's nest." His dad knew all too well what happened when you did, but that was about all Finn knew about his involvement and who had really started what.

Nobody had ever bothered filling in the younger Harts on everything that had happened all those years ago. Even as the oldest of the four, Finn had been just nine when the fishery collapsed once and for all. He and his little siblings had been mostly sheltered from the harsh reality of life until after the fact.

Only now did he know how petty things had gotten. Tidbits had been dropped here and there, like the fact his grandfather Floyd once publicly accused his dad and Uncle Roy of peddling false hope by keeping their side of the business open despite the impending fishery crash. No more town-wide beach barbecues after that blowout.

"I hear there's someone new in town looking to buy downtown."

"Oh! Yeah. That's Jesse." The words spilled from Finn's mouth before he put two and two together. His dad was telling him something here. Any association with him and... well, Floyd would be reluctant to part with property that enriched *their* side of the family.

"So you do know him."

Finn sighed. How could he explain it? He wasn't about to tell his dad what was going on between them. "He's my new neighbor. He only wants to set up a little artist studio and art gallery to sell their work."

Dad made an approving noise. "That doesn't sound like a bad idea. I hear Floyd's considering it." Finn didn't ask where his dad got such reliable gossip from. Finn just tried to keep his nose clean and avoid contact with anyone, really.

"A reasonable idea? Floyd's considering it?"

"I know. I looked up and the sky's full of prize hogs." His dad's tone was dry, making him laugh. He'd dealt with his own dad's ego for too many years to be polite about it.

"You think they have a chance of getting the property?"

"Buying or renting?" Dad shrewdly asked.

"I think he's good with either. Honestly, Grandpa should be paying *them* to take it off his hands."

It was a reliable go-to line when they wanted to vent about the other Harts: how little care they took for their property, and how bad it made the town look.

"He should. But he's thinking about letting it go to them cheap since they're hustling so hard."

"Really? Jeez." Finn's heart lifted. Maybe there was a chance for his new neighbors. They deserved to get a break, and Jesse was right. His own business would only lift up the whole town.

"But if Dad—sorry, your grandpa—gets a hint that you're friends... Monty and the kids will throw a shitfit that their inheritance is going to you."

Dad and Roy, Finn's uncle, barely acknowledged the other brother, Monty. Monty had taken their father's side and wound up on the other side of the family rift. And Monty's kids—Rain included—were a spoiled bunch.

Finn sighed. He'd long since accepted that the politics really were this petty. "Yeah, I know. It's not like we're strolling through town together."

"Just don't poke the bear, that's all I'm saying. Things have been good these last few years."

"What do you mean?" Finn pressed. "What's poking the bear?"

His dad paused for a few long moments before he finally said, "You know what caused the very first argument between your grandpa and us boys?" His voice was quiet and deliberate.

A chill ran down Finn's spine. He sat up straight. At twenty-nine, he'd never heard what happened two decades or more ago, and he'd resigned himself to it being a dusty secret too old to brush off in the telling. "No. Nobody ever told me the whole story."

Dad's sigh was quiet. "I didn't want to ever have to tell you. But Uncle Roy came out, and Dad—I mean, your grandpa —didn't take it too well."

Finn's jaw dropped. He couldn't remember Roy dating *anyone* in the last few decades. Everyone around town seemed to assume he was gay, as a permanent bachelor, but he and his uncle had never even talked about it.

"Then Floyd struck a few low blows. Monty took his side. They decided his sexuality was the main problem around here, not declining fishery stocks. I think it gave them something to latch onto that they felt like they could control."

Finn couldn't hold in his snort. Like anyone could control their own sexuality, let alone someone else's. "Right."

"I know," Dad sighed. "But that's why Floyd's always been so cold to you."

Finn bit his lip. "But I came out way after that..."

"He was there when you came running into the room at all of four years old in Mom's high heels and lipstick as eyeshadow." Dad was clearly trying not to chuckle. "Coming out was a formality."

It was funny, looking back at how he'd seen everything back then compared to everyone around him. "Yeah," Finn admitted. "I guess so."

"And I turned out to have a surprisingly gay bunch of kids," Dad said, but he didn't sound even a bit regretful. No— he sounded proud. "Nothing could piss Floyd off more."

Finn burst out laughing. It was a strange kind of revenge, but it felt like he'd never loved his dad more than that moment. His mind was spinning. No wonder everyone had hidden the truth from them.

Finn nodded to himself, staring through the living room window like it held all the answers. "Thank you for telling me all that."

"It's long past time," Dad said, and if Finn wasn't wrong, he sounded sheepish. "I just didn't want to put all that crap on you while you were figuring yourself out. And for the record, we all had Roy's back, even back then. Nobody else in town cared, except his own so-called dad."

This put a different spin on everything. "Well, I don't give a shit what he thinks," Finn told his dad. "But yeah, I can see how Jesse and me would ignite that all over again. We'll keep our heads down for a while."

He gently guided the conversation toward what his mom was making for dinner. But the whole time, his mind spun. He wanted to get off the phone and tell Jesse the good news right away—and the mixed news. Wanted to tell him to hang on a little longer and push a little harder and keep his head down a little more.

But he couldn't get involved. The more he meddled, the more reason Floyd would have to back out if he found out. So it was Jesse's work to do, and Finn would avoid steering it at all.

Then they could honestly say there was no conspiracy between them to get the bad Harts to release their stranglehold on the town. Or to gay up the town, like Floyd was probably thinking.

Even though I'm pretty sure the guys do want to gay up the town. It made Finn grin to think about Jesse's friends irritating Floyd without even knowing it.

"Okay, I better go," Finn finally told his dad. "Oh, wait. Did Dash tell you he's thinking about moving out here?"

"Is he really?" His dad sounded as surprised as he'd felt. "But what about his job back there?"

"I dunno. Sounds like he has itchy feet and wants to be closer to home."

"It'd be good to have another of my boys back," Dad said, which made Finn's heart swell with pride. Finn was protective of all his little siblings, but maybe Dash most of all.

His dad hadn't always been as accepting of Dash as he should have been. But Finn coming out had helped Dad open his mind, and... well, they were all in a good place now.

Now the key was not to disturb the balance.

It all made more sense now: how Dad had been so unsure about Dash, the only supposed girl of his four kids, coming out as trans and gay all those years ago. But he'd come around to be more protective of his fourth son than even Finn and the boys. And Dad had stuck by them the whole time, never batting an eye when they'd all come out as gay, bi, or queer in turn. Plus, like he said, he'd stuck by Roy through thick and thin.

Dad had never steered Finn wrong. Which was what made him hesitate to answer the door after he hung up from the phone call, even though he'd recognize the knock anywhere.

It was Jesse.

When he pulled open the door, Finn pushed back all the thoughts until later and winked at Jesse. "Sorry, you didn't catch me in the shower again."

"Damn. I'll time it more carefully next time," Jesse said, but he was glowing—in fact, bouncing up and down on his toes. It was adorable.

"What's going on?" Finn opened the door wider and stood aside.

Jesse's voice was a high-pitched squeak. "We got it!"

Finn's jaw dropped. He hardly dared to hope. "You what? Got... the..."

"The property! Floyd's going to lease to us at first and then talk sale next year when we're sure if we can afford it. And it's totally affordable. I talked to the agent and the people and the other people and they all said we can sign the contract and then he's willing to hand over the keys right away which is one big advantage of leasing rather than buying, and—"

Finn squeezed Jesse's shoulders and shook him gently until he stopped and took a breath. "Whoa. One thing at a time."

Even as he led Jesse to the couch, Jesse kept talking a mile a minute, waving wildly as he outlined his plans for renovations and opening within a month—just with bare-bones furnishings, of course. They could add more display units and decorate the place as they started bringing in money.

"And I'm an actual adult with an actual adult lease on a *commercial* building!" Jesse couldn't sit still.

Finn remembered the feeling well: when his house sale had gone through, he'd spent an afternoon gobsmacked that he'd locked himself into a long-term financial commitment.

But he also remembered feeling deeply proud of himself and his own space to do what he wanted. And that had just been a house—not even the foundations of a whole business.

"I think this calls for celebration." Finn grinned and glanced toward the corner shelf, where he kept a few spirits. Mostly for when his dad and uncle were visiting.

Jesse surged toward Finn and grabbed his shoulders as he collapsed onto his lap, kissing him hard.

The breath left Finn's lungs as a wet, hot mouth sought his own and claimed it. Jesse kissed hard, with teeth and tongue and fire in his blood. This was a whole new level of boldness, even for him, and his body responded with pure joy.

He wrapped his arms around Jesse and pulled him against him, wrestling for control of the kiss. Finally, he managed to suck on Jesse's lower lip, making Jesse whimper and go limp in his arms. He did it again and Jesse gave a mewling whimper and then panted for breath.

Everything Finn did made Jesse press forward against him, eager and hungry.

And Finn felt that same insatiable thirst for him, but it was tempered with just a note of caution.

Don't get too close.

Once again, his name was a double-edged sword. Just being born into the right part of the wrong family could undo Jesse's hard work if they weren't careful.

But why should they have to be? He was fucking sick of tiptoeing around town like he should be ashamed of anything.

He hadn't done a thing wrong.

Finn growled and flipped Jesse onto his back on the couch, crouching over him. Finn kissed the whimpering, squirming man until his nails ran down Finn's back. Then, he pressed light kisses along his jaw and cheek toward his ear.

A tongue flick against Jesse's earlobe made his whole body arch in one fluid rippling wave. He tried it again, and Jesse hooked a knee around his waist, locking their bodies together.

Within moments of kissing behind Jesse's ear and down his neck, Jesse was already squirming, trying to rip his shirt off. Finn let him do it, raising his arms while Jesse pulled off his work shirt and threw it aside.

"You know, I could use that shower soon." Finn grinned playfully.

Jesse was disheveled already, his hair messy and eyes glassy, lips swollen with kisses. Red marks on his neck where Finn had just been kissing and sucking led down to his collarbone, and Finn itched to carry on down his body.

Head to toe, he wanted to lick Jesse all over, turn him on and leave him wanting until he was screaming in pleasure at the slightest touch. And then he wanted to fuck him hard and fast until they exploded with ecstasy. And then—scariest of all

—he wanted to hold him close and stroke his hair and tell him how fucking beautiful and strong he was.

How grateful Finn was that Jesse had blown into his life and this town and put down roots.

How much he wanted Jesse to stay here, with him.

Whatever the consequences, here he was—stirring the hornet's nest. Sticking not just a foot in it, but jumping up and down, waving *come and get me*.

Because Jesse? One kiss from him was enough to make Finn tear down everything he thought he'd known about his life and build it again from the foundation upward. And whatever was going on, Finn knew enough to know that didn't happen every day.

Damn the risks. Some things were worth it.

And increasingly, Finn was starting to suspect that his heart knew the truth of it: Jesse was one of those things.

Or could be, if Jesse agreed to it. That was the great unknown, and it would remain unknown until he had the balls to find out.

But not yet.

First, the shower was calling.

Finn peeled himself off Jesse and stood, never breaking eye contact as he stretched out a hand to Jesse.

"Come."

9

JESSE

Finn's house was about exactly what Jesse had expected. It was small and cozy, but decorated well. Like he was well settled in the place, and comfortable.

It was fascinating to catch glimpses of his life in the rooms: framed photos of people Jesse assumed were family members or friends in the living room, potted plants on the windowsills.

Navigating the stairs took a moment since Finn seemed unwilling to drop Jesse's hand. He went first, pulling Jesse up after him. Which gave Jesse a fantastic view of that firm ass half-hidden by his tragically loose work jeans.

"Eyes up here, mister," Finn teased when they got to the landing upstairs, but he leaned in to lap at Jesse's lips in another sensual, openmouthed kiss.

Jesse moaned and kneaded Finn's chest before pulling back. "Which way?" Looked like maybe two bedrooms upstairs, not as big a place as the house next door.

"Here. I have an en suite."

"Oooh. Fancy." Jesse winked. After trying to get ready in

the morning with five guys and two bathrooms, he was actually a little jealous. "Can I make a reservation?"

Finn grinned. "You can share mine anytime. We can save water and shower together."

"How responsible."

"I try."

Jesse followed Finn into the bedroom, their fingers locked tightly together in a silent promise of what was to come, and took the chance to look around before he got too distracted.

The bedroom was sleek and masculine. All matching dark wood furniture and a huge, cozy bed with pillows, an extra throw along the foot, and a sitting ottoman chest thing at the end of the bed.

The walls were painted, too, not the standard white that he'd come to expect from every rental in his life. It was a dark, soothing room with blues and greens, but not oppressive.

Just like the seaside where they'd first gotten to know each other.

"You like the ocean?"

"I like the sounds of waves lapping against the shore. Gulls crying. Sand or rocks underfoot." Between each sentence, Finn punctuated them with kisses.

"You like hearing me moan, too," Jesse pointed out with a wicked little grin up at him.

Finn's eyes widened. "You noticed."

Jesse giggled. Kind of hard to miss the way Finn's breath caught and his grip tightened whenever Jesse made a loud sound. "Hell, yeah." He dropped his voice to barely a whisper of the moans he expected he'd be making later. "Show me the shower you texted me about earlier."

"Fuck." Finn let go of his hand at last and shoved open the

bathroom door. It was a simple three-piece suite, but the shower was a great open one with a rainfall head.

"Nice," Jesse whispered. No slipping around in the tub while trying to grope each other, or embarrassing 911 calls. Last thing he needed was to be the talk of the local hospital.

Finn grinned. "Big enough for both of us," he murmured. He pulled Jesse in by the hand and pressed a kiss against the back of his hand, then sidled behind him and turned them both toward the counter.

The mirror stretched the length of the wall behind the sink and taps, and one glance was almost hypnotic. Jesse's gaze fixated on Finn's hand as he felt it slide around his side until it rested in the middle of his chest. Finn pulled him back, supporting his weight and grinding his cock into his ass.

Fuck. Jesse squirmed against him, his toes curling as he watched his own reactions.

"See how hot you are?" Finn breathed out. His other hand was on the move, grazing up Jesse's thigh until he paused to squeeze the hard line of Jesse's cock.

Jesse gulped and closed his eyes for a moment, trying to keep himself in check. He was going to come in three breaths flat if he wasn't careful. "I wanna watch you jerk off first."

He hadn't been able to shake the image from his mind since their texts earlier that day. He'd played it over and over in his head, and now that he could see the wall Finn had suggested leaving his load splattered across, the desire to see it burned through him.

"Oh?" Finn's grin over his shoulder was wickedly broad at the suggestion. "You do?"

"I do," Jesse breathed out. "Please?"

Finn let go of him and pulled his belt open, slowly turning on the spot while Jesse watched. His eyes flickered between the mirror and Finn's body in the flesh, enjoying every angle of the striptease.

Finn pushed down his jeans and stepped out of them, bending over to pick them up and toss them out the door into the bedroom. Jesse gulped as he reached out for a quick grope, sliding his hands up those strong thighs and over the firm, rounded flesh.

"Tsch." Finn winked, smacking his hand and dancing away. He turned to face Jesse, palming the bulge between his own legs.

Jesse moaned in protest. Knowing he wasn't allowed to touch made it all the worse. He backed up against the counter, curling his fingers around the edge as he watched Finn squeeze himself.

Fuck, that big cock looked perfectly sized in Finn's hands. Long fingers wrapped around the line and pulled up the shaft, plucking a few times before Finn hooked a thumb in his underwear and dragged it down, too.

Jesse's gasp was impossible to muffle. Finn was hard as anything, his shaft flushed pink and perfect. He wanted to drop to his knees and suck him off again. Even thinking about his lips stretched around that thick length made his mouth water.

"Mmm," Finn moaned, the sound echoing sharply off the tiled walls. "God, imagining you pressed up against the rock face with the sea lapping against the beach... or you on your knees on the kitchen floor..."

"I was just remembering that, too," Jesse whispered. "What else do you want?"

Finn stepped into the shower and turned on the water, fiddling with the dial. All the while, Jesse couldn't tear his eyes from the length jutting up toward his chest.

"I want," Finn breathed at last, "to spread you over my bed and kiss every inch of you. To find out what makes you tick. To make you so hard you're begging me to touch you. To make you come so hard you forget your own name."

Jesse's knees were definitely weak now. The steam rising from the shower had nothing on the heat rising in his cheeks. He kept his hands firmly on the edge of the counter as his cock throbbed in his pants. "Oh," he managed, his voice choked. "Fuck."

Finn smoothed his hands down his body all the way to his thighs and then took hold of the base of his thick shaft, his hand curled around in a practiced motion. He jerked toward the tip in a few sharp thrusts. "I want to bend you over that counter and fuck you while I make you watch every little twitch of pleasure crossing your face—listen to every sound that spills from you."

His hand sped up on his shaft, pumping up and down as Finn leaned back against the wall. The glass between them gave Jesse a near-perfect view at first, but it was rapidly steaming up now that the shower was on.

All he'd be able to see when Finn came would be his load splattered across the glass. Not the tension in his body, or the way his lips parted and formed a perfect O.

That wouldn't do.

Jesse nearly stumbled as he stripped his shirt and pants off, ignoring Finn's low laugh. Once he was naked, he hovered in the gap that served as a door in the shower. Without the glass between them, a wave of damp heat struck.

"You've had me turned on for days," Finn breathed out, his voice low and rough. "Especially imagining you in that ripped shirt. Stumbling home all turned on and needing me."

"I'll wear it again for you," Jesse promised, giving Finn a

grin. He was waiting for the right moment to pull that trick out. "But I need you right now." His hand slid down toward his cock, but Finn stopped his jerking and reached out to grab his wrist.

"No."

Jesse whimpered in protest, staring at Finn. But however many noises he made, Finn didn't relent until he let his hand drop to his side. "Okay."

Finn let go of him and smiled, leaning back against the wall again and spreading his feet. "You said you wanted to watch. So you get to just watch. It'll be your turn next, if you're patient."

Fuck, those words sent another jolt of static through his brain and need through his belly. It was all the self-control Jesse had not to just grab himself and start jerking off, but he didn't dare push it.

So he stood and watched the pink, stiff flesh pumping in and out of Finn's tight grip, and the way Finn's body stiffened and his breaths grew short and quick.

By now, he could tell when Finn was getting close. And when he tried to turn side-on to face the glass, Jesse made his move.

"No," he told Finn, his voice just as bold and certain as Finn's had been.

Finn froze for a moment with surprise, his brows climbing. "Huh?"

"Like I said earlier: don't waste a drop." Jesse stepped closer, until the spray coursed over his back, and dropped to his knees. A little shifting and his chest was out of the direct spray, leaving it a bare, wet, blank canvas. He tilted his head back, exposing his throat.

Finn stepped closer, gently cupping the back of Jesse's

head. "Beautiful," he whispered, his voice barely audible over the rush of water. His hand was smoothly pumping along his shaft, hard and fast. "So fucking gorgeous."

"Come for me," Jesse begged. "I've been waiting for so long. Show me how much you want me."

The first jet of Finn's hot load hit his chin as Finn cried out in a loud growl. Drop by drop, he coated Jesse's throat and chest while his nails dug into Jesse's shoulder, keeping him on his knees.

When he was done, he gulped for breath, stepping into the stream for just long enough to rinse himself clean.

Jesse whimpered as he shifted from knee to knee. All he wanted was to jerk off hard and fast, but Finn had said he had plans for him.

"Come here," Finn whispered, gripping him by the biceps. He gently drew Jesse to his feet and turned him around until he hugged him from behind, his softening cock still pressing a line against Jesse's ass. He steered Jesse into the spray, letting Jesse roll his head back against his shoulder to keep his face out of the water.

Jesse let Finn wash him clean, but he wasn't contented with just that. No, Finn's other plans became obvious all too quickly.

He was touching Jesse all over, his palms gliding from thighs to stomach, sides to chest. Jesse's back still pressed against Finn's hard body, and he knew Finn would catch him if his knees gave in.

Which was good, because the slightest accidental graze of Finn's wrist against his swollen shaft made Jesse cry out and stumble.

Finn just guided him out of the shower instead, grinning as he shut off the water.

"Hey!" Jesse grunted, squirming as cool air hit warm, sensitive skin. Especially his cock, which was straining toward his stomach. "Fuck."

"Sorry," Finn whispered, kissing his shoulder as he grabbed a towel and wrapped it around Jesse. Now he stood in front of him, gently patting him dry and draping the towel around his shoulders.

The fluffy fabric made the lack of pleasurable contact almost bearable. Jesse pouted but grabbed the edges of the towel to take over drying off while Finn toweled himself.

He was so turned on that it nearly hurt to ignore it any longer. But all he had to do was cast Finn one pleading glance, and Finn dropped his towel and took Jesse by the hand to lead him to the bedroom.

Jesse tumbled onto his back on the bed, scooting up the silky sheets until his head rested against the pillows.

Best of all, Finn followed, crawling over him and not letting Jesse get away. His eyes were dark and hungry, like he'd spotted his favorite prey in the world.

Jesse whimpered at that look and spread his hands and feet apart, burying his arms in the pillows and pressing his feet into the bed.

"Gotcha," Finn growled, swinging a knee over him and running both palms up his flat chest and stomach.

Jesse would have blushed at that look if he weren't so flushed and needy already. Even though Jesse didn't have a six-pack or pecs to rival Finn's, Finn was drinking in the sight of him.

"You like?" Jesse finally managed. He was quivering at the slightest touch, which meant Finn's wandering hands across his stomach and chest were almost painfully erotic.

"More than like," Finn breathed out with a sudden smile at

him. But his eyes were veiled, like there was something else on his mind. Whatever it was, he was keeping it to himself.

Jesse's skin was cool now, so every touch of Finn's lips against his chest and neck made him flinch with the pleasant heat that ignited under his skin. Still, all the moans in the world wouldn't make Finn hurry up his explorations.

Minutes passed as Finn found spots that made Jesse groan: behind his ears, the edge of his collarbone, between his ribs, just above his belly button. And that was just the beginning, because the destination of these wanderings became apparent when he started kissing circles around Jesse's nipples.

"Fuck," Jesse panted, squeezing his eyes shut. "Finn…"

"Mmhmm?" Finn's lips closed around one perky nub, and Jesse felt like he nearly bucked off the bed. In truth, he couldn't go anywhere fast with Finn's weight on his legs, but Finn slid a hand under his back when he arched up.

"I need… I need… I need you," Jesse managed. His cock was about ready to burst, especially when Finn's tongue flickered rapidly across his nipple. He gave a full-throated cry of pleasure.

"That's more like it," Finn breathed out. But even so, he didn't move down to suck Jesse off—or even touch the hard length that bobbed in midair between them. At this point, Jesse would have ground himself against sandpaper for a hint of relief. It was enough to almost bring tears to his eyes, but despite his protests, it only turned Jesse on more.

Finn had no mercy, and as much as Jesse hated it, a deeper part of him loved it.

Nobody had ever taken this much care with him—or turned him on this much. Jesse had never felt agonizing pleasure like this, and now that he was in the midst of it, he didn't know what to do with himself. This was somehow better than any sex he'd ever had with a boyfriend.

Maybe it was because their relationship was focused on sex. Not anything else like pesky romance and commitment and that kind of fantasy.

But no—his treacherous bastard of a brain reminded him that this whole encounter started because he'd wanted to share his good news with a friend. His news about the future. And just earlier that night, Finn had so closely listened to his past.

Something deeper was building between them, and it terrified Jesse.

Easier to focus on squirming and thrashing under Finn, begging for any kind of pleasure Finn would deliver.

Oh, fuck. Finn shifted and his cock was a hard weight against Jesse's leg. Had he really been tormenting Jesse for that long? Or was Jesse turning him on that much? Jesse's breath caught as he glanced down and then moaned.

Finn was hard again and grinding slowly against Jesse's hip to make sure he knew it. When he saw that he had Jesse's attention, Finn grinned. "Look at that. Your fault."

"Okay. Credit, blame, whatever. Just fuck me," Jesse begged.

"Mmm." Finn grinned and shifted off him.

Oh, fuck. No, he couldn't leave him like this. "Please!" Jesse gave a moan of protest and rolled to the side to try to grab him and haul him back.

Finn laughed. "Patience," he whispered. "I will, babe."

The pet name sounded too good. Jesse squirmed and caught his breath as Finn pushed his shoulder, rolling him onto his front.

"Yes," Jesse gasped, pressing his face into the pillows and

shoving his hands under them, too. He stuck his ass up in the air, spreading his legs as he shifted onto his knees.

He expected Finn's hands running across his cheeks, spreading them open and kneading gently, waking up every sensitive nerve.

He didn't expect a hot, wet, firm tongue running from his balls up to his tight hole.

"Fuck!" Jesse almost slammed into Finn's face, but Finn had a hand on his lower back, keeping him down on the bed. Jesse could trust him enough to let go, so he did.

Oh, God. The wet, warm licks against him shouldn't have felt so irresistible, but they did. He found himself whimpering, pushing back against Finn, spreading his legs as his cock throbbed heavily in the air under him.

"Please, please, please," Jesse panted at last, when that tongue had invaded him and pushed him past where he'd thought the edge might lie. Still, no relief came. "Please fuck me."

Finn ran his hand slowly up Jesse's side to cup his face as he kissed between his shoulder blades. "Since you asked so nicely," his lover murmured, his voice low and steady.

He listened to Finn ripping open a condom and opening the lube.

Fingers came first, wet and thick but gentle as they slid inside him, opening him up and preparing him.

When they weren't enough for him, all he could do was moan in a broken voice, and Finn's hand smoothed down his skin. A gentle rub told Jesse that he was listening.

A hard weight pressed against him, and then slowly—too slowly—into him.

Finn was deep inside him within a few thrusts, and his palm cupped the back of Jesse's neck, keeping him in place.

"Yes!" Jesse gasped, pushing back into him as much as he could. "Now, babe. Now, please!"

Harder and faster, Finn drove into him, stoking the fire that burned through him. With every damn surge, he lit up the nerves inside Jesse that seemed fine-tuned to Finn alone.

He was almost too big to handle, but in the best possible way. Jesse was pushed to the edge of his endurance, thoughts buckling under animal sensations and primal need.

Finn grabbed his cock and jerked, so hard and fast that Jesse couldn't even be shocked enough to beg for mercy. It was all he'd needed for long minutes now. A few skilled flicks of Finn's wrist later, Jesse spilled over the edge, exploding in an orgasm that shook his whole body. A cry ripped from his throat as pleasure spilled from him.

When the sweaty skin finally cooled again in the air and he could almost breathe, Finn slid out of him. Jesse twisted to look over his shoulder as Finn yanked the condom off and jerked himself off for the second time in an hour.

This time, he marked Jesse's back instead of his front with his sticky mess, and Jesse's toes curled with satisfaction at the hot droplets painted across him.

"Oh, fuck," Finn groaned, shifting until he lay next to Jesse, a hand on his upper back. "You're all messy again. You better get in the shower."

Jesse gave a breathless giggle. "If I do that, I'll only start the cycle again."

"Mmm. Okay." Finn's voice was heavy and thick with the same sleep that tugged at Jesse's eyelids.

He barely wanted to move, so he just listened to Finn get up and then return. A warm cloth ran along his back as Finn cleaned him up. Then, hands tugged at the covers under him, pulling them down to his feet and back up over him.

Jesse hummed, still feeling the ache deep inside him from where Finn had just been. Maybe in the morning, they could do it again. He daydreamed about how sexy it would be to wake up in the middle of the night for a quick fuck. With Finn's body wrapped around his, anything felt possible.

"I meant it earlier, you know." Finn's voice pierced the sleepy haze, and Jesse cracked his eyelids to find that the room light was off now. The darkness was nice.

"Mm?" Jesse pressed back against Finn's chest, squirming until he fit just right.

"When I said I admire you. I really like you, Jesse." Finn's tone was a little too careful and measured to be flippant conversation.

Jesse froze and stiffened, his eyes flying open. He stared ahead into the darkness, where he could just make out the shape of the dresser in the corner of the room. "You do?" he murmured, trying to keep his tone casual.

"Mmm. I know you said you're not looking for more, but... you're a hell of a guy. It takes a brave man to do something like you've done. Are doing." Finn's strong arm snaked over his side as he pulled Jesse into his chest and then loosened his grip.

Jesse could wriggle free if he wanted—climb out of bed and head back home.

But he didn't want to.

As much as the words scared him, he wanted to stay here in Finn's embrace. He just didn't want to promise something he couldn't give, and he wasn't sure his heart was available.

Jesse drew a deep breath and let it out before he weighed his words. "Thank you. That means a lot to hear."

"But you're busy starting your new business." Finn's perception surprised Jesse. "It's okay. I get it."

"You do?" Jesse tried to turn to see Finn, but that would

mean giving up the comfortable position they'd found, so he gave up and peered over his shoulder at Finn's shoulder.

"Mmhmm." Finn rubbed his chest in long, soothing strokes along his ribs and down his stomach. "I'm just saying... we could be great together."

We already are.

Jesse's breath caught in his throat. Really, what would be the difference in dating versus what they were doing now?

Besides commitment, and vulnerability, and long-term planning? No, thanks. He didn't want any of that. Not so soon after being burned. But Finn wasn't Dominic. Not even close.

Jesse nodded slightly, wanting to let Finn know he heard.

And as much as he was afraid to say it, that he agreed.

Long after Finn's breathing evened out into deep, slow breaths, Jesse gazed through the darkness at the moonlight spilling over the thick carpet. And he thought about those words, whispered so carefully by the man who held him like something precious.

Even when they weren't fucking—just sitting on Jesse's bed earlier tonight, talking about his past, Finn had held his words safe in the air between them. It had been a long time since Jesse had felt so safe. Not to plan, not to be in charge, not to dream of something more, not to strive to improve himself.

Just safe to *be*.

Finn's words were a challenge to one kind of safety—the stability of knowing there was nothing on the line between them. But it was too late for that. Because there was, it was now clear: Finn's heart.

And... maybe Jesse's heart was already on the line, too.

10

FINN

Finn tipped his head back as he lapped the last few drops from his coffee cup like the elixir of life. The burnt taste trickling across his tongue to the back of his palate invigorated him like the caffeine about to hit his bloodstream.

"That first cup," Jesse murmured. When Finn lowered his mug, he found Jesse leaning on the counter next to him, watching him with his head tilted in interest. His eyes flickered from Finn's throat up to his eyes. "Nothing like it."

"You can say that again." Finn set aside his mug and took Jesse's hand, squeezing lightly. "Thank you for staying the night."

Jesse's grin brightened as he gazed up at Finn. "My pleasure."

Every damn time he smiled, something fluttered in Finn's chest. He didn't want to put a name to it, because if he did, that meant thinking about it.

It meant admitting what was growing between them. And he'd come so close to that last night. He'd grazed the subject, and Jesse had stayed silent.

Worse—he'd gone rigid in Finn's arms for the first time ever. Though he'd quickly relaxed, Finn couldn't forget that first reaction. The first rejection.

"I've gotta get going." Finn tore his gaze from Jesse's with difficulty. It was hard not to get lost in those bright eyes.

The flash of disappointment crossing Jesse's face was hard to witness, even if it was just a twinge.

Finn couldn't bear the idea of ever seeing disappointment crease those beautiful lips. Letting him down... or betraying his trust.

No more pushing him, he decided on the spot. He'd tried to ask, and Jesse had shut it down.

Whatever Jesse wanted, Finn would give him. Or try his damnedest. If that was just friendship and sex... if he was afraid of what romance would mean for him... Finn would be patient and wait a little longer.

"Okay," Jesse said a moment later, smiling at him again. "I'd better go explain myself to my friends."

Finn grinned. He couldn't deny how curious a part of him was. What would he say? Would he admit to wanting more, or would he call it just a fling?

Was it just a fling, to him?

"Good luck," Finn said, keeping his voice strong and steady. "See you later."

"Later," Jesse said, stretching onto tiptoe. He kissed Finn once and then headed for the door.

Finn waited in the kitchen as he heard the front door open and close, brewing himself one more cup of coffee for his travel mug.

This man was going to lose him a lot more sleep, no matter how this played out.

Sitting in town, on the edge of the square, he replayed last night in his mind for the dozenth time that morning. What had it meant?

Then he jumped, patting down his pocket as his phone rang. It was Mike, and the distraction was welcome. His boss probably wanted to check in on their status before the weekend.

"Heyo," Finn greeted, rolling down his truck window to rest his elbow on the sill. "Bright morning out here."

"It is. It'll be a good one. How's the site looking? I won't get any nasty surprises?"

"Not one," Finn promised. Truth was, building always threw up nasty surprises. It was a miracle anything really got built, the number of obstacles that found their way to any given site.

If it wasn't materials taking longer than expected or clients changing their minds, the tiniest blueprint mistake could cause a domino effect. Even the weather caused chaos on a regular basis.

It was strangely satisfying to oversee it all. The responsibility had been overwhelming at first, but Finn had quickly adjusted. Even if he stressed out on the job sometimes, Finn was able to leave that behind after work hours. He liked to pick up again in the morning with fresh vigor to push through whatever problems they faced that day.

"Hey, I got good news. We got a local job."

"No kidding." Finn raised his eyebrows. "Where?"

"Remodeling a place on the east edge of town, by the docks. He's turning the floor above the grocery store into two apartments. Guess he thinks he can rent them on Airbnb or whatever."

"Huh." Finn always liked work in their own back yard. "You'll have to give me the scoop today."

"I'll send an email with everything. Wanna drop by the office later for a look at the plans?"

"Copy that." A new project starting—just in time. They were about ready to wrap up on this site. "Catch you later, then."

"Later, Finn." Mike hung up and so did Finn, tossing his phone into the cupholder.

He closed his eyes for a minute to bask in the sunshine. Soon enough, he'd be juggling timescales and costs in his head. For now, he was happy to sit back and enjoy life.

"Hey."

The voice startled Finn. His elbow hit the steering wheel, sending a momentary honk through the air. "Jesus." He'd recognize that voice anywhere.

But no, it was younger. Smoother or softer, perhaps. Not Floyd, his grandpa. Rain, his cousin.

"Sorry," Rain added. A smile twitched at his lips as his dark eyes met Finn's through the truck window. He raised both hands momentarily for emphasis. "Didn't realize you were asleep at the wheel."

"Not asleep." Finn pulled his coffee mug out of the cup holder. "That's what I've got this for."

"Just daydreaming?" Justin's cheerful voice cut in. Following behind Rain, carrying his own coffee cup, he gave Finn a wave. "Morning! Guess what today is?"

"Huh?" Finn eloquently grunted. Instantly, he regretted it. No doubt Rain was judging. All the fancy, privately educated Harts would have looked down their noses at him.

"Payday!" Justin answered. "Which means getting my own car this weekend. No more bumming rides off you!"

Right—it was Friday.

"Oh, sweet." Finn managed a glance at Rain, but Rain was

smiling as he moved around to the passenger side. "Just in time for us to get a job in town."

Rain climbed into the narrow bench seat at the back without complaint, which kind of surprised Finn. As he got settled, pulling the seat back into place for Justin to climb in, Finn's phone chirped.

Justin kept chattering. "In town? No kidding."

"Yep," Finn said. He slid his phone out of the cupholder and checked it, then opened the message.

It was from Jesse.

GETTING KEYS THIS MORNING. XOXOXO

Finn grinned and tapped out a quick response. *Send pics!*

They'll be dirty. ;) A moment later, Jesse hit with the punchline. *The interior is AWFUL. Dustier than my ass before we met.*

Finn laughed and pocketed his phone with a shake of his head.

"Someone special?" Justin was watching him with a grin.

Finn nodded once. "Sorta. A friend has big news. I'm happy for him."

"Friend, huh," Justin echoed with a nod, sipping his coffee and looking out the front windscreen. "Mmhmm."

"Hey," Finn protested with a laugh. Justin knew he was gay, as did most of the town, so at least there was no *who is she* bullshit to put up with.

Then he caught his breath and kicked himself. Rain was in the back seat, listening in. And he could put two and two together to make six all too easily.

"Anyway, yeah, the new site's in town." Finn diverted the conversation as swiftly as he could, his eyes flickering sometimes to Rain in the rearview mirror as he drove them to the job site.

It was impossible to hide his sunny mood, though. Justin kept giving him smirks that meant *you stud*, and Finn couldn't deny it.

Luckily, instead of teasing him or gunning for the crude details, Justin talked with Rain on the drive, leaving Finn to let his thoughts drift as his eyes skimmed the asphalt ahead.

Last night had been wonderful. Better than wonderful. He'd finally gotten his chance to show Jesse how good it could be between them, and he'd left Jesse limp with the best kind of exhaustion.

Who wouldn't be proud of that? Or of the way Jesse had snuggled into him this morning, burying his nose into Finn's neck as the morning light peeked through the curtains?

For a moment, Finn had been able to fool himself into thinking Jesse was his. That they were just waking up for another morning by one another's sides.

The very first time they'd slept together, and he already wanted more.

As much as he told himself he was going to let Jesse take the lead, every bone in his body ached to ask Jesse out. Properly. Like he deserved. On a date and everything.

Jesse wasn't the only one holding himself back.

Finn's eyes flickered to Rain in the rearview mirror again. He was busy talking to Justin, his face animated in a way it usually wasn't when he talked to Finn.

The distance between them was noticeable, but Finn knew better than to think this rift could heal with a little time spent banging at things with hammers side by side.

Work was one thing. Getting personal was altogether different.

For most of the other Harts' lives, they'd been privately educated, but for some reason, Rain had switched from private school to public high school. By then, he hadn't known any other kids, but they'd sure known about him. His cousin was about four years younger, so they'd only been at school together for one year before Finn graduated. Their paths had barely crossed.

But even Finn had heard the whispers. Rain was aloof, mysterious, and if not for his family name, that would have made him a target. Finn had always prided himself on not acting like that. He'd made friends—and tried to make as many as possible, from all the different social groups in school.

Finn had become a kind of social chameleon, making it clear that everyone was welcome in his school. And yeah, it had been a bit egotistic to think of it as *his* school, but he'd at least been able to use his name to set an example for the other kids.

The worst of the bullies had stopped pretty damn quickly when Finn made it clear that his parents would talk to their parents. Or worse, *about*. Because Finn's side of the family might not have much money, but they had a lot more respect from everyone in town for what they'd done.

It was one of the few times he'd been able to use his name for good. Similarly, Finn found himself glad he'd been able to hook up the guys next door. They'd even gotten the gallery and work space they needed without calling on his name, just his knowledge.

He kind of wished he could boost the whole thing more, but it was better to keep his distance. It would do Jesse no good to get the landowners of the town dead set against him before they even met him.

Oh, here they were. On autopilot, Finn had found a spot outside in the line of construction crew vehicles. He pulled in and scrambled out, then leaned his seat forward and unhooked the belt so Rain could climb out past him.

"Thanks for the lift." Rain stepped out, but as he came level with Finn on the ground, Finn spotted the moment the mask snapped back into place. He'd gone from any other guy to that unknowable man again. Polite, yet cold.

So did Finn. Instead of joking around and clapping Rain on the shoulder, he just nodded once and busied himself with the seat. "No problem."

"The garage says they'll have it fixed up by tomorrow, so if I could get a ride back, too…"

"Yeah, of course. I'm not gonna leave you stranded," Finn said, laughing and slamming the truck door shut.

Their eyes met and he could feel the unspoken comment Rain was holding in. And it was Finn's mistake, too. Any little hint of letting someone down, of fracturing a family, or of greed was off the conversational menu.

"Yeah. Appreciate it," Rain said. He followed Justin toward the framed house, and Finn watched after them, shaking his head.

Whatever Rain was looking for from him, he wasn't going to find it. Finn was here to work, and work hard.

11

JESSE

"Oh my God, we actually did it!" Aaron clung to Jesse's arm like a panda to bamboo.

"Open it up, open it," Ezra urged Jesse, flapping his hands at him.

Jesse laughed, his hands shaking as he sorted through the key ring. When they'd signed the contract and picked the keys up, the agent had explained: front door, back door, dividing door, windows...

"I think this is it." Jesse fumbled to get the key in the lock as all five of them clustered around the narrow opening in the building.

The key turned, the door swung open, and a small billow of dust greeted them.

Beau sneezed down the back of Jesse's neck. "Sorry!" He gasped, then did it again.

"Aaaargh!" Jesse squirmed away from them all and swatted at his neck as he stumbled into the building. "Gross, dude!"

"There's a less than ceremonious entrance," Ross gloomily observed. He shielded his eyes to squint around the space.

"You'll have to light incense to get the bad juju out," Beau teased Ross, who flipped him off.

It was surprisingly bright given the double layer of newspaper lining the windows from the inside. There was a large window that would overlook the square as soon as those were torn down, and a window along the side overlooking the ocean, too.

In the middle of the shop sat a counter, and a couple of empty metal shelving units were stacked against one wall. One door in the back wall led to the stockroom.

Overall, it looked like nobody had rented this place in donkey's years.

They'd been in here once before, walking through it with the agent before the contract was negotiated. But now it was real—the keys in their hands, their signatures on paper, and all.

Rent was dirt cheap, the landlord was willing to let them modify it as they saw fit, and they might even get him to sell—if they showed they were eager to look after it.

"There's a lot of family memories here," Floyd Hart's agent had explained to them. "He wants to make sure the best people get a hold of it."

This was their chance to prove themselves.

Once they'd finished cleaning, anyway. How were they supposed to evict eleven years of dust?

"We're gonna need masks," Ezra immediately decided. "I've got 'em in the car."

They'd brought some of their supplies to start loading into the shared workshop at the back of the building, but they might have been hasty in doing so.

"And bleach. A lot of bleach," Beau said.

Ross wrinkled his nose. "And window cleaners."

"That's us." Jesse grinned at his friends and spun on the spot, throwing his arms out as he twirled. "This is ours!"

"Fuck yeah! We forgot the champagne." Beau mock-gasped. "We should be christening the place."

Jesse could feel the comment coming from Aaron before it even left his mouth. One look at his face told him that. "Oh, Jesse can take care of the christening."

"Fuck off," Jesse told him with a laugh and went to find the right key for the stockroom and workshop.

"Can't afford the champagne until we get the shop open, more like," Ross muttered, which made them all laugh.

The mood was light as they checked out the space, and it didn't take long for them to get ahead of themselves.

"We could have a nice table here in front of the window, and put a higher one behind here for the bigger stuff, like pottery. A standing screen to hang paintings on..." Ezra gestured to the front window while Beau stood by his side and mapped things out with his hands.

"Whoa, guys." Jesse held up a hand. "Let's get the place clean first. Then we'll figure out what we need."

"There's some old fixtures back here," Beau called from the workshop.

Jesse nodded. "I saw them on our walk-through. I'm glad they left them."

"Agent said anything in here is ours," Beau added.

"Ours to find garbage disposal for, probably," Ross sighed.

Jesse cracked a smile. "Ever the optimist. You wanna go check those out, Beau? Ross, you're in charge of windows. The rest of us will work top down. Get the cobwebs down, then walls, then the floor..."

Excitement made the work of cleaning the place up fly by

—as did nerves. Jesse was hyperaware that he had both a home and a storefront to pay for, and no tourists to show for it yet.

He had to trust that if he built it, they would come. But it definitely meant he had no time to spare on things like romance.

Even if Finn's excitement for him was palpable in his responses to every photo Jesse sent. And even if Jesse wanted to grab Finn by the hands and dance around the place and kiss him as he thanked him for encouraging him to just ask Floyd.

All it took was a little elbow grease to smooth the way, apparently, and Finn had been more than kind to him.

He was nothing like Dominic, and Jesse knew it. That wasn't what was holding him back from romance, was it? Thinking that Finn might turn out to get bored with him and shack up with someone else?

Jesse's gut ached, and he scrubbed the floor all the harder, mopping like it had personally attacked him.

No, Finn wouldn't do that. But that didn't mean Jesse felt worthy of his attention.

Why would he be interested in little old me, anyway?

Sure, Jesse had started a business—plenty of people did. He'd moved in next door—that was just convenience, not a good reason to like someone. They had hot chemistry—that didn't mean they could build a good life together.

"We should take a break for lunch," Aaron finally suggested. "I'll go grab something from the store."

"And more window cleaner. And another dustpan," Jesse added with a sideways glance at Ezra. He and Beau had been horsing around, and one of them had stepped on the dustpan, cracking it.

Just managing his friends and this whole project was a full-time job in itself, much less *making* anything. He'd barely made four pieces all week. That wouldn't cover rent.

No, he told himself, his resolve firming again. He couldn't afford the distraction. Not until the shop was open.

As if reading his brain waves, Beau spoke up. He sat on the now-clean countertop, reading his phone. "When should we hold our opening party?"

"As soon as possible. We can do a real minimalist space," Ross pointed out. "Say hi to the townspeople, let them know what we've got to sell—maybe find more people to join in."

They'd talked about it before: making it a proper co-op. Welcoming new members would strengthen them. A lot of handicrafts weren't yet represented in their little group, after all.

Beau nodded. "Bump up the excitement of seeing this building open for business again."

They all glanced out the window at Aaron, who was coming back from the store with loaded bags dangling from his arms. He waved and gave them all two thumbs-up through the huge window, and they waved back.

Compared to even a few hours ago, the place looked great. Better every minute, in fact. Already, they'd had a dozen people stop in their tracks and look inside when they noticed the work going on inside and the paper gone from the windows.

The sooner they were open for business, the better.

"Okay," Aaron panted as he arrived with drinks and sandwiches. "There's one more thing."

"What's that?"

"If nobody else will do it, we should. We gotta do something to make it clear we're here not just to get their money, but to... you know, make things better."

"What's that?"

Aaron pointed with his sandwich out the shop window, toward the overgrown, grassy square with its shabby wooden bench and weed-filled flower beds. "Clean that up. All in favor?"

One by one, they nodded as the wisdom of Aaron's suggestion sank in.

It was going to be a long day.

* * *

"Who knew we were so good at starting parties?" Beau's grin was absolutely delighted, and Jesse had to laugh. "Here, grab this. Aaron? Give us a hand!"

They clustered around the small metal barbecue, shuffling together as they carried it toward the center of the town square. Even emptied of its charcoal, it was solid, but Jesse was used to carrying crates of clay.

"Phew," Beau panted. He dusted off his clothes and sighed. "Good thing I'm in work clothes." The charcoal had gotten all over him, giving him weird, smudged outlines like a living Lichtenstein piece.

"I'm sure Ezra would scrape that off you and reuse it," Jesse teased. "Don't let him near you."

Beau beamed back at him, folding his arms as he looked around them. "Look at this! Isn't it amazing?"

Jesse had to agree. After they'd finished scrubbing the inside of their new space, they'd moved the work party outside. They didn't have many tools, but that didn't turn out to be a problem for long.

One by one, people had dropped by. Some had offered to lend them lawn tools. Others had come by with their work boots on and shears in hand. Cutting down the bushes and piling the greenery into the back of someone's truck had made a huge difference. Then, they'd picked over the site to clean off stray garbage and bottles.

One task at a time, the square had started to shine. The more it did, the more people came to help out.

Better yet, they'd gotten to chat with people: art hobbyists wanting to get in more practice, or knew people who might be interested in selling things. That would help make the rent even more affordable for everyone, if they could bring in a couple more people.

A guy called Scott, who'd brought a lawnmower, had said he was the editor of the town newsletter and he'd promote them in it.

It looked like they were going to have to form that co-op sooner rather than later, and Jesse was thrilled.

"Who owns this place, anyway?" Jesse asked Victor, the owner of the grocery store on the corner. He'd come by in old jeans and a T-shirt just twenty minutes ago to join in the work party.

"Oh, it's town property. But nobody ever seemed to look after it these last few years. What an eyesore it's been!" He beamed and clapped Jesse's shoulder. "Bless you all for digging in and doing something about it."

Jesse watched Ross pulling weeds with surprising speed. He'd been the first to get into the muddy garden beds, and they were already turning bare. Ready for replanting with something else. Something flowering, and bright, and sunny.

"When did you say your gallery is opening?"

It must have been the tenth time they'd been asked that question, and Jesse grinned. "As soon as possible. We're aiming for next weekend. It'll be a bare-bones spot, but..."

"Oh, bare-bones is where everything starts." Victor reached out to shake hands vigorously and smiled at Jesse. "Welcome to town, kiddo. You won't find a better place to live in this whole state. Hell, the whole damn coast."

Jesse laughed. "I hope you're right."

"Mind you." Victor glanced around and then lowered his voice. "Not everyone's gonna be so happy to see this town polished up."

"Really?" Jesse feigned ignorance of the town politics, waiting to see what else would come out. Already, he'd heard an amusing handful of anecdotes and rumors from everyone here—about everyone else.

Betty said that Gregory's business was on the rocks. Gregory said that Victor liked dressing up on weekends in his home. Victor said that Darrell and his twin brother, Dan, had dated the same woman. The twins said people deliberately mixed them up just to wind them up. And on it went.

Most of it, Jesse figured, was a thin approximation of the truth. People always needed something to talk about, or else blown-up whispers would pass for news.

"Uh-huh." Victor nodded and lowered his voice. "Some people like the town the way it is, so nobody is higher and mightier than them."

Jesse's danger flags pricked up. He folded his arms and rubbed them, squinting up at the sun. Not much time left in the day before people started getting off work.

"Good to know," Jesse told Victor, trying to play it cool. He just hoped Victor didn't have stories about Finn acting that way. "Thanks."

His attention was distracted now. A pickup truck had just pulled up outside the grocery store, and a dark-haired man slid out and headed inside.

A familiar pickup truck.

"That's... well, I'll be." Victor squinted. "That's Finn Hart, isn't it? And his cousin Rain. *In his truck.* Cher will never believe this..." He strode off.

Jesse leaned on his rake and watched as someone else got out of the truck, too, and walked off.

Then the driver's door opened and his heart lifted, all other troubles forgotten: Finn was coming to say hello.

A few steps into the road, Finn stopped short. His eyes widened and his jaw dropped. Instinctively, Jesse's heart raced because he was in the middle of the road—not even at a cross-walk—but he reminded himself that this wasn't Portland. There was no such thing as traffic.

He headed to the edge of the square to greet Finn when he started walking again.

"I've..." Finn trailed off, his voice thick.

It took Jesse aback. His heart pounded at the sight of Finn wide-eyed and almost tearful. He hadn't expected this kind of reaction, and now he wasn't sure what to do. Hug him? Apologize? Celebrate?

"I've never seen the square like this." Finn cleared his throat, his gaze finally straying from the people gathered around the barbecue, leaning on the single bench and sitting on the newly shorn lawn together.

Jesse offered a tentative smile. As long as Finn wasn't mad at them for taking over and making this happen, he was happy. "Good?"

"Good?" Finn echoed in disbelief, his laugh short and sharp. "This is... I had no idea you were planning this."

Jesse cast him a sheepish grin, still holding his breath. That wasn't an answer. "It wasn't quite planned. We got done early with cleanup inside. Then we figured we should do something about the view."

"Inside—" Finn turned quickly and looked around the square until his eye landed on the storefront without paper or boards across it. The window gleamed in the sinking sun. The exterior was still shabby—for now—but inside...

"Wanna see?"

"I'd love to." Finn fell into step beside Jesse, casting him little sideways looks. "Goddamn, you don't waste time when you decide you want something."

Jesse burst out laughing. "You should know that by now." He cast Finn a sideways glance of his own.

"Mmm. That impatience has a silver lining," Finn said, his voice quiet and pitched for Jesse's ear only.

Jesse grinned and held the shop door for Finn. "Voila!" He gestured around. "Not much for now, but..."

"It's beautiful," Finn said, but he was looking at Jesse. His eyes were gleaming again, his lips quivering slightly. "Jesse, I've never seen the square or any of the buildings refurbished. Only in photos. By the time I was old enough to remember, the fishery collapse was... well underway. Half the town had already closed." He looked around at last, as if to distract himself from crying, but his fist was curled tightly.

Jesse reached for Finn's hand and stroked it lightly until his fingers uncurled. "I'm glad you got to see this, then."

Finn grabbed him around the waist and hauled him in. This time, instead of a kiss, he hugged Jesse long and tight. Those strong arms enveloped Jesse and crushed him against his chest, and his hand rubbed Jesse's back slightly—like he didn't even know he was doing it.

"It's okay, sweetie," Jesse murmured, his arms around Finn's waist. "Things are looking up." But before he could properly hug him back, Finn pulled away and laid a hand on his cheek.

The warm heat against his skin made Jesse go still. The clamor in his head subsided. He closed his eyes for a moment, resisting the urge to lean into it like a cat.

"Thank you," Finn murmured. When Jesse reopened his eyes, Finn's gaze flickered between them.

"For what?"

"Giving me hope again." It was Finn's turn to smile sheepishly. "I guess I thought this town would slowly dwindle and die off. Everyone my age or younger moves out of town. It feels like I'm personally failing them by not... you know, helping."

Jesse shook his head. Finn was a good man, but he clearly had too much invested in this idea of his responsibility to the town. "It's not your job to reboot an economy just because you're related to someone who founded this place."

"I guess not," Finn agreed with a slow nod. He hadn't dropped his hand from Jesse's cheek. "But I want to see other people discover this place. People like you."

Jesse swallowed hard. Was this a proposition? Was one coming now? Did Finn think this was all a romantic gesture? Because yeah, part of it *was*... not necessarily romantic, but aimed at making Finn feel better about the square named after him, and...

Fine. It was a little romantic. But he wasn't ready for everything that came attached to that word.

"I'm not asking you out," Finn told him, his eyes gleaming with amusement. It was like he'd been listening in on Jesse's worries. "I know you've got a lot on your plate, and I don't want this to stress you out."

He finally dropped his hand to Jesse's shoulder, and Jesse shook his head, resting his own palms on Finn's sides. He stepped closer. "You don't stress me out," Jesse murmured. "Just the opposite. I'm tired out around you."

"Oh, no." Finn frowned.

"No!" Jesse quickly added. "I mean, in a good way. Like I can relax and let down my guard. I'm safe."

That frown vanished, and instead, Finn smiled at him. "Yeah. You are," he promised.

Already, just Finn's presence made Jesse feel more certain. More grounded and focused, and less scattered around all the little tasks he had to do.

He believed in himself just a little bit more.

Jesse and Finn leaned in, meeting each other halfway as their lips pressed together. Right here in front of the window, in the middle of the shop.

Not exactly public, but not private. Anyone could look in and see them. Draw the conclusions they wanted. Whisper to each other until the rumors blew up.

Jesse didn't care. Finn had hope in his eyes at last, and he adored that expression—like he adored every one of Finn's expressions.

Suddenly, Finn pulled back hard and took a step away from Jesse.

Jesse caught his breath, his heart rising into his throat. Had he done something wrong? Said the wrong thing? Had Finn just realized he wasn't that into him?

But Finn was gazing over his shoulder. Jesse twisted to see what had caught his eye.

The dark-haired man who'd climbed out of his truck was walking past the window, a bag in each hand. He looked straight ahead, his lips pressed together, almost like he was deliberately avoiding looking at the square. He did cast a glance toward the shop, but he didn't seem to see them inside.

"Who's that?" Jesse murmured when he'd passed by. He tried not to make it sound jealous or needy, but Finn's whole body language had shifted instantly upon seeing him.

Finn sighed, the sound heavy. Even his shoulders slumped. "Sorry. Lifelong habit. That's my cousin Rain. He works on the same construction crew as me now, but I... I don't trust him."

"Is he bad news?"

Finn was silent for a long moment. His expression was too complicated to read as he stared out the window like Rain was still standing there.

Finally, just when Jesse wondered if he'd even heard him, Finn looked back at him. "I don't know. I hope not."

Jesse bit his lip and nodded, then took Finn by the hand to lead him back out to the party.

He had nothing to hide. If Rain was a Hart, he should be glad they were clearing up Hart Square and bringing people together.

A good dozen people were gathered now, and more were walking toward the square carrying what looked like bags of food. Jesse was proud to be a part of that.

And this time, Finn didn't step away from Jesse like he'd been zapped. They walked to the square hand in hand, and Jesse smiled as he heard the strumming of a guitar.

The tools had been cleared away, the barbecue had been lit, and the smell of roasting food drifted across the open air.

"We used to do parties like this down by the beach," Finn murmured, his voice quiet. Reminiscent. "Bonfires. Again, they stopped when I was just a kid."

"Maybe they'll come back." Jesse squeezed Finn's hand. "Tell me about them."

As Finn talked about roasting marshmallows, hunting

seashells in the surf with his brothers, picking up sea glass with his grandpa, Jesse found himself hanging on to every word.

Even when they dropped their hands, they stayed close together, and nobody else approached to disturb them. Which was good, because Jesse wanted this time with Finn. He wanted to learn about his past and what he dreamed of in the future.

Jesse was certain of it: he liked Finn. And Finn liked him back. He was just waiting for Jesse to be ready.

A week lay between them and the soft opening of their new gallery. On the other side of that week... a whole possible lifetime lay ahead.

The thought was terrifying, but only in the way that a hermit crab settling into a newer, bigger shell might find the space intimidating. And for the first time, Jesse could see himself maybe sharing that shell with Finn.

Yeah. He'd like that. Hart family drama or no, Finn might just be the kind of guy who was worth it.

12

JESSE, A WEEK LATER

"Should we swap those around?"

Jesse wiped his brow and resisted the urge to glare at Ezra. Sure, he had more experience creating displays to show his art. The only displays Jesse had built were towers of bean cans in the grocery store he'd worked at in Portland.

But it had been a long week. Even though they'd set up their new shared working space so they weren't in each other's way, they'd been working side by side getting this place ready to open.

"Fine," Jesse said shortly. He tried to hold his temper in check. They were nearly there—just a few minutes to get through before they all piled into the hatchback and headed home to shower and change clothes.

A shower would do them all a world of good. Jesse couldn't wait to see the transformation from a bunch of young guys in sweaty T-shirts to a group of artists in nice clothes. Not all of them would wear collared shirts and nice jackets, but they had to dress consciously now.

Not that they were trying to look like art collectors, but

image was everything. People would value a piece of art more from someone who looked put together, or at least crazy artistic somehow.

Yet another lesson Jesse's mom had taught him by example. She'd sold the same pieces for twenty bucks at a local farmer's market in a floaty sundress and straw hat, and a hundred bucks at an exhibition in a cocktail dress.

"There." Jesse stepped back for a look, but Ezra ducked around him and walked outside to see the display from that angle.

Smart, Jesse had to admit. He followed, his stress raising a notch or two when he saw the signs over the door.

Arts Bay Gallery soft opening! Come for wine and nibbles, walk away with a new family treasure! 6pm tonight.

In other words: the wine isn't free, please buy something so we can make rent. Now to hope the message was received loud and clear.

They'd had three other artists offer their work for sale on commission already. Given their sparse fixtures, the space was still too open, but they'd filled all they could for now.

"Perfect." Ezra put a hand on Jesse's shoulder as they looked at the window display. "What do you think?"

Jesse had to admit it was tasteful, appealing, and classy as fuck. "Damn. Don't know how you do it," he said, shaking his head.

Ezra gave a self-deprecating laugh. "I've got all those student loans for a reason. Are we good to head home?"

Jesse gave him a sympathetic, almost guilty smile. He always felt a little bad for the majority of his friends who had gone to higher education. Sure, some of them had gotten better jobs than him, but four or more years later. Unlike Jesse, they were trapped there now.

The day's setup work had been a collaboration between the five of them, but they kept looking to Jesse for direction. It was almost uncomfortable now. Jesse didn't want to hog the spotlight or become a control freak. He hadn't expected to make this his own project.

But somehow it had become his—and maybe it was no wonder.

He'd been the one throwing every waking minute into the place over the last week, firing new pieces, staying up late painting and glazing. Always the first in and last out.

Anything to avoid being at home during the evening, just a few steps away from playing with fire.

It had hit him crystal clear after the impromptu square cleanup party: he couldn't keep leading Finn on. With everything Finn said—or more to the point, didn't say—he made his interest clear.

He'd only said yes to being friends with benefits because Jesse had shut down the chance at more. Smoking-hot sex was one thing. But who knew how long he'd be contented to wait around for someone to love him?

A week was a long time to wait, but it hadn't cooled off Jesse's interest one bit. Hell, he'd deleted Grindr and ignored the IKEA cashier who'd tried flirting with him on Wednesday.

No other guy was like Finn. It wasn't just about sex, it was... something else. Something he couldn't put a finger on, because he hadn't let himself.

Until now.

His excuses had run out. Sure, he could keep making them about how he had to make sure it was successful, but that was only delaying the inevitable emotional processing. With the shop open, it was time to put up or shut up.

Jesse's mouth went dry as he nodded. Going home meant changing into his outfit for tonight and getting ready.

He wasn't going to hide his feelings any longer. He'd made up his mind, and no amount of warnings could persuade him otherwise.

It was taking sides in a war he'd never known to date a Hart, but Jesse was ready to plant his flagpole in Finn's soil.

So to speak.

He grinned at Ezra and half hugged him as he waved everyone else out to look at the display and head for the car. "Let's do this."

Jesse's hands shook with nervous tension. It was five minutes to six. A few people had been milling around the town square for the last few minutes, but that was all.

And no sign of Finn yet.

Part of him had hoped that Finn would show up before the opening. His presence would have been a wave break against the tide of anxiety that threatened to flood Jesse.

This was it. Their futures were tied up with this one night, and Finn had to know Jesse was crawling out of his skin with anxiety.

Again, he strode up to the window and shielded his eyes, looking at the handful of parked cars. No red pickup trucks.

Wait. He hadn't noticed that before.

Nobody milling around the park was sitting down on the shabby old bench. Because it was gone.

"Hey, uh. Come look at this." Jesse waved the other guys over. "What's missing?"

"Did someone steal the bench?" Aaron yelped with laughter. "Oh my God."

"I don't think it was stolen by accident," Jesse disagreed. He glanced around at his friends. "We just cleaned up the square. *Then* it disappears?"

Couldn't they see? This was a sign. A subtle one, but clear nonetheless. If they were going to come here and tidy up without asking anyone's permission, they couldn't expect support from the other Harts.

But his friends were all grinning at each other as they moved back to walk around the space once more. The jokes and laughter had reached a halfway frantic tone. Hell, they probably didn't know anything about the town politics. He wouldn't if not for Finn teaching him.

"Come on." Ezra touched his shoulder again. "You should do the honors of unlocking the door."

"Why me?" Jesse's brow furrowed as he looked at Ezra. "I mean, all of you are just as much a part of this."

"Why *not* you?" Aaron had come up behind them, his tone serious. He rested a hand on Jesse's other shoulder.

"It was your idea. You deserve this moment. And we're behind you. Every step of the way." Beau gestured Ross over and then slid his arm around Ross's shoulder. "Come on. Group hug!"

Jesse groaned, but he didn't seem to have much choice in the matter. His friends piled in around him for a hug.

"Dammit, can't I be moody for no reason?"

"I wouldn't say for no reason." As everyone peeled away from the hug, Beau hung on, looping an arm around his neck. "You miss Finn."

"What?" Dammit, Jesse's voice almost cracked. Had one of

them seen them holding hands last weekend? They hadn't been subtle, but was it that obvious?

"We see the way you look at each other. Not just at the square, but since we moved in." Beau smiled. "And yeah, we were a little worried about you rushing into things. But he seems nice, and it's been too long since you dated anyone... nice."

Jesse let a long sigh out and leaned into Beau's shoulder. He was right. Dominic had just been the latest in a string of failed boyfriend attempts, and Jesse's confidence had been sliding down for more reason than just a breakup. "It just seems too easy to be around him. Like there's a catch."

"Why haven't you had him around this week?" Aaron wanted to know. "He's hot as fuck, and ripped. He would have helped lift heavy things, you know."

"I don't want to use him," Jesse said quickly, looking over at him.

"No... you want him to use you." Aaron smirked and looked pointedly at Jesse's shirt and back up to him.

Jesse went bright red while the others chuckled. "Yeah, we saw that. You fox."

Damn it, of course his friends had noticed. He'd taken the ripped T-shirt from a couple weeks ago and upcycled it.

A few stitches in loose pink thread, widely spaced along the gap, held the material together in such a way that it looked like it had been intentional.

Art, and a personal touch at that.

"Easier access, huh? Will we see this shirt again after tonight?" Aaron tried to pinch one of Jesse's nipples while Jesse yelped and swatted his hand away.

"Asshole."

"The best in the state," Aaron told him with a cocky smile.

"Anyway, it couldn't be more obvious who's on your mind. And we like him. We approve, don't we?"

The rest of his friends murmured and nodded.

"Yeah, well," Jesse mumbled. "We'll see if he comes."

They'd swapped texts every morning and night. He'd kept Finn up to date on every stage of the remodel. But there was one thing he hadn't done.

"Did you ask him to?" Beau's gaze was way too perceptive.

Jesse bit his lip. He didn't need to answer. His guilty expression gave it all away to his friends. "Um," he mumbled, his gaze dropping to the floor.

How could he explain it? He hadn't wanted to pressure Finn into attending, especially when he was so clearly worried about the town and what people would think of them being together.

His family, that was. He'd been all kinds of confident around locals, except when his cousin was concerned. And, as their landlord, Floyd Hart was invited tonight. Recipe for disaster, right?

"Lord!" Ross exclaimed. "Get on that, man."

Someone shushed Ross, and then Beau said meaningfully, "I don't think that's necessary."

Jesse looked up so fast he might well have given himself whiplash. And there, outside the window, stood Finn.

Holding a bunch of flowers.

He could hear the barely restrained squeeing from the men around him, and it didn't help him contain his own emotions. His heart leapt, and tears sprang to his eyes.

Maybe it was a gift to all of them. He shouldn't jump to conclusions. It would look like a real asshole move if he assumed this meant more than...

Than what? A neighbor bringing flowers to the opening of

their art gallery? A neighbor looking at him through the plate-glass window like he was a priceless work of art?

Jesse unlocked the door, his fingers trembling on the metal, and pulled it open. Finn met him in the doorway, his smile broad.

And oh Jesus, did he look gorgeous. A crisp white shirt and navy blazer, dark jeans that fit him perfectly. His dark blond hair was slicked back, the front swept to the side, and he looked freshly shaven. He even smelled like a dream, all sweet and spicy. Jesse wanted to bury his nose in Finn's neck and breathe him in forever.

"Congratulations. I hope I get to be the first one invited in," Finn greeted Jesse with that warm smile of his.

Jesse's heart melted. He grabbed Finn around the waist and hauled him in, bouncing onto his toes for a kiss. It was a stretch, but Finn bent down to meet him, one hand flattening against his back.

He tried to ignore the whoops and catcalls from behind but swiftly realized it wasn't just behind him. The handful of people who had been waiting in the square—Cher, Victor, even Gregory—were there, and they grinned.

See? We've got this, he wanted to say, but he was busy catching his breath as Finn pressed the bouquet into his hands and swept him off his feet, stepping over the threshold.

"I'm so glad you came," Jesse whispered, looping his arms around his lover's neck. "For us."

"I came for you." Finn's eyes glinted with a touch of wicked humor. "Over and over. And hopefully many more times."

Jesse restrained his giggle and flicked his nose. "Hey. Behave."

"If you insist," Finn said, steady and mellow as always.

"But only for now." He set Jesse on his feet and looked around, his brows climbing as he raised his voice again. "This place cleaned up pretty good."

"Well, you clean up... pretty good," Jesse managed to retort as his friends moved for the door to greet their guests. He wasn't quite done with Finn yet. Wasn't quite over the fact that he'd shown up despite Jesse's best efforts to give him an easy out.

"And so do you." Finn hooked a finger around one of the threads spanning the rip in Jesse's shirt. His grin was one of recognition.

Jesse beamed at him and took his hand. "Stick around 'til the end?" He glanced up at Finn. "I have something I want to ask you."

From the million-megawatt smile Finn gave him, he already knew what it was.

"I'd be delighted."

"My feet are killing me." Jesse sat on the counter and rubbed his face, looking around once more. They'd at least cleared out the trash—empty cups, snack bags—and returned the tables they'd borrowed from Cher's bar.

The place still had to be swept and probably mopped before they opened tomorrow, but at least they'd set their opening hours to start at noon on weekdays.

They had time in the morning, and since it was near midnight, that was a good thing.

Jesse and Finn were the last ones in the building; the others had walked home together a few minutes ago after meaningful winks and nudges.

Like they'd really do it in the workshop, he'd wanted to protest—and then he'd remembered their first time together. Yeah, he wasn't above a little workshop action.

"Come on out to the square and sit with me. Let's get some fresh air," Finn suggested.

Through the long night of entertaining guests, managing the music, talking about his own art and the co-op concept, and selling pieces... Jesse had forgotten to mention it to Finn.

"There's one problem with that," Jesse said. He beckoned Finn toward the door as he hopped down from the counter and led him outside.

"What's that?"

Jesse locked up and pocketed the keys, then silently took Finn by the hand and led him across the street to the newly vibrant square.

"Oh." Finn spotted it when they reached the path where it had once sat. "Wait, what?"

Jesse lifted his shoulders in a shrug and turned on the spot where the bench used to be. He glanced around, then breathed in a deep lungful of fresh air.

His whole week of stress and worry couldn't be further away now. Just the touch of Finn's hand made it all melt into insignificance.

All that mattered was that they were here together, under the moonlight, breathing in the cool evening air with a hint of salt on their tongues.

If they were silent, past their breathing and the thudding of Jesse's heart—always quicker with Finn touching him—they could hear the lap of waves on the harbor shore.

"It's beautiful here anyway," Jesse told Finn. Then he took him by the hands, twirling himself around and then back again.

Finn grinned and took over steering him, moving in a circle with him as they shuffled across the grass.

Jesse dissolved in giggles a few moments later, letting Finn sweep him into his chest.

It was ridiculous. He'd barely gotten any wine for himself, saving that for their guests, but he felt drunk. Must be the exhaustion—early mornings and late nights—and the sheer relief.

They'd counted the cash before they'd left. Everyone had sold at least half of the pieces they'd displayed.

It was a good start. They weren't home and dry yet, but the signs were there. A few guests tonight had even come in from out of town.

One step at a time, they'd get there.

"You had something you wanted to ask me," Finn murmured, his voice thrumming through his chest and Jesse's cheek.

Jesse pulled away from him. "Mm," he agreed. "I don't want to keep holding myself back. I haven't let fear stop me doing all of this. I won't listen to it now."

"What are you afraid of?" Finn's voice and touch was soft, reverent. The way he looked at Jesse—the way his eyes gleamed in the light, full of understanding and curiosity...

It made Jesse feel special. More than that, feel *seen*. Like Finn understood him.

"Me, I think." Jesse's brow furrowed as he gazed up at Finn. "Does that make sense?"

Finn nodded. "I think so. But if it helps, I'm not." His warm palm cupped Jesse's cheek, and this time, Jesse let himself lean into the touch and close his eyes.

"Why not? I could just... take off back for Portland. All of this could flop. Or I could ignite some new argument between all the Harts."

"Maybe," Finn conceded, but he didn't sound like any of those options scared him. "But maybe it's worth it."

Jesse looked up at Finn, his hopes rising.

The time was right. The way Finn watched him, Jesse knew there was a net under him, waiting to catch him. So he stepped off the cliff.

"Finn... would you go on a date with me? A real date?"

Finn leaned down and pressed his lips against Jesse's for a long moment—then several more.

The kiss was warm, gentle, but firm. With Finn's hand still cupping his cheek, Jesse let himself melt into him. Let himself be weak at last, for just a moment, and trust that he wouldn't be left behind.

When they finally pulled back, Finn's smile was playful. "I think that was answer enough, but in case it wasn't clear... I'd like nothing more. Thank you for trusting me."

Overcome by a hot, tight emotion that knotted his chest and closed his throat, Jesse just threw his arms around Finn and hugged him as tight as he could.

Into the darkness, he whispered, "Thank you for believing in me."

"Always," Finn promised.

And in this moment, Jesse could finally believe it.

13

FINN

Finn flicked hangers aside as he riffled through his closet. He didn't have a lot of formal clothes, but he knew how to mix and match the staples of his wardrobe for the required events.

The Christmas tree lighting, the Easter dance—though the town had fewer events every year, a few were still social calendar staples. And, as his father had told him, they would not be outshone by the *other* Harts.

So the boys had grown up learning to dress well and talk fancy. Not pretentious, like their cousins, but polite.

Finn had suggested visiting Millie's for a nice Sunday supper, so he didn't have to dress up too much anyway. It was kind of a relief that Jesse had agreed. The closest truly classy restaurant was a half-hour drive out of town, so they weren't going there. Besides, there was no better food than at the family restaurant run by Mildred's girls.

Mildred had founded the place forty-odd years ago, and since then, it had been a staple. Her daughters still ran Millie's, and although they were both married now—with college-aged kids—they were always proudly "Mildred's girls." Finn was weirdly excited to show the place to Jesse.

Whatever he dressed in, he'd be overdressed compared to some and underdressed compared to others. So Finn just grabbed the dark red shirt closest to hand and shrugged it on, then tucked it carefully into his dark jeans.

"Perfect," Finn told himself in the mirror and grinned. He combed his hands back through his hair. Even seeing his own face in the mirror reinforced the excitement that coursed through him. He was glowing like he hadn't in a while.

Time to go pick up his date.

Finn grinned as he locked up the house, patting his pockets to make sure he had everything. He strolled next door, heart already pounding. It was tempting to coast down his driveway and then drive up the guys', then honk. But the driveway was filled with two cars—the battered hatchback from before, and another sedan.

"Hey!" Jesse was waiting on the front porch, phone in his hand. He pocketed it and trotted down the steps with a smile.

"Well, hello there." Finn wolf whistled playfully. Jesse had chosen a silky, floral cream shirt. It clung to him beautifully, just like his skinny jeans. They might as well have been sprayed on.

Jesse twirled in the driveway and primped his hair before giggling as he approached Finn and took his hands. "You look handsome, too," he greeted Finn and stretched onto tiptoe.

Finn recognized his cue for a kiss. He leaned in and down, crossing the gap between them to press his lips against Jesse's for a few long moments. Then he pulled back and smiled. "You ready?"

"Always," Jesse answered with a playful wink. He scooped

Finn's hand up and laced his fingers between his, then strode across the grass toward the truck.

"Need a boost?" Finn teased as he walked Jesse around to the passenger side.

Jesse gasped and yanked his hand away from Finn's, then flicked his nose. "Cheeky!"

Finn burst out laughing. He opened the truck door and bowed, grinning as he finally got a blush out of Jesse for it.

Jesse muttered, "Show-off," under his breath and stepped up into the cab. When he was inside, Finn shut the door and headed around to the driver's side.

But despite his reluctance, Finn caught the glow of pleasure on Jesse's face. He'd had a feeling he wasn't used to being spoiled, and Finn planned to change that.

"Any plans coming up?" Jesse asked as Finn pulled out of the driveway.

Finn explained that he was expecting phone calls from a couple of his siblings, and he was also planning on calling a solar panel guy to talk shop.

"You keep in touch with your family?" There was a question that could easily fill the whole five-minute drive to the restaurant. "I mean, I guess you do since... all the stuff you've said before."

"I'm lucky," Finn agreed with a nod. "We're all close on my side of the family. Most of my siblings moved away for work, but my parents still live here. And my uncle. My dad and uncle own the construction company where I work."

"Oh, of course. Cool. So you have some relatives really close to you."

Finn nodded. "What about you? Everyone in Portland?"

"Mom lives about an hour south now, in some little up-and-coming hippie commune." Jesse shrugged casually.

"So it runs in the family." Finn winked. "Co-ops, house shares..."

Jesse's laugh was quiet and sheepish, but still as musical as ever. "Yeah. I like sharing space with people, but I dunno. Mom's much better at it than me. I keep getting all prickly from being around them so much."

"How so?"

Finn listened sympathetically as Jesse talked about arguments over morning showers, window displays, and even what to cook for group suppers.

"If I just lived with them, that'd be one thing. Or just worked with them. But..." Jesse finally trailed off, clearly refraining from venting. His breath was slow and measured. "It's good. I'm happy."

Finn smiled and reached across the console to pat Jesse's thigh. He left his hand there for a minute, until he found a parking space. "I get it. I've lived alone since I moved out from my parents' place. It'd be hard to change that now. Here we are."

Jesse scanned the outside. To his eye it must have looked pretty generic, for a restaurant, but the shutters were painted in the same Creamsicle orange that they always had been. "Okay. I brought my appetite. I hope you did, too."

"Oh, yes." Finn let his voice drop to a quiet growl and smirked when Jesse blushed and scrambled out of the truck. Turning him on was far too easy and a lot of fun.

They took hands as he steered Jesse into the restaurant.

"This is it?"

Finn hadn't expected the tone of Jesse's voice. Disappointment.

"Uh, yeah. This is the place." Finn glanced around the familiar setting—fake plants twined around a few columns inside, light wood tables on one side and booths around the edges. It was set on the coast, and the ocean-view booths and tables were the best. You could watch the waves washing up on the shore below. Like a five-star experience, but at neighborhood restaurant prices.

"Hey," Finn greeted the waitress. "Could we get an ocean table, please?" There were only a few of them, in front of full-length glass windows. That was code for *fancy date* here.

She flashed a grin. "Of course. Right this way."

Finn's guard was up now as he pulled Jesse's chair out, then dropped into his own seat and accepted the laminated menu.

Jesse was polite as he thanked her, but after they were alone, he glanced across the table at Finn. "I thought it was more of a... steakhouse or something."

Defensiveness made Finn's answer quick. "No, it's a family restaurant. Best we've got for miles."

"Oh, I bet it's good if you like it. I just..." Jesse trailed off, then frowned and leaned over the table to touch Finn's hand. "Shit, sorry. I'm not judging *you*."

Even the touch wasn't much reassurance. Finn smiled awkwardly over the menu. "Yeah, it kind of feels like it anyway, though. Everyone in town loves this place. It's not just a restaurant, Jesse." He kept his tone gentle, but he also didn't want to brush it off and let that awful feeling simmer inside him.

Jesse's eyes went wide. "Oh. Shit. I didn't realize. I just wanted to treat you to something fancy."

Finn laughed. "This *is* treating me," he explained. He set aside his menu and took Jesse's hand, his gaze fixed on Jesse's face. "This is where you go no matter what the occasion."

It was hard to figure out how to explain it to Jesse, because so much of his emotional connection with the place was his own memories.

Folks headed to Millie's after a day at the beach, walking the coastal path, or fishing in the harbor. First dates, prom events, and family reunions happened there. It had first become special because of what it meant to the people of Hart's Bay, not because of its menu. But the nostalgia factor was strong now, too. You could go with your parents for their wedding anniversary as a grown-up, but eat the same baked mac and cheese that every kid in Hart's Bay remembered.

There was no other choice, really.

"Oh," Jesse said softly, his gaze flicking across Finn's face. He squeezed Finn's hand and let go, leaning back so the waitress could bring them water. He thanked her.

"How do you feel about garlic bread?" Finn asked Jesse.

They brought out baskets of soft bread that melted in your mouth, but the specialty was the garlic butter. There was nothing like it, and Mildred and the girls guarded the recipe fiercely.

The only catch was that both people on a date had to eat it. They weren't kidding about the garlic.

"I love it."

"Phew," Finn breathed, which made the waitress laugh. "Can we get that, please?"

"Of course."

When she left, Finn grinned at Jesse, who was casting him a slightly alarmed look. "You'll see."

Jesse laughed before his expression went serious. He leaned in. "I'm sorry. I didn't realize you had so many memories here. I was getting all self-conscious, like I should be treating you to something better after keeping you waiting."

Finn just blinked at Jesse a few times. Keeping him waiting? He'd been waiting on the porch outside.

When he saw the confusion on Finn's face, Jesse winced and elaborated. "This week, I mean."

Finn's brows climbed. "Ah." He shook his head. "You told me from the start that your priority was getting this open. Waiting a week or two for a date isn't a big deal, man. I just wish I could have helped more."

"I didn't want to take advantage of you," Jesse said, shaking his head. "And I wanted to wait to ask you out until it was right."

Finn clicked his tongue and smiled fondly at Jesse. "That's not how neighbors act. I'd have helped you out even if you never dated me, babe. You're in Hart's Bay now. I bet a lot of people would have helped you out inside as well as in the square."

"Really?"

"Yeah," Finn chuckled. Jesse's naivety was adorable. *He might not understand yet, but he will*, Finn thought. *As soon as times get rough and people are there for him.*

"I... oh. I don't know how small towns are. People are friendly in Portland, but not *that* friendly. I never thought I'd leave it, even five years ago."

Finn saw the chance to steer the date to more first-date conversation and ask the things he'd been curious about. "Were you born there?"

As he listened to Jesse talking about his life story, the date seemed to reach surer footing. But it didn't take long before the question came back at him.

"I guess you lived here all your life?"

Finn nodded. "Born and raised. I have a photo of myself

sitting at that booth"—he pointed at the corner—"in a high chair. For my grandpa's birthday, I think."

It was the last time the family had gotten together. Back then, without all the cousins, they'd filled the booth and two tables beside it. He'd heard vague references to that day since, but nobody would quite tell him what had gone on.

"Oh." Jesse lit up and glanced at the booth he'd pointed out, then back to him. "I hope I get to see photographic proof."

"I'll show you when I'm home," Finn promised, laughing. "I was an ugly baby, though."

"What?" Jesse gasped and laughed. "No! There are no ugly babies."

Finn raised a brow. "That's a nice fiction."

That made Jesse burst out laughing. The sound was absolutely gorgeous—it filled his heart.

"And I came here for my first date," Finn told Jesse with a slow smile. "And prom. And my first gay date..."

"Oh, wow," Jesse breathed out. Now Finn could see him getting it—the meaning in this place, far more than the tacky decor and plastic menus.

Finn smiled. Even though it was sometimes a pain in the ass to have such deep connections to the place he lived, it was also special sometimes. Every street in town was imbued with layers of memory from his years here.

Hanging out with friends and playing in the park; family trips to the beach; graduating high school and getting his first job at Hart & Hart Construction.

As embarrassing as it was to have his whole life on display for the curious onlookers, Finn also knew them—their kids and families, their past, and, for some of them, plans for the future.

They had a beautiful community, and it had always hurt

his heart watching it slowly disintegrate like sand washed away by the relentless tide of life.

The garlic bread wowed Jesse, and so did the Parmesan pork chops and mashed potatoes with fresh green beans. They kept chatting about their lives, sharing tidbits that Finn meticulously stored away.

Everything Jesse said just fascinated him. From the anecdotes of Jesse's mom running into trouble with the HOA for her wildflower meadows in the yard to Jesse talking about the forums where he'd hung out as a young teen, trying to find people like him...

Finn couldn't stop thinking about how Jesse had been bullied, a constant background hum behind all these stories. That was fucking hard to think of. Sweet, kind, loyal Jesse being treated like shit just because he was brave enough to know who he was at an age where most people didn't? Finn just wanted to sweep him away from the world.

"I came out a lot later, it sounds like," Finn told Jesse. The dishes were cleared, and they were waiting for dessert. He was holding Jesse's hand over the table, stroking along his thumb gently. "Ten years ago now, so I was nineteen. God, I was so different back then. I had my first gay date at one of these tables. I don't remember which. I was a nervous wreck," Finn laughed.

Jesse laughed, too, but not in a mean way. "How so?"

"I wouldn't even hold his hand under the table until the very end." Finn smiled fondly, shaking his head.

"Who was he?"

"Oh, I barely remember him. A guy who lived farther up the coast. He was the classic surfer boy. We met at a gay bar in Portland and swapped numbers. Then we met here." Finn laughed sheepishly. "Totally wrong for me, but I realized I could never go back to trying to date girls."

"Did you think you were straight? Or were you fighting it?" Jesse's voice was quiet and understanding, and even though Finn had never shared these details with a love interest before, it only seemed natural to spill now.

He could trust Jesse.

"I was fighting it," Finn admitted. "Apparently everyone knew when I was four. But I was so worried about what they would think. Even though I knew we're on the friggin' West Coast, in a whole bubble of happiness where nobody cares... somehow it was different because it was me. I'm the oldest kid. I was supposed to continue the family name."

"Luckily you have siblings for that." Jesse grinned. "And besides, who says you can't?"

"Back then things were different," Finn said, though it was hardly necessary. His lips twitched into a smile. "And I have more gay siblings than statistics would support."

Jesse laughed. "I'm twenty-four, and even I remember how growing up, gay adoption wasn't even on the radar. Starting a family..." He trailed off and shook his head. "Do you want to now?"

Finn hesitated before nodding. "I think I'd like that."

"I think you'd be a great dad," Jesse said quietly. "As long as you stop holding yourself to higher standards than everyone else."

Finn blinked a few times. Jesse's words cut right through years of self-realization. "You're pretty damn smart, you know that?"

Jesse laughed and shook his head, waving Finn's comment off as their slice of cheesecake arrived. "I'm just good at reading people. Especially when they're good people."

Finn blushed. "Yeah?"

"Yeah." Jesse let go of Finn's hand and thanked the waitress, then picked up one fork. "So here's to us. To living with less fear, with more... us."

"To us," Finn echoed and dug into the sweet slice of dessert, blinking back the heat in his eyes.

In the air between them, a whole new beginning blossomed.

14

FINN

The air was still electric on the drive home. In fact, it was even more charged now. Finn rested one hand on the steering wheel as he drove, and the other on Jesse's thigh.

"And I'm planning this new series for the shop on the coast still." Jesse was chattering about work, and he'd lit up in a way that Finn found simply precious. "I promised the owner, so I can't let him down."

"Mmm," Finn hummed. "I'm sure he'll appreciate it. Are you working with all of them while keeping your own gallery stocked? That's going to be a lot of work, isn't it?"

Jesse's groan was theatrical, and it made Finn chuckle. "It sure will. I'm gonna be working long hours." He covered Finn's hand, his thumb gently rubbing shapes into his skin. "I hope you're okay with that."

Finn smiled at him. That was Jesse's fear, wasn't it? Driving him away? Well, he wasn't so easy to rattle. "Of course," he said. Jesse had been clear about his priorities since they'd met. And one of the things he loved about Jesse was his work ethic. It wouldn't be fair to complain about that now.

"You're a hell of a guy," Jesse said softly. Finn glanced sideways as he waited at a stop sign, and he caught Jesse watching him. Studying him.

It was rare that he blushed, but his face definitely went all hot there. "Uh. Thanks."

"No, really," Jesse chuckled. "You've been nothing but patient with me. Except in bed."

Like that, a jolt of heat interrupted all rational thought. "Uh-huh." Finn kept his eyes firmly on the road, but Jesse's touch slid from Finn's hand up his wrist and along his arm.

Inch by inch, the warm pressure of Jesse's hand lit up nerves under his forearms, the crook of his elbow, and along his biceps. By the time Jesse's hand reached his shoulder and slid forward, over his chest, Finn's breath rasped.

Pulling into his driveway came on autopilot, thankfully, because he was already painfully hard in his pants by the time he fumbled to shut off the truck and unfasten his seat belt.

Jesse unbuckled and slid over the seat in one smooth motion, shoving his way past the console until he squeezed between Finn and the wheel.

"Fuck," Finn gasped. There were suddenly too many limbs to keep track of, and Jesse's lips were on his.

They kissed hard and fast, mouths seeking each other in the dark stillness of the parked truck. Finn grabbed Jesse's ass to haul him closer. The slender little thing might fit in the gap, but it was a squeeze.

Just like how Jesse fit into his life.

"Inside," Jesse whispered. "Before I suck your cock here in the driveway. I was debating road head there. Shame that drive's so quick."

Finn seemed to have forgotten how to say anything besides the all-purpose sound of agreement and horniness.

"*Fuck*," he gasped and shoved his shoulder against the door to open it.

He lifted Jesse down first, keeping his arms around his chest and waist until he was sure Jesse had his footing. Then he followed. The truck door was barely closed when Jesse shoved him up against it.

And he kissed Finn again—right here in the driveway, one knee sliding between Finn's to keep him there as he braced a forearm across Finn's chest.

Finn ran his fingers along the bare skin of Jesse's forearm all the way to his shoulder and then grabbed the back of his neck, hauling him in to devour his mouth.

When Jesse went weak, Finn caught him and then tossed him up like a load of lumber over his shoulder.

"Finn!" Jesse gasped, but Finn kept a tight hold around his thighs.

"You trust me not to drop you?" Finn started walking toward the front door, adjusting to the feeling of Jesse's weight on his shoulder and the hardness undeniably pressing into his arm.

Jesse was quiet for a moment. "Yes," he whispered from behind Finn's head, and he stopped squirming.

"Good." Finn smacked that firm little ass on his way up the porch steps. The low, yearning groan that elicited made him try it a couple more times before rooting in his pocket for his keys.

"Hurry up," Jesse groaned when Finn missed the lock the first time.

Finn grunted and tried again, then nearly kicked down his own door when the lock finally slid open.

Inside they stepped, and he tossed the keys aside, shut and locked the door, and headed straight for the stairs.

Jesse gasped as he bounced on Finn's shoulder, his hands tangled in Finn's shirt. "Not even pretending to invite me in for coffee?"

"Do you want coffee?" Finn stopped at the top landing and swung Jesse down from his shoulder again, setting him on his feet. "Or do you want something else to drink?"

Jesse's eyes were dark, pupils blown with desire. "I want to swallow your load. Almost as much as I want your cum smeared on me again."

Finn growled and stepped into Jesse's personal space, and Jesse didn't move back. He took another step, and now their bodies were crushed together so tightly he could feel Jesse's heart hammering.

"Clothes off," Finn ordered, pushing Jesse backward with his bulk. It was easy to steer Jesse into his bedroom with the size difference between them. He could have knocked Jesse over with a finger.

Jesse didn't resist. When his knees hit the back of the bed, he went willingly, tumbling onto it and gazing up at Finn with such beautiful wide eyes. "Strip me down," he countered.

Finn grinned at him, letting his hunger consume him as he tore at Jesse's clothes. "Gladly."

It took next to no effort to peel his shirt off, but he struggled with those skinny jeans. Finn growled, fighting them down over Jesse's thighs and knees while Jesse squirmed, trying to be helpful.

"Careful," Jesse whispered when Finn pulled on the hem to get them off his feet.

"I *am* being careful. You're lucky I don't just rip them off." Finn gazed up the length of Jesse's body, admiring every sleek inch of skin he intended to lick before the night was over.

Jesse whimpered and closed his eyes, tilting his head back and exposing his throat.

When those jeans were finally off, Finn pounced, crawling over Jesse and kissing the exposed lump of his throat, then the hollow at the base of his neck. He licked each side of his collarbone all the way to his neck, then kissed behind Jesse's ear.

Every touch of his mouth made Jesse tremble and press toward him in nonverbal desperation. It certainly wasn't silent, though, because his movements were accompanied by soft whimpers and squeaks of pleasure.

The sheets rustled and the mattress squeaked whenever Finn shifted his weight to kiss a different spot on Jesse's body. That trembling body under his was so sensitive that the slightest graze of Finn's hand or mouth wrung sounds from Jesse.

Finn wished Jesse could see himself through his eyes right now. He'd never, ever see himself the same again.

"You're the most gorgeous man I've ever laid eyes on." Finn grinned as he pulled back to rain a few more kisses on Jesse's thick, swollen lips. "And laid."

"I'd better get laid fast," Jesse whispered back, his voice cracking. Even through underwear, his cock was straining against the fabric. "Touch me, Finn."

Finn smirked. "I am touching you," he murmured.

"My cock. Touch my cock. If you edge me again, I will..." Jesse trailed off, wordlessly shaking his head.

"Come in your pants? Can't have that." Finn softly laid a hand on the bulge, enjoying the warmth and weight in his hand. He squeezed until Jesse whimpered his name, rubbing the heel of his palm into the length, then up and down until his underwear was damp across the swollen tip.

"Yes," Jesse cried when Finn finally peeled his briefs off

and tossed them aside, leaving him naked. "Fuck me, baby. I need you. I need you so bad I can't think straight."

Oh, Finn knew the feeling. Part of him needed Jesse in a way he couldn't explain with words—only with his body. And he intended to.

Finn wrapped his hand around that length and rubbed Jesse's cock slowly, letting him feel every ridge of his fingers with each jerk of his wrist. "I need to finger you first."

"Please," Jesse whispered. That one syllable spoke of so much desperation and barely restrained pleasure. He shuddered under Finn with every quick, hoarse breath. "Please open me up with your cock. Make me forget my own name. I need you, Finn. I need you in me."

How could Finn resist? He flicked on the lamp and grabbed a condom and lube on autopilot. Then, he knelt between Jesse's legs, wetting his fingers. Even when he let his fingers dance around Jesse's hole to tease him, Jesse's whimper won him over.

In he slid, opening Jesse and enjoying every writhe of his body, every squeeze of pressure around his fingers. Fuck, he was going to feel incredible.

When Finn finally slid his zipper down, his cock burst free. He treated himself to a few strokes of his own hand as he rolled the condom on, just to warm himself up before he pressed close.

"In me," Jesse begged when his tip pressed against him. "Now, baby. Don't wait."

Finn stifled his moan. The hot, frantic desperation between them was only building. This was no tender lovemaking like he'd expected after the intimacy at the restaurant earlier.

It was even better. They were so into each other that they

barely needed to say a word, but they did anyway. Every pleading syllable that dropped from Jesse's lips made Finn want to spread him out and tease him for hours.

But he could do that later. The desire Jesse had awoken under his skin had no patience.

First, Finn wanted to plunge deep inside him and fill him up. He wanted to be so deep inside Jesse that neither of them could think straight. Animal pleasure and no inhibitions, just like that time on the beach. Or in the kitchen. Or last time in bed.

He pushed himself inside, and he nearly lost his mind with the pleasure. There was nothing like the heat and vulnerability of Jesse under him.

As Jesse gave way to his tip and enveloped his throbbing shaft, Finn groaned. His fingers curled tightly into the bedsheets next to Jesse's beautiful face. He couldn't look away as Jesse's mouth fell open and his eyes squeezed shut.

Finn pushed Jesse's knees up against his chest, and Jesse shifted until his knees hooked over Finn's shoulders. That made the angle fucking divine for Finn, Jesse's tightness wrapped around the tip of his aching dick.

"Yes!" Jesse's breath was ragged and his voice thin, but his cry was surprisingly loud. Apparently that was just the spot for him, too.

Finn's mind spun as he plunged deep inside, deeper with every thrust. Inch by inch, he made himself at home inside Jesse, and they were joined together. Body and soul just briefly intertwined until nothing else mattered but the two of them.

It *was* making love—and maybe love wasn't soft and timid all the time.

"That's it, baby," Finn whispered, watching Jesse's expression relax. His body softened just a bit, but his cock twitched even harder.

Jesse's nails raked up Finn's back to clutch at his head, and Jesse pulled him in for a kiss. They kissed in sloppy, open-mouthed motions, tongues and teeth clashing. Soft growls and grunts served as their shared language.

At last, Finn filled him up completely, and Jesse's grunts and gasps turned sharp and desperate against Finn's mouth.

"More," Jesse hissed. "*Fuck* me."

Finn braced himself on his knees, his muscles tight and every movement sharp now. In and out he went, losing himself in the divine heat and tightness that squeezed around him. Every slap of his balls against Jesse's hot skin sent an extra little shock wave of heat through him.

"You feel so fucking good," Finn gasped. The bed creaked under them, and skin smacked skin. The sweat beading his skin only heated him up more. Deep inside, he needed release just as badly as Jesse, but he wanted to wring his orgasm out of him first.

So Finn shifted his weight to brace himself on one forearm. With the other hand, he reached between their tightly pressed bodies to wrap his fingers delicately around the sensitive shaft. Then, he tightened his grip with each stroke, until he was jerking him off just as hard and fast as his hips drove into him.

"Yes!" Jesse's face screwed up again, his eyes squeezed shut. "You're so big it almost hurts. But so good. So fucking good. You fill me up just right."

What man didn't love hearing that? Finn grinned and nipped Jesse's bottom lip, bending him in two with ease. Damn, he loved how flexible he was.

"I want to come inside you," Finn whispered, letting his tone go low and filthy. "I want to watch my load dripping out of your hot little hole. I want to bend you over and use you every damn day until you can't walk straight."

Jesse's whimpers turned to moans, and his moans to cries. Each time Finn twisted his wrist on the upstroke, his whole body shuddered with need.

"I'm so close. Don't stop," Jesse gasped, and then he shivered and gave way, his head rolling back against the pillow. The line of his throat had a sweat-soaked sheen, and his lips moved silently for a few seconds, spelling out curse words.

Then Jesse squeezed hard around Finn in an uncontrollable, stuttering rhythm. They were both hot and sticky as he spilled his load in a few big gushes, and then a few drops at a time. His whole body writhed and squirmed under Finn, but he couldn't go anywhere. Not with Finn's weight on him.

And certainly not with the whole length of Finn's cock driving into him, pinning him to the bed.

"Yes!" Finn gasped, finally letting go of Jesse and grabbing the sheets by his head again.

This was it—blissful, sweet release approached in a thunderstorm of pleasure that started from the inside and worked its way out.

Finn came hard and fast, a cry ripped from his throat by the sheer force of it. Everything else disappeared but Jesse. Just his sweet face, tight body, and hot little hole still shuddering and clamping around Finn's cock.

"Jesse!" Finn growled, his thrusts shallow and quick now as he pumped into him a few last times.

Waves of pleasure gradually calmed, sapping the energy from his bones as he started to go soft enough to pull the condom off and toss it.

"I loved that," Jesse gasped. His hands ran all along Finn's body, smoothing along his muscles and the flat planes he could reach as his knees dropped to the bed again. He lay splayed under Finn, covered in a streaky mess and grinning like the cat who'd gotten the cream.

Finn shifted his bulk off Jesse and rolled onto his side next to him, but Jesse quickly slid a foot over Finn's thigh and threw a leg over him, keeping him in place.

"I was gonna go clean you up," Finn murmured with a laugh.

Jesse's response was soft, breathy. "Not yet. Hold me first."

Oh, he could do that.

Finn slid one arm under Jesse and pulled him gently closer, turning onto his back until Jesse's cheek pressed against his chest, their legs tangled together, Jesse's palm softly caressing his now-soft cock.

It was intimate and sensual and everything Finn had ever missed from sex before.

Vulnerable. That was the word he'd been looking for. He'd thought that was just during the act, but strangely, he felt even more vulnerable now.

Even though he was still dressed—and his jeans and shirt were going to need washing—it was more intimate than lying skin to skin with anyone else had been before. Their hearts seemed to be beating in rhythm.

It took Finn a few minutes to realize what Jesse was up to when he slowly started to peel off Finn's clothing. He chuckled gently and helped, sitting so he could shrug off his shirt. His jeans came off easier than Jesse's had.

"Better," Jesse whispered, pressing his cheek against Finn's bare chest. The hum of contentment that vibrated through his chest was impossible to misinterpret.

That same deep contentment drew Finn's eyelids closed,

and it took all he had to resist until Jesse's hold loosened and he let him grab tissues to clean them up.

They didn't have to exchange a word to agree that Jesse was staying the night. Finn drew the covers gently across them both and turned out the bedside lamp.

Listening to Jesse's deep, even breaths in the darkness, Finn closed his eyes and knew peace like he never had.

One thing was for certain: there was no turning back now.

JESSE

"Well, good morning, sunshine."

Jesse tried not to laugh as he strolled into the kitchen to find Ezra and Beau by the coffeemaker, their brows arched in nearly identical expressions.

"Good morning," he answered and headed for the cupboard. He grabbed a mug and braced for the questions from his friends.

Instead, Ezra just smiled. "Had a good time?"

Jesse didn't ask how they knew where he'd been last night. He hadn't told them it was a date, but Beau had spotted him getting dressed in his best outfit yesterday and sneaking out of the house to wait on the porch.

"Um, yeah." Weirdly, they didn't even tease Jesse for his blush. They did grin at each other, though.

"Are you on your way to the shop?" Jesse asked.

Ezra nodded. "Ross is walking down later, and Aaron's got the early shift at work. We can drive together."

"Perfect," Jesse agreed. He grabbed cereal while Ezra filled his mug, then nodded his thanks and crashed at the kitchen table.

Monday brought its own challenges—they were going to have to figure out how to man the shop while fairly splitting the work time. All of them had their own working rhythms to figure out how to fit together plus covering the cash register.

"I was thinking we should set a grand opening date ASAP," Beau told him, sitting opposite.

Jesse grunted around his mouthful of Cheerios and nodded for Beau to go on.

"Then we can get more attention through the summer. Write to the local newspapers. Invite our parents. Maybe invite the mayor... you know, that kind of stuff." Beau gestured as he spoke, underscoring his words.

Jesse's mind was already on the practicality of inviting his mom to town. She'd need at least a few days' notice to figure out whose car she could share. The mountain community where she lived now split vehicles.

That life was too isolated for Jesse, and even his mom hadn't sounded entirely happy about being far away from him. Jesse still wanted to have friends and a life of his own.

And maybe a boyfriend.

Jesse's cheeks flushed. "Yeah. Sorry for dropping the ball, I should have thought that."

"You've been a bit distracted this weekend." Beau grinned.

Jesse cleared his throat and looked down into his bowl. He should really tell them about his date, but it still felt too vulnerable. He was handing his heart to another guy already, and it felt too soon. The last thing he wanted was for them to think he wasn't serious about Finn.

They wanted him to have a hookup, a bit of fun to get

Dominic out of his system. Not a boyfriend—not again, so soon.

"I'll arrange the grand opening," Beau promised. "Maybe at the end of the summer? Last weekend of August?"

Oh, man. That was barely over a month away. They'd barely been able to afford the wine for the soft opening! Jesse inhaled the last of his Cheerios and coughed while Beau smacked his back.

But Beau was right. The sooner, the better. They only needed a few weeks to build up the hype.

"Perfect," Jesse managed after he gulped coffee to clear his airway. "Then we can see if we can get a beach bonfire going."

"Beach bonfire?" Ezra thoughtfully nodded. "That would be fun."

"The town used to have them." Jesse stood up to toss his bowl into the sink and finish his mug of coffee.

"Oh yeah?" Beau rubbed his hands together. Jesse could see him already planning posters and sourcing chairs. There was nothing to build community like a good party.

Ezra grinned. "Someone's been studying their history books. Sneaking out to do extra homework."

"It wasn't that long ago," Jesse said with a shake of his head, pretending desperately not to understand the teasing. "Actually, I bet if we talk to Cher or Victor, they'll help sponsor it."

"Everyone was really happy about the cleanup at Hart Square," Beau agreed, clapping his hands once and standing up. "It's a plan."

"Not everyone," Jesse murmured, his mind drifting back to the bench that had suddenly gone missing. It hadn't shown up all fixed again, Grinch-style.

While he hadn't asked Finn, not wanting to rub salt in old

wounds, he could only assume it had been sponsored by the Harts. They seemed to own everything else in this fucking town.

But his friends ignored him as they chattered about plans for the grand opening and beach barbecue. They quickly decided they could set up some workstations of their own on the beach to show townspeople how their art was made, or else do an open house of the workshop.

All Jesse wanted was to have a lump of clay in his hands while he pumped the foot pedal. He daydreamed already of using his fingers to sculpt it into something perfectly individual, yet part of a cohesive group... just like himself and his friends. Especially after a bit of time with their feet to the fire, and a different splash of paint on each of them.

Maybe something inspired by the town. His mind cast over color choices and thematic possibilities. Fish would be too obvious, wouldn't it? But people here still felt deep ties to the ocean and the fishery, as much as it reminded them of better days.

Jesse let them plan the event out loud while he did the driving. It only took a few minutes before he pulled into their parking spot alongside the gallery.

The town was laid out for far more industry than happened these days. Each side of the square had a row of shop fronts—the grocery store took up half the length of its side, and the bar took up about a third of its own building. All four buildings were uniform, two stories, and clearly built at the same time.

Their side of the square backed onto the waterfront, with a scrubby field and concrete dock area between them and the waves. The way to the harbor was between their gallery and the grocery store.

Warehouse buildings and docks were about all that was left, so the few people who lived above the empty storefronts or came here seemed to use the area as free parking.

Seagulls were screeching today over the rush of waves. A few boats bobbed in the harbor, but they seemed to live there. The marina was certainly never full. The local seal, apparently named Lucy, was the most active resident these days.

He lingered behind the others for a few moments, looking at the vast open stretch of blue behind the docks and rusty gangways.

It was easy to imagine its former glory—loads of fish being delivered for processing and packing, townspeople spilling out of the harbor toward the grocery store and bar and whatever else had been in this square back then.

"Shit."

Beau's tone brought Jesse back to the present in a heartbeat. He spun on his heel, looking for the other two. Something was wrong.

Jesse's friends were just out of sight at the front of the building. His steps sped up, and he almost pirouetted as he rounded the corner.

It didn't take long to notice what had drawn Beau's ire: raw egg splattered across the front glass. It had dried into an ugly mess, bits of shell stuck to the glass.

Ezra swiped the keys from Jesse's hand and unlocked the gallery, pushing his way inside. A moment later, he was back in the doorway. "The window's intact, I think."

"Well, thank God for that much," Beau said, drawing a deep breath and letting it out.

Jesse was still frozen on the spot.

Gradually, after Beau took his hands and squeezed, he

became aware that they'd been shaking. So was the rest of him. His lips felt numb, and his stomach was roiling with emotion.

"Jesse? It's okay. There's no damage. Just a bunch of dumb teens, I bet," Beau told him.

Jesse's throat was tight and hot. Just a couple of days after their soft opening? No way was this coincidence. What were teens doing cruising the town on a Sunday night looking for trouble, anyway?

That didn't fit.

"They don't want us here." Jesse's heart hurt. "Someone doesn't." His hands were still shaking, even as Ezra came up by his other side and squeezed his shoulder.

"Look, I bet it'll be easy to figure this out. We call the cops, they ask around, and someone will talk." Beau finally managed to make Jesse's feet come unstuck from the concrete of the sidewalk and led him inside. His eyes were blazing with fury, but he seemed to be keeping it together better than Jesse.

"Maybe," Jesse muttered, his gaze turning to the inside view of the window—smeared all over with egg now, blotting out the view of the square. That had to be a dozen eggs, all carefully aimed for maximum impact.

His friends' voices rang around the empty gallery while Ezra switched on the lights. "You get him sitting down," Beau said. "I'll grab something sweet for him from the store."

"Yep," Ezra said. "Oh, and ask them if they sold eggs last night."

"Great idea." Beau strode for the door, and it rattled, and then it was the two of them.

"Come on, Jess," Ezra said softly, steering him for the stool behind the cash register. He was no bigger than Jesse, but he bodily planted Jesse on the stool. His grip was surprisingly firm and reassuring.

With his weight on the stool, Jesse finally felt like he could breathe again. He leaned into Ezra's chest, and his friend silently hugged him. Ezra's eyes were wet, too.

A few seconds passed as tears burned hot in the corners of his eyes. Jesse felt just as pissed off at himself as he was at whoever had done this.

He shouldn't take it to heart. It wasn't the worst thing. No bricks through their window, no spray-painted slurs, nobody driving by their house to tell them to get out of town.

But it felt like an assault on the last week's work. After pulling so many dawn-to-dusk days in a row, after all the wonderful things people had said in the square cleanup party and at the soft opening...

It seemed to come from nowhere.

Fuck. Not from nowhere. Jesse's breath rasped as Ezra finally let him go. He rose to his feet just long enough to wriggle his phone out of his pocket. "I should call Finn. No, wait. Maybe not."

If they cleaned this mess up, Finn didn't have to know. Because guaranteed, he'd interpret it as a response to...

Well, to the two of them.

And who was Jesse to say it wasn't? Finn knew the town better than him, and he'd been worried from the very start that people would find out.

Was this an attack on Finn, then? Using Jesse to get to him?

There were too many possibilities, none of them good. Weirdly, for a moment, Jesse found himself wishing there had been a note slid through the door or a voicemail they could play back.

Some explanation of what to expect.

"Victor's gonna talk to the guy who was working last

night," Beau burst through the door to say, out of breath. He brandished a chocolate bar and strode up, peeling it open and shoving it into Jesse's hand. "Eat."

Jesse didn't argue. And the sugar melting across his tongue did help jolt him back to his senses.

No matter what caused it, they had to keep their chins up and keep on going. Buckling would make whoever it was happy, and Jesse wasn't going to have that.

Hell, no. Not after working his ass off to make this happen. They were on the hook for a year's lease. They'd signed the paperwork just a heartbeat ago. They still had fifty-odd weeks to make it through.

If every week was a fight, Jesse would fight.

"We're not going down quietly," he finally said when he was done the chocolate bar, licking his fingers and tossing the wrapper in the trash. "Come on, let's grab buckets."

Beau clapped his back and held up sponges. "One step ahead of you. Let's go."

They filled two mop buckets and carried them outside while Ezra carried cloths, sponges, and the mop to get some of the high bits.

It was going to take a good few minutes to clean up this mess, but at least the shop didn't open for hours yet. They had time to make the window gleam like new. By the time customers came by—if anyone did on a sleepy Monday morning—they'd be sparkling like new again.

Jesse splashed a bucket over the window and started picking bits of eggshell off.

Like hell would they back down first, but if this was about them, it was going to keep happening. As long as he and Finn dated, he was choosing sides, and that made all of them a target.

Maybe being with Finn *was* going to be trouble, just as Finn had told him. He hadn't quite believed that the rifts could run that wide and deep in a tight-knit little town like this.

Jesse ignored everyone, pouring his energy into scrubbing every last bit of egg away. What the hell was he going to tell Finn?

And then a voice broke through his haze, deep and piercing. "What the hell?"

Finn stood there in faded blue jeans and a gray T-shirt, his expression the mirror of Jesse's just minutes ago.

Shit. Looked like Jesse didn't have a choice in what to say or when.

16

FINN

It was a pleasure to work in their own town, but this was the first time Finn had ever worked on the roof of one of the Hart Square buildings.

The only buildings *not* owned by Floyd were Cher's bar and Victor's grocery store.

The windows of the apartments above Victor's grocery store were ancient now, and the roof had started to leak. The ground floor had been kept up well, but Victor hadn't had the money to maintain the apartment above it. Now, he wanted to remodel it, fix up the roof, and make a nice place to live.

At least the downstairs was in good shape. As long as they were careful with load-bearing walls, they shouldn't need to disturb the business too much, aside from scaffolding.

Victor had never come out on any particular side of the family feud, but he'd said to Finn's boss that he knew this crew would take care to do a great job.

And Finn planned to. He whistled on the short drive down to town. Perhaps the best unintended side effect was that Jesse didn't know he was working here today. Starting this afternoon, he planned to spend his lunch breaks with Jesse at the art gallery for the next couple of weeks.

Visions of sharing sandwiches while sitting on the dock watching the waves danced through his head. Everything was coming together.

And then he rounded the corner and threw on the brakes.

Jesse and two of his friends—Ezra and Beau—were standing outside the store with buckets of water. And this wasn't just a normal window-cleaning session. Something was splattered across the glass.

As Finn parked and climbed out of the truck, he watched Jesse picking fragments of eggshells off the window.

His gut dropped, and too many things clicked into place at once.

Only one person knew enough about Finn and Jesse to pull this off. Only one person would want to send this message on the morning they started work here.

And now he knew that Rain had the same bitter, spiteful plan for the long game as all his goddamn family. Finn had even been starting to like him, spending as much time as they did together.

Even if he got fired today, he could go back to living comfortably on Daddy's bank account, having sent the message to reignite the war between them.

What was the fucking point of it all, anyway?

Maybe it wasn't Rain, the thought occurred to him. *Maybe it isn't even about us.* But the coincidence was too strong to ignore.

Finn strode across to the art gallery, wasting no time covering the ground between the grocery store and the art gallery. He came up behind the guys, his nails biting into his palms.

"What the hell?"

Jesse turned, and his eyes widened in unmistakable trepidation. "Finn," Jesse whispered. He gulped, sliding his rubber gloves off and draping them over the edge of the bucket.

Finn took a moment to scan the damage. It looked like they were mostly clean now, just a few spots of egg left.

Ezra and Beau both nodded at him but made excuses to send Jesse inside. "We're almost done," Ezra assured Jesse. "Go make sure everything's fine in there."

Finn took Jesse's hand and pulled him into the gallery. He only had a couple of minutes before work began, but he'd use them to make sure the place was safe.

And make sure Jesse was okay.

Shit. He wished he'd left the house five minutes ago. He was expecting Mike to show up any minute, and he couldn't be late to get the work started on day one.

"I didn't know you were coming."

Damn, Jesse sounded out of it. Finn's chest felt tight, and he squeezed his hand hard. "I wanted to surprise you. I'm working across the road for the next couple weeks." He pointed at the grocery store. "Looks like you surprised me, though."

The laugh that bubbled from Jesse was small and sad, and it broke Finn's heart clean in two.

He was going to tear Rain a new one the minute Mike arrived.

"It's okay," Finn murmured and pulled him in for a hug, crushing Jesse against him. He kept his voice soft, even if he wanted to spit fire. No way had Jesse made enemies of his own in town yet. And anyone who targeted Jesse because they wanted to get to Finn was a lowlife.

"No, it isn't."

Finn shook his head firmly. "It will be. I know who did it, and we're gonna outsmart him." He rubbed Jesse's back gently. "I've gotta head across the street before Mike arrives. But I'll be back at lunchtime, okay? You get to work, and I'll join you for our very own *Ghost* moment."

"If you want, we can do that. Please stay alive, though," Jesse murmured, finally cracking a little smile as he pulled away from Finn. "It's a lot hotter that way."

"I'll do my best," Finn teased. He slid two fingers up Jesse's chest to raise his chin, then leaned down and kissed him.

Jesse relaxed in his arms, letting a soft breath out as they kissed like they had all the time in the world. Even though Finn knew he had just a minute, he didn't let his own stress bleed through. Jesse needed him more right now.

When Finn finally pulled away, Jesse smiled up at him. "Go get to work. I've never gotten to ogle hot construction workers out my office window before. I'm looking forward to it."

Finn cracked up laughing and winked at Jesse. "I'll give you a show," he promised. "If not at work, definitely afterward."

Jesse bit his lip and looked up through those long lashes. "I hope so."

When Finn finally left him—several kisses and dirty promises later—he nodded to Ezra and Beau, who had finished up the window. Now, they were dumping buckets of clean water over the sidewalk.

"See you later," he told them and crossed the street to the

building site. Already, the familiar trucks and cars had arrived and parked by the harbor.

Today's task was scaffolding and starting on the roof. Without a watertight roof, nothing else mattered. And that meant Rain was a critical component of their crew—the very man Finn least wanted to see.

It was a couple more minutes before Rain showed up. Finn watched Justin's car drive past and folded his arms tightly as he waited outside the side door. The guys were walking around inside while Mike talked them through the work to be done.

Rain had caught a ride with Justin today, because both of them climbed out together and headed toward Finn with smiles. Treacherous, two-faced smiles.

They leaned in to murmur to each other, and Justin glanced across at the gallery before they reached Finn.

God, don't tell me Justin's in on it, too. Finn had liked him, too. But now he spent all his lunch breaks talking to Rain, and it felt an awful lot like choosing sides.

"Morning," Rain greeted.

Finn couldn't help his snark. "Late night?" he shot at them.

"You know how it is," Rain said with a smirk. It only underscored the fact that he knew. He knew about them, and no doubt he'd told Floyd by now.

Well, fuck him. Finn wasn't hiding his feelings for Jesse. He wasn't going to be ashamed of what they had together, however much Rain gloated.

He wasn't going to let Rain see that he was getting to him. That would only be letting him win.

So he silently turned on his heel, ignoring his dark-haired cousin and striding upstairs.

It was hard to focus on the plan as they joined the other guys for a walk-through: ripping out windows and replacing them, checking exterior walls for water damage, fixing interior walls and ceiling, tearing down some interior walls for an open-plan apartment, and re-roofing...

They had a lot to do in a couple weeks, so Finn had no choice but to shove his feelings about Rain into a box, put it on a shelf in his brain, and get started.

Maybe sweating over some hard labor would help him keep the animal in his chest under check. The part of him that wanted to launch itself at Rain and show him a lesson. The half-formed plans of telling Mike that Rain was fucking up, or even of letting him fuck up by not teaching him something properly.

It was hard to be the bigger man, but Finn had to try. Otherwise it would just give the other Harts more ammunition to fire back, and Finn wasn't going to give them an inch.

If this was the first shot of the war, he wasn't letting them find justification for it after the fact. He was going to fight clean and politely.

Finn was going to work hard and blank Rain. Sooner or later, given enough time, his cousin would end up the one with egg on his face.

And then he'd be sorry.

***

"So to make it skinny, do you just put your palms in like..."

"Whoa!" Jesse exclaimed as Finn suddenly brought his palms together.

The clay flying around between them wasn't quite even. What had been a short, round bowl was rapidly developing a weird clay growth.

"Damn it, I suck at this," Finn laughed and pulled his

hands away from Jesse's. He was sitting behind him, his knees spread and Jesse's body tucked against his.

His chin rested on Jesse's shoulder when he slouched a little, and he easily framed Jesse's body with his own like the scaffolding they'd spent the morning building across the street.

Finn loved being wrapped around Jesse, just like they'd woken up that morning, spooning in his bed. Finn still remembered the warmth of his leg tossed over Jesse's, his arm across his shoulders, hand flat on his chest. The slow, even rhythm of Jesse's breathing changing into a yawn and stretch as Finn stirred.

The heat of his morning wood pressed up against Jesse's ass, and the way Jesse had pushed back against his boner as he stretched.

And the way Jesse had rolled onto his front, tugging at Finn's hip silently until Finn understood: he wanted him to grind against his ass.

Minutes later, his juices coating Jesse's back, he'd reached around under Jesse, stroking him off while Jesse whimpered and pushed himself up onto hands and knees.

The slow, steady, needy rock of Jesse's body against his...

"Finn," Jesse murmured, his voice alight with amusement.

Finn gulped and dragged his focus back to the man between his legs, whose back his erection was pressed insistently against. "Fuck," he murmured for Jesse's ears only. "I was thinking about this morning."

"Mmm." Jesse craned his neck around to peer at him, a mischievous smile on his lips. "I can tell."

Finn tried to bring his attention back to the present. His friends were working just on the other side of the room, and even for them, that would be too bold. It *did* give him ideas for the future, though. "I'm a terrible potter."

"You're great for a beginner," Jesse countered and patted his thigh as the wheel slowed and stopped. "So that's how it works."

"You do that all day? Man, my job feels easy now." Measuring, cutting, laying tiles... those were all methodical, almost mindless. But watching Jesse work—before Jesse had tried to teach him the ropes, anyway—had been something else. Something magical.

The slightest twist of his wrist could turn one shape into another, and he could tell Jesse delighted in the shifting shapes in front of their eyes.

"Thank you for showing me," Finn murmured, kissing the muscle between Jesse's neck and shoulder and easing away. A quick pluck of his jeans hid the semi that gradually faded when he lost contact with that sexy body.

Jesse just beamed up at him. He was splattered in clay, the stuff under his short nails and a small spray of it across his cheek. "You're welcome. Thank you for spending your lunch break with me."

"Trust me, it's my pleasure." Not only did Finn get to spend more time with Jesse, but he didn't have to spend half an hour trying to shoot lasers from his eyes at Rain.

It was a good distraction for both of them: Jesse doing what he loved best, and Finn admiring him work. But once he'd kissed Jesse goodbye and headed back to the work site, that awful, sick feeling settled in the pit of his stomach again.

It didn't help when he showed up and saw Rain sitting on the second-floor scaffolding next to Justin. They'd been looking across the street at the front of the gallery, and they'd definitely seen him come out of the workshop entrance around the side.

Finn glanced up at them, trying to keep his emotions in

check. But all Rain had to do was wink at him and raise the crust of his sandwich in a little toast, and Finn's chest was on fire with the injustice all over again.

The fucking nerve of him.

Of course Rain was in a great mood. He was gloating over his victory, but without ever saying a word.

He didn't have to. They both understood each other perfectly well. There was more than enough family history for that, even if he barely remembered Rain from years ago.

Finn fumed as he climbed up to the roof and strapped in to get back to work.

"How was your lunch?" Rain joined him, apparently ignoring every one of Finn's signals. They'd been silent all morning, and that had worked just fine.

"Good."

"Anything exciting going on in there?"

"Nope."

The second one-word answer Finn gave *did* seem to send Rain enough of a message. He shut up and got to work, and they stayed largely silent for the next hour as they worked on removing the old roof.

He kept an eye on his own safety harness all day. Not that he thought Rain would stoop that low, but you never knew.

At least the next few days were supposed to be pleasant. Rain was a year-round problem in Oregon, but a little better in the summer.

Once, Finn had appreciated summers for the beach barbecues and time off school. Now he liked them for easier construction scheduling. And even on the roof in full sunshine, it rarely got too hot—especially a place like here, right by the ocean.

If the tension building in his chest as the hours dragged by in silence got to be too much, he could always stop for a look across the roof to the wide expanse of the ocean.

The sheer scale and beauty of the nature all around town was a reality check. None of the petty bullshit between their families mattered in the end.

"All done," Finn told Rain at last. "You can head down."

Roofing was a job for tomorrow. Assuming Rain didn't take the chance to climb up here with a hose, it should work out great.

"Thanks," Rain said as he headed to the edge to clamber down the ladder and make for the ground.

Finn stayed silent, not even giving him that much. The more he blanked Rain, the less chance he'd lose control of his tongue and let Rain see how much he'd gotten to him.

It was just like the first day of Rain being on the crew all over again, only now that Finn knew Rain's endgame, he was fighting to work through the fury. He hated being two-faced, so he wasn't going to pretend anything was fine between them. He just wasn't gonna give him the time of day.

And definitely no more rides to jobs. He could rely on Justin for that.

Finn glared down from the roof as the two took off a few minutes later for Justin's car. Finally, after one more walk around the naked roof, he made sure the tarps were secure and headed for the ground himself.

He paused at the edge of the roof, gazing down at the art gallery across the road which was just closing now, too. Whatever Jesse said, he had to be realizing what he was going to lose by being involved with Finn.

It was too late for warnings. God only knew where the escalation was going to lead. As much as Finn fought to keep it in check, family drama spread like a wildfire once it got started.

And word was going to spread. By tomorrow, no doubt everyone in town would know that shit was about to go down.

Finn sighed and gave up his vantage point, stepping down the ladder one rung at a time.

Taking the high road was bullshit sometimes.

17

—

JESSE

"We can't just ignore it." Ezra flipped the sign on the door to *Closed* and turned back to face the other guys.

All of them stood clustered around the cash register. Jesse and Aaron were sitting on the counter, Beau was on the stool, and Ross was pacing the room.

The window was beautifully glossy now, but every time Jesse saw it, he thought of the sight this morning: yolks, whites, and shell bits streaked across the whole length of the glass, ugly in their silent message.

Get out, it had said. *We don't want your kind here.*

"Well, what else do we do?" Jesse raised his shoulders in a shrug. "Release a public statement?"

Aaron snorted. "It's just dumb kids, I bet."

"No way." Jesse folded his arms tightly. "There looked like a whole dozen eggs. Kids might throw a couple eggs, sure. They'd hit all the buildings around here. They don't care what's abandoned or not. Why weren't Cher's bar or the grocery store hit?"

188

"As a former delinquent youth," Ross raised his hand, "I agree with Jesse."

Jesse hadn't expected the support, but he was glad someone was listening to him, at least. He smiled at Ross. "*Thank* you."

Ross shook his head. "I'm still not sure what it's about, but it's not random."

"Okay, but what else can it be?" Ezra pressed his lips together and folded his arms. "It's homophobic. No matter what they intended, they hit up a store full of gay guys."

Jesse groaned and rubbed his face. They'd been debating this all afternoon and hadn't made any headway.

For his part, he was still sure it wasn't that simple. If it were, why wouldn't they have taken the chance to share their thoughts about the men who'd moved into town? Hell, why hadn't they targeted their house?

It didn't add up. His gut instinct told him that wasn't the solution—that it was too simple.

"No way. Finn's gay and they've never done this to him."

"Honey," Ezra murmured, flapping a hand at him, "I don't know if you've noticed, but Finn's built like a brick outhouse. Only a moron would pick on him for being gay."

"So it's because we're a bunch of pansies?" Beau burst out, a cloud of fury written on his face, but Jesse interrupted.

"No, Beau. It's not about you guys. I keep saying this!" Jesse turned to Aaron, whom they were filling in. He'd dropped by after his work shift and nap to catch up on events and figure out what they were all doing next. "It's me."

Aaron looked as skeptical as the rest of them had been about his theory. He was willing to hear Jesse out, though, because he gestured at Jesse to continue. "What makes you say that?"

"Oh, come on. Our landlord hates my—" Jesse broke off. Fuck.

Jesse blanched. He'd been about to say *boyfriend*, without even thinking twice about the word. He and Finn had never even talked about dating yet, just *going on dates*.

And yet part of him was already thinking of Finn like he was attached to him. He couldn't very well tell the others that until he'd asked Finn. And while all this was hanging over their heads, he was afraid of the answer he might get if he asked.

But—this whole situation aside—it was kind of nice.

It had been so long since he'd actually been *happy* at the idea of being with someone. Dominic hadn't made him happy in months by the time they split. The butterflies in his stomach were familiar in a long-forgotten way.

The smirks his friends exchanged might have made Jesse blush with pleasure if not for the fact that this relationship was the problem. He was sure of it.

"He hates Finn, and people have seen us in public together," Jesse picked up the thread of his argument. "Finn knows who it is."

"Orrr..." Aaron drawled. "Someone's a homophobic douchecanoe and the two of you getting together has made them angry because Finn's the town favorite and you're the gay guy coming in here like you own him. In which case, it's still anti-gay."

Jesse's stomach rolled. Now, that was a real possibility, and it made him just a little afraid. If that were the case, what was coming next? Also, why did the idea of having a claim on Finn make him feel so damn giddy?

"If only our pet asshole had left a calling card regarding his intentions." Ross sighed. He leaned on the counter next to Jesse. "Someone around town has to know."

Ezra just shrugged. "No matter what, we can fight back." His face lit up. "I know. I've got it. We make our window display the gayest shit we've got. Rainbow flag and all. I've got some homoerotic paintings. We find Jesse's pink pottery."

"I have rainbow earrings," Beau chimed in, a smile growing.

"No," Jesse argued. His chest was tight with fear.

Even if it was about him and Finn being two men and not who Finn's parents were, Jesse didn't want to spotlight this. He wanted to hide in a hole—by Finn's side—and wait for the storm to blow over.

But his friends shook their heads. They weren't letting him shrink away from dealing with this.

"We don't just hide from bigots. Whether they're biased against us because we're from out of town, or because you're dating Finn, or because we're gay... that doesn't matter. We need to stand up and show that we won't take that shit quietly," Ezra spoke up fiercely. "That we're here and queer, so get used to it."

To Jesse's dismay, the others were all nodding.

"I mean, clearly someone has a problem with us. That bench? You were right," Beau told Jesse.

"Huh?"

"You said back then that it wasn't just kids messing around and stealing it or something. One of the construction guys came in earlier. Looking for something for his wife's birthday. I sold a whole set!"

They paused to high-five him, and then Beau went on.

"He told me the bench showed up down by the beach. Or

the metal pieces did, anyway. It's all burnt out like it was lit up."

A chill ran down Jesse's spine. He swallowed hard and folded his arms. "Right. You believe me now that that was a warning? Then where is this going? A rainbow display will only make them break a window."

Beau snorted. "We're in the Pacific Northwest. Nobody cares if you're gay out here. If anything, people will rally around us."

"And I can put that painting in the window," Ezra gasped. "The one I finished yesterday."

Jesse eyed him. "Which one is that?"

Ezra pointed over to the wall, and Jesse's jaw dropped. He hadn't even noticed the new painting, but it instantly sent a chill down his spine. Two men—unmistakably, from their silhouettes—stood, back-on, holding hands. They were close to the edge of the cliff overlooking Hart's Bay.

One man had broader shoulders and a frame like Finn's, and the other man's short, spiky hair looked... an awful lot like Jesse's.

"That's some gay shit," Ezra declared in a self-satisfied tone, folding his arms.

Jesse shook his head and pushed himself off the counter. He started to pace around while Ross leaned where he'd just been. "I don't like it."

It felt like his friends were using him and Finn as pawns. For all he knew, for models in their paintings, too. Surely nobody had seen him and Finn there, had they?

Finn didn't want to be used for his family name, and with Jesse's relationship with him now known, it felt like trading on that indirectly.

"Let's vote on it. Who thinks we should change the window display to something obnoxiously proud?"

All four of the others put up their hands, and Jesse blinked away the tears that instantly sprang to his eyes.

"Fine. Do what you want."

Jesse knew he was being childish, but he didn't have any more fight left in him. He'd tried his hardest to get through to them, and it hadn't worked.

This felt like it was targeted at Finn or Jesse, or both of them. What little Finn had said today made it clear he knew more than he was saying yet.

The only thing Jesse could do was take on the responsibility of making sure the place stayed safe. And keep his distance from his friends for a few days, until his temper cooled off. Or until it escalated and they realized they'd been wrong about this.

It was spiteful, but so were they. They'd been so damn smart until now. Why did it all have to fall down around this, their first big test?

"Jesse—" Beau started, but Jesse wouldn't let him try to smooth this over.

"No," Jesse cut him off. "Don't talk to me yet."

He was perfectly entitled to be pissed. They were acting like it was an attack on all of them, not Jesse and Finn. While they were technically right, they were totally wrong about the cause.

But nobody would listen for long enough to believe that. They'd never even asked Finn what *he* thought about this before reaching this decision. And Jesse had the awful feeling that they were only about to inflame the situation, no matter who was right about the cause.

He stood and headed for the workshop door to let himself out.

"Let him go," he heard Ezra stage-whisper.

Jesse breathed a sigh of relief when he reached the salty seaside air without anyone following him. He needed space to himself to collect his thoughts and figure out how to ask them not to tank his new relationship before it even started.

His steps took him automatically along the path behind the building. He joined the coastal trail that ran through the trees and up a steep slope.

Without Finn's hand in his, the climb up to the cliffs was much less fun. But at the same time, Jesse needed the outlet, so he poured himself into the exertion.

By the time he crested the hill and the now-familiar sight loomed into view, not only did sweat bead his forehead, but tears pricked his eyes.

Ezra was only being difficult because... well, God only knew why. Lately, it didn't seem like they could agree on anything. But all the rest of them, too?

Sure, Jesse hadn't believed Finn when he'd said how petty this division was, and that it would affect Jesse if he got involved with him. But now that it had actually happened, his friends were still refusing to see it.

Did nobody trust his word?

And now Finn was going to see that display and think that Jesse was using their relationship as a shield, or a token of... town approval.

Using him for his family name.

"Fuck," Jesse groaned. He kind of wished he'd taken over control of the damn gallery. They were all happy to let him take charge of starting it up, but now they could gang up on him in a vote.

Damn it, that was what he was feeling: taken advantage of. Maybe he was projecting in thinking they were using him and Finn as tokens, then. But maybe he was right. He wasn't thinking clearly enough to be able to tell.

He took a minute to lean on a tree by the top of the cliff path, looking around the dark rocks and the water that slowly lapped the cove below. The sheltered bay was a breath of peace, but Jesse could find no peace in his troubled mind right now.

He stumbled down the path to the rocky beach and paced down to the ocean, trying to clear his mind by crouching and scooping up a handful of rocks.

God, he was awful at skipping rocks. Jesse tried for a couple of minutes, searching out flat stones to try. The best he got was three bounces.

He sighed and kicked his toes against little rocks, sending them flying. Slowly, Jesse made his way past the wreckage of the bench that had once sat in the square. It was little more than charred wood and nails now.

Jesse headed up to the sheltered little cove they'd shared just a few weeks ago. As he sat on the rock in the middle, Jesse's shoulders slumped. He hung his head and let the fear that was nibbling at the corner of his brain take over for a few minutes.

The slow, steady wash of waves calmed the anger in Jesse's chest, but sadness only replaced it. A day of hard work throwing new pieces hadn't erased his feelings from that morning—just hidden them.

And here they were, spilling forth again: maybe this was the beginning of the end for the relationship. What was special enough about Jesse that Finn would want to put up with this shit?

Worse yet, maybe this was the town turning on them. Today had been quiet. Their first Monday in business was hardly a reliable barometer, but only a couple of customers all day long was a bad sign.

"Stupid," Jesse mumbled, kicking a rock down the beach.

He'd been stupid to think he could succeed at this whole crazy idea: the art gallery, the workshop, everything. And now it was going off the rails before it had even really gotten *on* the rails.

Just like his relationship with Finn. They weren't even properly dating. But that was no shield against whoever the fuck had such a problem with Finn's relatives that they were willing to take it out on Finn—and Jesse, by extension.

You're just a stupid little boy running after dreams.

Like a brick to the stomach, Dominic's words crashed back into his brain. He'd almost forgotten, after the initial sting had faded.

But that had been Dominic's response when he'd called him out. Like any boyfriend had the right to, he'd demanded to know whose cologne was on Dominic's shirt—who had left the mark on his neck.

The boldness of Dominic's next words had only been matched by their cruelty: *I met a friend and we had fun. It's been going on for a couple months. I can't believe you're pretending you didn't know.*

Jesse, holding in his tears, had told Dominic that monogamy was nonnegotiable for him. So Dominic had come out with those breathtaking, cutting words next. Told him he was chasing dreams for wanting a guy who shared a vision with him. Who told the truth to him, and not half-truths designed to obscure what he really wanted.

Finn had been that guy. Over the last few weeks, he'd

gotten to know him. Well enough to know that Finn wasn't going to like Jesse's friends spotlighting their relationship.

But his friends were so sure they knew best. And they usually did. Hell, if not for Finn, Jesse would have agreed with them. Bullies didn't back down because you quietly cleaned up their mess for them.

Fuck. He kind of agreed with his friends, didn't he? They were doing the right thing, and it scared the shit out of Jesse to be dragged into that with them.

Jesse swiped at his eyes, but the fat, warm tears were trickling down the edges of his nose.

Stupid of him to cry for shit that had already long ago happened.

Stupid of him to want more for himself and everyone else.

Stupid of him to be sitting here crying about it when he could be talking to the others—Finn and his friends.

Why did he just feel like a stupid lump of clay that hadn't been formed into anything useful? That never would be?

Jesse slid onto the ground and rested his back against the rock, stretching his legs out until his heels settled into divots in the rocks underneath. Then, he dug out his phone and dialed without even noticing.

"Hey, Mom."

His mom had picked up within a few rings, as always. "Hi, darling," she greeted.

She always sounded mellow, like nothing in the world could possibly bother her. Jesse drew strength from it, sitting straighter against the rock.

His mom sensed that he had a problem right away. "What's on your mind?"

Oh, God. Where did he even start?

Jesse swiped at his face. "Things are tough right now." He

didn't really want to explain that he was crying over broken eggs. Mom would chuckle and point out that he could use them for scrambled eggs.

"Oh, Jesse. Do you want to talk about it?"

"Not really." Jesse just wanted to hear from someone who would always believe him. He closed his eyes and rolled his head back. "I just met this great guy, and... I don't know. I'd do anything for him, but I'm worried he doesn't feel the same about me. That I'm more trouble than I'm worth."

His mom didn't let that stand. "You're worth all the trouble in the world, Jesse. Any man worth his salt can see that."

Jesse smiled to himself and swiped at his face. "Thanks, Mom." He knew she had to say that, as his mom, but it did help. "I know what I should do. I just don't want to."

He had to talk to his friends and tell them the problem: he was thinking about way more than the egging right now. He was scared to stand up to bullies, and that it would lead to Finn leaving him, and that he was still aching from Dominic. Then they'd think Finn was nothing more than a rebound.

And he didn't know how to explain to them everything he'd found in Finn that had nothing to do with Dominic. But his heart was still bruised from old words, and they'd just poked right at that bruise without even knowing it.

"We all do that, avoid things that aren't pleasant, even if we have to do them," Mom told him. "I'm avoiding chopping these onions right now. Do you want to stay on the phone and cry with me?"

Jesse chuckled. The offer meant a lot to him, but his tears were drying up now. If only he could get a great big Mom hug from her. "I'll be okay," he told her. "I just needed to get that out of my system."

"Okay, honey. If I let you go, will you go do what you need to do?"

"Yes, Mom." Jesse's smile lingered on his lips. "Thank you."

"I'm proud of you, Jesse. Now, you call me tomorrow night, won't you? It sounds like there's a lot to talk about."

"So much." Jesse chuckled and let his breath out. Mom would like Finn. If all this shook out well, and they did get to have their grand opening, and Finn did turn up as his boyfriend... Mom would like Finn. "And can you keep the last weekend of August free for a trip here?"

"I'd love to!" Mom hummed. "It's been years since I last went to the coast. It's a date, honey."

Jesse chuckled. "Great. Thanks, Mom. Talk tomorrow!"

As he hung up, he drew a lungful of air and sat still. In fact, he was so still that he could hear voices in the distance. The close distance.

"Need to bring more firewood down here."

"Sounds like a lot of effort. We'd be better off gathering driftwood. You don't get scrap benches every day."

"You never know. There might be a whole pile of scrap wood nearby real soon."

Jesse's breath caught in his throat.

Rocks clinking against rocks indicated that nearby foot-steps had reached the beach. His adrenaline spiked until he found himself frozen on the ground, staring at the retreating back of a dark-haired man.

One glimpse at him was enough to remind him where he'd seen him before: it was Rain, Finn's cousin. Another man with light, sandy hair was at his elbow.

And as they both reached the seaside, he thanked his lucky stars that neither turned to see him. They were just far enough away at the edge of the tide that he couldn't hear what the other guy said to Rain to make him laugh and grab his ass.

The other guy didn't pull away from the touch like two straight guys joking around. He leaned into him instead, grinning at Rain.

Jesse's eyes flew wide. He eased himself to his feet as slowly as he dared and tiptoed across the rock, one step at a time. When he was close enough to the cliff path, he broke into a run and sprinted.

His heart pounded in his ears so loudly he didn't even know if he'd imagined them shouting after him. Or worse, chasing him.

Jesse's lungs burned and his face burned, but he didn't dare look back until he'd stumbled down the last grassy knoll to the side door of his workshop.

Oh, thank God he'd pocketed the keys before he left. He risked a glance behind him—the coast was clear, but who knew if it would stay that way?

The door was locked up and the car was gone, so his friends had gone home in the time he'd spent crying by himself on the beach like a loser.

Jesse slipped inside the building and locked the door before deactivating the burglar alarm. Here in the darkness and quiet of his own space, he was safe.

For now.

18

FINN

It was hard to miss the change in the art gallery window.

Before, they'd had an understated display: paintings of the seaside, families with kids in floaty rings, and seashells. Jewelry with pearls and bits of shells, or elegant twisting metal designs. Pottery with patterns of vines, elegant flower vases, and the likes.

Now, the display reached out and grabbed Finn by the balls.

A rainbow flag hung behind the stand on which the paintings hung in the backdrop. Two men gazed at one another in one painting. In another, two pairs of hairy, muscled legs stretched into the frame and toward the ocean on a beach. A third was a painting of a peach and cream, and it made Finn's cheeks flush. Even the pottery in the display was pink.

Then, he saw the central painting: two men overlooking the cliff, holding hands. They looked an awful lot like Finn and Jesse.

What had Jesse told his friends? Finn's stomach lurched. It wasn't like he was ashamed, but all the things they'd done had been between them. He didn't like the thought of them gossiping about the wonderful, private spot they shared.

Finn shook his head slowly, trying to come to terms with what he was looking at. The town already knew the newcomers were gay. But this was a statement if he'd ever seen one.

Was this Jesse trading on his relationship with him? Banking on his connection to the Hart family name? Finn's eyes lingered on the painting as Blake's name popped back in his head. Even though he knew one guy screwing him over didn't mean another would, the suspicion was hard to shake.

Jesse was going to be sorely disappointed if he thought that would prevent the storefront from another attack.

It wasn't that Finn was ashamed of what he had with Jesse. He was still going to hold Jesse's hand in restaurants and park cleanup parties. But Finn's dad and uncle would be pissed. They'd worked hard in the last dispute to negotiate a truce between the factions. Jesse getting a rental agreement and immediately setting up a display like this looked like he was gloating.

Like he'd gotten hold of one of Floyd's properties and immediately bragged about it. Anything that benefited Finn or his family would leave a bitter taste in Floyd's mouth. This was going to bring the evil eye to bear on Jesse.

Everything had seemed so perfect at lunchtime when he'd wrapped himself around Jesse and pressed his hands over Jesse's, watching and feeling him work.

No doubt Rain had seen them together. He'd walked right past the gallery to Justin's parking spot. Trouble was brewing, and Finn wasn't sure if it was his job to protect Jesse, or if he'd just been knifed in the back himself. Jesse knew damn well how vulnerable Finn felt, and how hard he worked to keep things smooth around here.

"Fuck," he breathed out, rubbing his face for a few long moments. It was quiet in the square tonight, no sign of the bar opening.

He had plenty of time to think what to do. And as he squinted toward the back of the gallery, he spotted a beam of light streaming across the floor. The gallery was dark, but there were lights on in the workshop at the back.

Finn headed around the side of the building to the workshop door and rapped on it.

When there was no answer, he sighed. "Jesse? Is that you in there?"

The door cracked open, and Finn grabbed the handle to yank it open, expecting trouble.

But Jesse stood there, arms folded over his chest, not even meeting Finn's gaze. He didn't move in for the hello kiss he might normally have.

Every ounce of his posture read that he knew damn well what Finn was here to talk about.

"I... can we talk?" Finn started. "I think we need to."

Jesse made a little sideways shrug and head bobble of an ambiguous answer. "Is this about the display?"

"Yep." Finn gazed evenly at him, but Jesse still wasn't looking at him.

"I knew it." Jesse bit his lip and shook his head. "Okay. Yeah. But not now. Please." Jesse glanced behind himself over his shoulder, and Finn followed his gaze to the gear still set up in the workshop.

As Finn's brain kicked in, it started to fill in the details of the scene, more than just Jesse's downcast posture. His hands and apron were covered in clay, and he was obviously in the creative zone. How late was he planning on staying up and making ceramics before he went to bed, anyway?

None of Finn's business, he reminded himself. He'd told Jesse he didn't mind. And it was true, he didn't—when there wasn't something as huge as this hanging in the air between them.

The elephant was back in the room, and he'd forgotten how awful it felt. Those brief few days of openness about everything had spoiled him. Nothing to dance around or fear saying.

Being forced to bite his tongue while Jesse avoided the conversation by working himself to the bone didn't sit well with him. They'd moved past that already, hadn't they?

"If not now, when?" Finn asked. It was reasonable to want work time to himself, he told himself. It wouldn't kill them to wait until tomorrow.

"I'll talk to you tomorrow," Jesse promised. His voice was quiet, and he glanced around behind Finn, too. He clearly had other things on his mind. "Before work?"

Finn sighed. He hated the idea of leaving now without clearing the air, but Jesse wasn't ready. Pushing him would make waves, and Finn found that hard. Too many years of smoothing things over kicked in.

So Finn swallowed his disappointment and nodded. "Come over tomorrow, first thing. Well, you know when I leave for work."

"I will," Jesse murmured. He hesitated, finally looking up at Finn. Uncertainty was written over his face as he tilted his face up.

Finn leaned in to bridge the distance between them with a little kiss, but it felt stilted and awkward. Something had shifted, and Finn had an awful feeling it might be forever.

It's one night, he reminded himself. He'd waited a whole week for Jesse to come around last time.

But, perhaps naively, he'd thought he never would have to again. It felt absolutely like he was being shooed away, and he didn't like it one bit.

Finn raised a hand in a little wave. "Right. Well, see you tomorrow."

"Good night." It sounded like a final statement, and the relief that bled into Jesse's tone was easy to hear. Before Finn had even reached his truck, Jesse shut the workshop door.

Which was good, because he didn't have to see Finn swipe at his eyes as he unlocked his truck door and climbed up into the cab.

It was probably a good thing Cher didn't seem to be opening her bar tonight. Finn wouldn't find the answers he needed at the bottom of a pint glass, but he sure wished he could try.

Evening turned into night as Finn sat out on the front porch, staring into the distance without seeing much at all.

He couldn't very well use Jesse's car to judge whether he was home—the other guys had obviously taken his car back home earlier, so they must share it sometimes.

Jesse had asked to wait until tomorrow, but Finn didn't mind staying up late to wait for him. He was going to lose sleep over this anyway, if they didn't talk.

Some of the other guys who lived next door had come and gone. Ross had popped out for groceries, and Aaron had come home with a few bottles of wine. Though Aaron had waved him over to invite him in, Finn had smiled and shaken his head.

He didn't want to be waiting for Jesse inside his own home when he came back, like a total creeper. He'd just give Jesse a chance to talk before bed. But even though he'd expected to be waiting a few hours, it was dark by the time he started to grow restless.

Finn could amuse himself by making lists and planning for work tomorrow, but even that amusement had run dry, and no sign of Jesse. That left him with far too much time for thinking, which was dangerous.

The night was a warm one, and the windows next door were all open. He heard Jesse's friends talking and laughing, and before long the guys spilled outside to the back patio.

The noise was a familiar comfort at first, but it started to irritate Finn before long. On Jesse's behalf, he found himself annoyed that they were having fun without him. While he worked, they drank and laughed.

A car passing by caught his eye, even though he knew Jesse wouldn't be in a car. And then he made a face. It wasn't just anyone—it was the humble little Ford Focus that Rain seemed to drive these days.

Not the usual ugly, fancy car his cousins usually splashed out on. For a moment, before all this had unfolded, he'd been dumb enough to take it as a sign that Rain was changing.

Well, that was bullshit.

Then, a thought occurred to Finn. He tilted his head and set down his glass of Coke on the little table next to the wicker armchair on the corner of his porch.

Rain was driving toward Hart Square. He couldn't be off to the grocery store—it was dark now, and he probably would have grabbed food from the store after work. And he wouldn't be driving to the bar if he was drinking. Besides which, most Mondays, Cher was closed.

Damn it, Finn didn't need an excuse to listen to his gut instinct. He was bored of sitting here doing nothing. And he *did* have it in for Rain now. Who could blame him?

Finn pushed himself to his feet and grabbed his truck keys, heading straight for the car. If Rain was planning on a repeat performance, it would be over in seconds. He was already wasting valuable time rather than following his cousin.

His phone was plugged in and charging as usual in the kitchen, and running for it would take an extra few seconds. The keys, however, hung by the door.

After a second of indecision, Finn swiped up the keys and left everything else behind. The house could stay unlocked with the other guys so close by. Hell, some people kept their doors unlocked all the time around here.

Finn's heart raced. The sick feeling in his stomach wouldn't leave. Rain was up to something, and Finn didn't trust that fucker.

Jesse might be trying to shut him out, but like it or not, Finn cared about him. He would never live with himself if any harm came to Jesse that he could stop.

The awful realization that his treatment of Rain might be making him escalate the situation cemented his decision. Because maybe this time, Rain wouldn't stop at egging.

The truck rolled out of the driveway seconds later, but enough time had passed that he couldn't catch up with Rain. But he knew where he was going anyway.

The square loomed into view, and just as he'd thought, Rain's car was parked next to the art gallery.

Here comes trouble.

Finn cursed under his breath. How long had he taken to

get to the truck? He'd been as fast as possible—but not fast enough.

His eyes widened. The workshop side entrance was wide open. Shit, was Jesse still inside?

Finn threw the truck into park and almost fell out of the truck in his urge to scramble out.

Please let me not be too late, he begged himself. *Please let Rain not be the man I fear he is.*

If he'd laid one finger on Jesse, there would be hell to pay. But more than that—Finn might never forgive himself.

19

JESSE

Fuck, Jesse's chest hurt as the door swung closed.

He stared at the closed door, so focused on listening that he stopped breathing. There: the faint purr of the truck starting up and driving past the building.

And then he was alone in the silence once more—just as he'd wanted. His only company was the faint hum of the kiln working overdrive in the corner of the workshop.

He whirled and glared at it like it had personally offended him.

"Well, that's me done," Jesse mumbled. No way could he focus on crafting through the night while keeping a watch on the store, as he'd planned.

But he didn't want to leave now and follow Finn to talk things out. If he was right, they were only going to aggravate things. The troublemakers would be back tonight, and this was his chance to catch them.

Jesse cleaned up after his work session, smashing the half-formed pot back into clay and returning it to his sealed tubs.

Scrubbing his hands clean gave him a way to focus his frustration, but before long, even his nails were spotless.

"Fuck," Jesse muttered. He shut off the water in the long trough sink at the back and dried off his hands, then sighed and turned to take in the space again.

He hadn't really come up with a great plan, now that he thought about it. It was still early—too early for anyone to try to make trouble. Darkness was considering settling in, but daylight still swept the horizon beyond the sea where the sun had just sunk.

If people realized someone was here, they wouldn't take the risk of being caught. So he headed over to turn off the lights, flinching. That meant he couldn't kill time on his phone, or the telltale glow would give him away through the store's front window.

And he couldn't listen to music, or he wouldn't hear the splatter of eggshells—or worse, the smash of broken glass.

Jesse could occupy hours daydreaming, but he could also think of way more fun options. Damn it, why'd he have to drive Finn away instead of just talking things out?

After pacing the workshop for another few minutes, letting his eyes adjust to the light, Jesse had to stop himself from pulling out his phone and just texting Finn.

Explaining himself over text was a bad idea. Relationships were face-to-face. Every time he'd tried to break that rule, no good had come of it.

But Finn was hurt right now. It had been written all over his face, so much so that Jesse hadn't been able to bear looking at him. He deserved a proper explanation, and Jesse would wake up at whatever godforsaken hour Finn did in order to make sure he got it.

If he left now and something happened to the workshop,

he'd kick himself. Besides, he wasn't in the mood to go home and reconcile with his friends. The sting of being voted down without anyone listening to him was still too fresh.

So Jesse settled in to wait.

He quietly made his way to the gallery, clutching a notepad and pencil. After pacing around for a minute, he decided to settle on the stool behind the counter. Less movement inside to catch anyone's eye.

By now, he'd adjusted to the low light. He could even squint and make out a couple of stars outside in the still quiet.

Without the bar open, it felt like the town had settled into a thousand-year slumber. Nothing stirred as long minutes bled together, one into another and then so many more.

Jesse lost track of time as he sketched new designs. They didn't have to be perfect, especially in this lighting—they just had to keep him awake.

And from thinking about Finn's look of resignation for hours on end.

It was worse than anger. That, Jesse could have taken. He could build a shield against it. Disappointment, even, was hard to stomach, but he could rationalize it away.

But the quiet, sad moment when Finn's shoulders had slumped?

Jesse's throat went tight, and he set down his pencil and notebook on the counter to drop his face in his hands.

Through the gaps in his fingers, he spotted a beam of light cutting through the darkness, traveling from the floor to the wall in moments.

Jesse froze. Then, boneless as a snake, he slithered to the floor and hid behind the counter, his breathing suddenly rasping loud in the still. He crouched there for a moment more before scooting to the side and peeking around the edge of the counter.

Just someone passing by. He wasn't sure which way. Maybe someone who lived in the apartment Finn and his work crew were fixing up.

Jesse let out a quiet breath and stayed still for a few moments longer, but there were no raised voices, and definitely no splintering crashes of cracking glass.

Against his better instincts, he crept forward toward the window, swallowing the sudden fear that rose in him.

This was a dumb idea. He should have left this to the burglar alarm and walked out of here tonight. Right now, he could be tucked up in Finn's bed, all their doubts cleared away, his head on Finn's broad chest.

Oh, how he wished Finn were here.

And not just because of the huge plate-glass window in front of him, and the glass front door, and the fact he couldn't keep the alarm on while he was sneaking around in here.

He moved in a crouch, staying as low as he could, even though his knees ached by the time he reached the window. When he did, he looked around. Nobody approached.

Jesse let out a breath again and rose to his feet.

That was when he heard the noise.

Jesse spun on his heel, choking on the gasp in his throat before it slipped past his lips. He pressed his lips together hard, trying to quell the dizzy wave of fear that swept through him.

He'd never known adrenaline like this. Not even walking into school on the first day of a new school year. Because there, at least, he knew what he was about to face.

Jesse slid his phone out of his pocket and dialed 911, his finger shaking as he held it over the call button.

Then, step by cautious step, he moved across the concrete floor of the gallery toward the workshop door. He'd left it ajar when he came through earlier, so he could get a look inside.

Light spilled through it now. Not much, but more than should be back there.

It's probably one of the guys. Or Finn. It has to be them. Nobody else has the key.

Shit. Now that he thought about it, had he locked the door after Finn left?

When he peered through the door to the back, he was at just the right angle to see the door outside, and it was wide open.

For a moment, he was relieved—but only a moment.

Maybe the wind opened it, his thought started, and then ground to a halt. As Jesse moved toward the workshop door, the beam of a flashlight swept toward Jesse. He gasped, reflexively dropping his phone. Like a goddamn idiot.

But he could clearly see now that someone was standing by his kiln. Which was now off, no more warm glow emitted by it. That sabotage could destroy two days of work.

No way was it a friend of his.

"Hey!" Jesse barked, bravery suddenly sweeping through him, steadying his hands. He stooped to grab his phone and shoved open the workshop door.

The man inside was already striding for the exit, his face turned aside. All Jesse could make out was his shoulder and the side of his cheek, and his gait, and the black jacket he wore.

He didn't recognize him. The man was older, with broad shoulders and graying hair. And yet... there was something familiar about how he walked.

Or rather, sprinted for the exit, shining his flashlight straight at Jesse's face.

"Ow!" Jesse hissed, making for the door. He was farther away, though, and half-blind now. "Wait! Come back here, you asshole. I don't even know you!"

"Good."

Stumbling for the door, Jesse jabbed at his phone. He got the flashlight on first and then the camera mode.

"Hey!" Jesse barked, hoping to get the guy to look at him.

And look he did—in time to see Jesse raise his camera.

Only a split second later, it occurred to Jesse that that was a monumentally stupid idea. Hitting the call button would have been better. But he couldn't switch back to his phone now, not fast enough.

Because the guy was walking toward him.

"You leave me no choice." He was suddenly there, wrestling the phone out of Jesse's hand with ease. "You're lucky I don't teach you a lesson, too."

Why did his dark eyes and furrowed brows look so familiar? Had he seen him at the pub? The art gallery opening? The square? Jesse's mind whirled as he gasped, trying to snatch for his phone.

"Give that back!"

"Maybe if you hadn't decided to play cop."

Two things happened at almost the same moment: first, with a crunch, Jesse's phone hit the ground and shattered into pieces.

And then light blinded them both, which made no sense, since the flashlight must have just broken, too.

It was the overhead light, and both the intruder and Jesse cried out, covering their eyes.

All Jesse could see was white sparkles bursting in front of his eyes, but his ears worked just fine.

And the voice he heard next was unmistakable. "Jesse! Are

you all right? Jesus!"

Finn was there, next to him—no, in front of him, shielding him from the intruder.

"Finn!" Jesse gasped, trying to sum up the story.

The intruder suddenly went still, and so did Finn. Jesse mirrored them both, not sure what was about to happen.

"Grandpa?"

Jesse's jaw dropped. His eyes were finally, painfully, adjusting. They were blurry and he squinted, shielding his eyes, but made out the features better now.

Yes—he looked more like Rain than Finn, but there were unmistakable similarities now that Jesse saw him in the light.

And he looked pale and furious.

"Finn," Floyd hissed. "What the hell do you think you're playing at?"

Finn's voice rose to what could only be described as a low bellow. "What am *I* playing at? It's you trying to threaten Jesse and his friends? I followed that car because I thought it was Rain's. How fucking dare you?"

"You don't understand, boy," Floyd snapped, his voice ugly.

Jesse was shaking, looking down at the pieces of his phone. The battery had come out, and the screen was shattered like a spiderweb. No way could he call the cops on that.

Of course! The gallery had a landline. All he had to do was make it to the front.

Floyd's eyes flickered to Jesse, and his grin was just as nasty. "Don't bother. Finn knows better. But you wouldn't, would you?"

Jesse was reasonably sure he'd just been insulted.

"You think the cops will take your side?" Finn snorted. "As if."

"Why don't we find out? The patriarch of this town—well respected by all—"

"Not all," Finn muttered.

"—versus two gay boys trying to stir up bad blood. Old wounds that should stay closed. Well, I don't know what your endgame is, but you can take it back to the big city and stop trying to ruin our town." Floyd stood in the doorway now, looking down his nose at them both like they'd just met anywhere, instead of in a break-and-enter.

"Ruin?" Jesse's voice nearly cracked. "I never wanted to ruin anything."

"And yet you have," Floyd snarled.

Finn's voice interrupted. He walked toward the doorway, his steps slow and surprisingly graceful. As he approached Floyd, his bulk seemed to grow, his square shoulders raising and hands curling into fists. "Don't you *ever* speak to Jesse that way again."

"I'll gladly never see his face again," Floyd retorted. "Or yours, or Roy's. Just remember, you started it. You haven't seen the last of me."

"If you don't get the fuck out—" Finn started, but Floyd was walking away now, almost as fast as he had earlier.

A car engine turned over and then, with a squeal of tires, he was gone. Finn grabbed the door and slammed it closed, then turned the lock on it.

Jesse slumped to the floor, tears pricking the corners of his eyes.

Instantly, Finn was there. His strong arms wrapped around Jesse, the smell of him driving back the fear in Jesse's heart. He pressed his face into Finn's chest and clung to his shirt.

At last, Jesse was safe.

FINN

God fucking damn it, the man was right.

Nobody would believe that Floyd Hart, money-grubber and selfish prick, would try to drive away his own tenants. Not even for their connection to Finn. And if they did press charges or try to report, it would only be starting another family feud. Against Jesse's own landlord, both of their gallery and home.

There were even more unanswered questions now than ever.

"Are you okay?" Finn bit his lip as frustration gave his words more of a bite than he meant. "You shouldn't have stayed here alone. What were you doing?"

"Trying to catch the vandals," Jesse answered, his voice small. His head was tucked against Finn's shoulder, his face turned away.

He sounded so miserable that Finn couldn't yell at him, much as he wanted to.

If it hadn't been Floyd—if it had been someone more agile,

more able-bodied, like Rain—Jesse could have gotten into a world of hurt.

"What happened?"

"He turned off—oh, shit." Jesse squirmed away from Finn and sprinted over to the corner of the room, fiddling with one of the big machines there. "My kiln."

Finn growled. "Asshole." He'd seen how hard Jesse worked and what skill and attention went into making these pieces. If they were ruined halfway through, the clay couldn't even be reused.

"I wanted to get him on camera. So he came and broke my phone. God, I should have called the cops."

"No point," Finn murmured, following Jesse over to the corner. There was a long counter along the back wall, and he leaned his hip against it, watching Jesse fidget with dials and buttons. "The chief of police is one of his best friends."

"Fucking seriously?" Jesse threw up his hands and turned to Finn, rage written across his features. "Does everything in this stupid little town have to be connected to you people?"

Finn sucked in a quick breath. It was hard not to take it as an attack. "I can't help being related to those jerks."

Jesse grunted and folded his arms, looking away now. "Yeah. I know. I meant him, and his people."

Did he, though? Finn shook his head to rid himself of the doubts. Jesse was angry and scared. He couldn't hold that against him. He just stepped forward, into Jesse's space, wriggling his hands under Jesse's folded arms to grip his fingers and ease his arms apart.

Jesse gave a reluctant smile and then chuckled. "Good thing you're so persistent."

"I don't know about that." Finn let go of Jesse's hands and

wrapped his arms around him, pulling him in to sway gently. "I just know a good thing when I see it."

"Even when I've screwed up?" Jesse's voice was small and afraid.

Finn shushed him and grabbed his hips, hoisting him up onto the counter. He sidled between his knees and rested his hands on Jesse's thighs, looking him square in the eyes. "Screwing up is human. I just want to talk to you about it when it happens."

"Yeah." Jesse held his gaze, though his cheeks flushed. Finn wondered what was going through his head as he parted his lips as if to speak, then stopped for a few moments.

Finn gave him a chance to talk. He said nothing, just rubbed Jesse's thighs as his gaze flickered between Jesse's eyes.

"I... I missed you tonight," Jesse admitted at last, hesitantly.

Finn smiled. "Me too." He didn't know how to explain that he wasn't sure he could keep going without Jesse by his side. As much as he'd worried at first... Jesse could show him off all he wanted now. Anything to keep him in his life.

"The other guys came up with the window display. They thought it was a homophobic act of vandalism, not because of us specifically." Jesse spoke low and urgently, like he was afraid Finn would dismiss him.

Finn tilted his head. "Oh." Suddenly, he felt foolish for jumping to conclusions. For assuming Jesse was trying to use him. God, he already knew Jesse better than that. "Of course."

"But I was so afraid you'd think—"

"Exactly what I thought," Finn finished his sentence, his lip crooking into an awkward smile. "Damn it."

"I'm sorry I didn't just say this earlier tonight," Jesse murmured, shaking his head. "I think a part of me is so afraid of talking to you because... well, then all the made-up problems that keep me from being with you will go away."

"And you'll have to be with me?" Given their very conversation right now, Finn held off taking it personally. He sure hoped he wasn't that bad to be around, though.

"No!" Jesse surged forward, nearly slipping off the counter, so Finn grabbed him and steadied him. "Whoa."

"Careful there." Finn pressed close—so close his body started to notice Jesse. It sure didn't help when Jesse wrapped his legs around Finn's waist to steady himself.

The smile Jesse gave him was full of mischief. Maybe it wasn't just to steady himself, then.

Jesse reached out to cup Finn's cheek, his palm soft and warm. "No, I'm... I'm afraid because then you'll have to be with *me*."

That made no sense at all. Finn just scrunched his face up as he tilted his head, looking Jesse up and down like the meaning was hidden somewhere on his body.

"What?"

Jesse's laugh was halfway to a groan. "Look, I... I didn't want to tell you this, but I guess I should. Last month, I got dumped by this asshole. That's why we moved here: I wanted a change, and everyone else agreed that guys are overrated. We made a no-men pledge and everything." His lips twitched into a smile. "That lasted so long."

Finn laughed. "Yeah, sorry about that."

"I'm not." Jesse smiled again. "They were all having problems—family, jobs, guys, you name it. The timing was perfect for all of us to make a fresh start. And I sure did." He drew a breath and let it out. "Especially in the relationship department."

"Yeah?"

"My ex was cheating on me with a bunch of guys. He claimed I must have known about it and looked the other way." Jesse's sigh was heavy, and he finally looked across the workshop. "And he said I'm just a silly boy full of dreams for wanting a man who only wants me."

Oh, Jesus. If Finn had been angry at Floyd, he was furious at this asshole. "What? No. He can suck a whole bag of dicks for what he did to you! You deserve a guy who wants you. And he doesn't deserve an ounce of your thoughts."

"I know." Jesse's gaze crept up to Finn's at last, and Finn almost held his breath as Jesse formed words again. "But I felt all wrong until I met you. You seemed to want me... body and soul. Nothing came that easy before. It had to be some kind of passing thing."

Finn shook his head slowly. "It hasn't passed yet," he murmured. He stroked his hand over Jesse's hair. "I want you even more now."

"Do you?" Jesse leaned backward on the counter, gripping the edge with his fingertips. "Show me."

"Right here?" Finn's grin spread across his face as he looked Jesse up and down. "Not even waiting to get to bed? Kinky."

"You're the one who fucked me on the beach," Jesse whispered, the words hanging between them. "God knows when I'll get to bed at this rate. I want to feel you here, to remind me I'm here. I'm safe."

Finn's chest swelled, and he gripped Jesse's thighs firmly for a few moments. "You're safe with me," he promised in a whisper. He pressed kisses along Jesse's neck as his lover closed his eyes and tipped his head to the side. "And I'll always want you."

"Always," Jesse echoed breathlessly, sounding dizzy. "How do you know?"

Finn ran his hands up the outside of Jesse's thighs, keeping his touch light as ghosts all the way up to his sides. "I just know," he murmured. It was a certainty deep in his bones that couldn't be put into words.

"Oh," Jesse sighed, rolling his head back against the cupboards.

Finn kissed Jesse's throat while he plucked his T-shirt out of his pants. When it was free, he glided his fingertips along bare skin, over his stomach and right up to his nipples.

Every time their bare skin touched, it was like a chemical reaction: predictable yet wondrous every time. And goddamn irresistible, like the compulsion to touch his tongue to a 9V battery.

Jesse's whimper was sheer bliss. It made Finn's length twitch and stiffen in his pants. He dove in, pressing close to layer kisses along his neck and throat, all the way behind his ear and down his neck to his shoulder again.

Finn kept his fingertips still on Jesse's nipples, however much Jesse squirmed. It wasn't until Jesse panted a breathless "Please" that he started to move them.

He drew slow circles around the sensitive flesh, and Jesse's cries echoed around the workshop while his body stiffened and ground against Finn.

Jesse clung to Finn, hands and feet locked around his back, grinding desperately against him.

"I'm going to suck you off right here," Finn whispered. He dipped his head to close his lips around one of Jesse's nipples. First, he planned to take him apart, one lick at a time.

Jesse's nails bit into his shoulders. "Yes!"

Every suck of the sensitive flesh, Finn alternated with

rapid flicks of his tongue across and around it. By the time he moved to the other nipple, Jesse's grunts were urgent.

Without a word, Finn got the message. He kissed the center of Jesse's chest as Jesse dropped his legs from his waist.

Sprawled awkwardly across the counter, it seemed to be all Jesse could do to hold himself there.

Finn grinned at the sight of him: disheveled, hair out of place, eyes glassy, lips parted.

"Beautiful."

Jesse flushed, his gaze flickering to Finn's. Knowing more about his past, Finn could now read the uncertainty, yet hope, in them. Again, his heart squeezed with anger at the asshole who'd ever made him doubt that.

"I want to swallow, Jesse." Finn licked his lips as he wrestled Jesse's jeans open like the only food remaining in the world lay behind them. He was ravenous for Jesse.

Jesse's jaw dropped, those pretty lips forming a perfect O. Then, he stuttered, "I—yeah. Please. Yes."

Finn fumbled with Jesse's underwear, shoving it down enough that his gorgeous, throbbing cock finally sprang free and upright. He groaned in appreciation, taking another moment to look over the sight.

Jesse's cheeks burned an adorable shade of red, but he watched hungrily as Finn licked his lips and leaned down.

Finn started by kissing the side of his shaft, draping his fingers along the length before sliding them into a gradually tightening fist.

He flicked his tongue around the head, enjoying the weight of Jesse against him. Finn was in love with the way he twitched, a shudder running through his body.

"Fuck," Jesse hissed. "More."

There would be plenty of time later to make Jesse beg for

it, so Finn smiled and obeyed. He wrapped his lips tightly around the tip of Jesse, his gaze flicking up to meet Jesse's eyes as he started to swallow him.

He let the length run along his tongue all the way to the back, the shaft wet and glistening as it slid out again. The second bob, he got even deeper, the tip just about touching the back of his throat. By the third or fourth, Jesse's whole shaft filled his mouth with the taste of him. With his need, salty and musky, precious and vulnerable.

Finn's hands slid to Jesse's hips, holding him on the counter as Jesse bucked and squirmed. He bobbed his head hard and fast, sucking in his cheeks.

He loved being in control of Jesse's pleasure, speeding up when Jesse seemed almost able to form words and slowing down again when he was coming along too quickly.

Keeping him hanging here in ecstasy, unable to do more than curse into the great open space of the workshop and squirm on the hard laminated counter.

"Fuck, fuck, fuck... Finn," Jesse gasped for breath. His hands had left the counter by now and were resting on the back of Finn's head.

Finn moaned and moved one hand to Jesse's, encouraging him to grip harder.

Jesse sounded adorably shy for a moment. "Are you sure?"

His mouth was a little full. In answer, Finn just moaned deeply, the vibrations coursing through his mouth and Jesse's cock.

Jesse's moan was incoherent in response. His fingers tightened on Finn's hair, and then he started thrusting his hips in short, sharp jerks.

Finn kept his head still to let Jesse fuck his mouth, and he didn't have long to wait.

The thrusts suddenly grew erratic, and Jesse's gasps for breath loud and rasping. "I'm..." Jesse choked out.

Finn pursed his lips even tighter around the head, wrapping his hand around the shaft to stroke him hard and fast. His tongue teased at the wet slit, and within moments, he felt Jesse swelling and giving in.

"Fuck...!"

With that, Jesse came, his load splattering across Finn's tongue. One swallow at a time, Finn sucked him dry, glancing up at Jesse's blown pupils and flushed cheeks.

He finally pulled back, mouth hanging open so Jesse could see him licking his lips slowly. "Dessert. Yum."

"Oh my God," Jesse mumbled, hands rising to cover his face. The shyness he'd developed was absolutely sweet, but it only made Finn want to do filthy things to him.

Finn grinned, pushing himself to his feet. He ran a hand up Jesse's stomach to his chest and leaned in to peck his cheek. "You're gorgeous, you know that?"

Jesse dropped his hands and smacked Finn's chest lightly. "Shut up and get your cock out." He dropped to his knees between Finn and the counter.

The sight took Finn's breath away. "Okay!" He laughed, but he couldn't undo his pants fast enough. His hands shook as he pushed his underwear out of the way and pulled his thick length free.

"Good." Jesse smacked Finn's hands away, so Finn braced himself on the counter instead and let him go wild.

And boy, did he have an idea of what he wanted to do. Jesse's gaze was intent and hungry. Had Finn looked like that just moments ago?

Finn gasped at the hot wetness that enveloped him, swallowing him to the base of his shaft. Jesse choked on his cock but didn't stop, pulling his head back and then pushing forward onto him again.

"Jesse," Finn gasped, his toes curling as electric shocks ran through his whole body. The stimulation was almost too much—going from the tight prison of his jeans to the tight suction of Jesse's skilled mouth.

Hardest of all to endure—yet most pleasant—was his tongue. Jesse's tongue danced around his shaft, twisting around his head.

"Mmm?" Jesse moaned around his cock. He spread his knees and shifted until the back of his head pressed the cabinet, pulling Finn's hips toward him. With his head braced there, he held still, his gaze flickering up to Finn.

Finn's breaths grew short and sharp as he realized what Jesse was doing. "Can I fuck your mouth?" he whispered, cupping Jesse's cheeks. His eyes were fixed on the pink, glistening shaft that Jesse's lips were stretched around. His cock had never looked hotter than when it was in Jesse's mouth.

"Mmmph." Jesse nodded slightly, his eyes wide and desperate. Like he needed Finn in his mouth so badly he couldn't imagine anything he'd rather be doing.

Finn growled, keeping one hand on Jesse's cheek while the other gripped the edge of the counter. He shifted his stance and started thrusting into Jesse's mouth in short, sharp jerks.

Did Jesse know how goddamn delicious the sight was of his own hardness sliding across Jesse's lips and tongue? "Fuck," Finn whispered, his voice rough with pleasure. "I could do this all day."

"Mmhmm." Jesse's eyes were wide and round but far from innocent as he moaned his agreement. He knew exactly what he was doing to Finn. Sexy, sly little fucker.

Jesse grabbed Finn's hips and yanked him closer, forcing

Finn's cock deeper into his mouth.

"I want you every damn day, in every way," Finn gasped, his thrusts growing harder and faster under Jesse's touch. "You're the sexiest guy I've ever known."

His balls were tight now, his body almost painfully so. Every muscle screamed for release, but he desperately wanted to make it last. But just the sight of Jesse on his knees in front of him made him want to blow his load.

Fucking his mouth like there was no tomorrow? Finn never stood a chance.

He gasped and threw his head back, his grip tightening on the counter to steady himself as his legs shook. That was it—the edge. And he'd just plunged straight off it, and now the water was rising to meet him fast.

For moments, the utter bliss of release was all he felt.

Then, like swimming to the surface, he gasped and broke free from the agonizing burst of heat that had enveloped him. He could think a little again.

His thrusts had slowed and stopped, but Jesse's throat still bobbed as he swallowed the last few drops.

"Jesus, you're..." Finn trailed off. Before Jesse could stand, he sank to his knees in front of him and pulled Jesse in.

Their bodies nestled together as Finn curled his legs up beside himself, wrapping his arms around Jesse's body and pulling him into his chest.

Jesse went easily, swaying into him with a contented moan. "S'was'good," he mumbled.

"Man, was it ever." Finn grinned at the fresh memory of Jesse, so bold and demanding and unapologetic. "I love you," he murmured with a fond smile and shake of his head.

It was only when Jesse's breath came sharp and fast that he realized what words he'd just spilled.

But Finn didn't want to take them back, because it was true. And goddamn it, he was tired of apologizing for the truth.

"That's..." Jesse trailed off, but he wasn't pulling away. "That's a lot to take in."

Finn laughed, the sound sharp and nervous even to his own ears. "I know. But... *I know*."

Jesse was quiet for a few long moments, but he rubbed Finn's thigh and his lower back, shifting to nestle his cheek against Finn's chest a little better. "I love you, too," he murmured at last. "And that scares me."

"If it scares you, we don't have to push it," Finn murmured. "We have time." He couldn't shake the glow of pleasure those words sent through him. He smiled to himself as he gazed toward the kiln, swaying gently with Jesse.

"Do we?" Jesse finally shifted until he could support his own weight, pulling back from Finn. He was still resting against him, but now he was looking at Finn, his gaze searching.

Finn wasn't sure what he was looking for.

"We have to do something about... what happened tonight." Jesse's voice wavered, but he didn't look away. "Report it to the cops or something."

Like fog struck by the sun, Finn's pleasurable high began to drift away. "I..." His chest was suddenly tight. "He was right, babe. Nobody will believe it."

"Both of us saw him," Jesse murmured. "Two against one."

If only the world worked that way. Finn rubbed Jesse's arm gently, then took his hand. He didn't have to say a word—Jesse could read his face.

"The smashed phone," Jesse continued, looking around. "And maybe someone saw him buy eggs."

Finn tried not to shake his head, but the movement—

however slight—attracted Jesse's attention.

And his scowl.

Finn swallowed hard. "I'm sorry. I wish there were justice. But if I start this battle, my dad and uncle will kill me. I'm sorry I brought this on you. If I'd known he'd go this far..."

Jesse pulled away from Finn and pushed himself to his feet, swaying slightly as he got himself decent again in quick, decisive movements. Whatever he was about to do, Finn wasn't sure he'd like it. He stood up, too, and zipped up his jeans.

As soon as he met Jesse's gaze, Jesse folded his arms and raised his chin, staring up at Finn. "That's not good enough."

Finn blinked a few times at the picture of defiance that suddenly stood before him. "Huh?"

"You keep thinking that you're the cause of all our problems." Jesse bit his lip. "You're not. Fuck that shit. Either stand up and be with me, or don't."

"I want to be with you." Finn hoped Jesse knew at least that by now. *Needed* to be with him was more like it.

"Then you can't let the bullies win." Jesse's lashes were wet. "Or else you're just accepting the same old pattern. Accepting your place. Like they won and you lost, and that's just the way it has to be."

Finn's chest grew tight. Jesus, he didn't even know half the family history himself, but he knew enough to know that these feuds were very real—and toxic for everyone involved. Jesse didn't know how bad it could get.

"It *is* the way it has to be," Finn rebutted, shaking his head slightly. "When you've lived here a little longer, you'll see."

"No," Jesse said firmly. "I *can't* live here if my landlord—at home and work—doesn't want me here. Don't you see? This is *your* story, Finn... not mine. In my story, I fight back. Because

I'm sick of slinking off and hiding from bullies. And you can either hide or you can stand with me, but you don't get to do both."

Finn's jaw dropped. He reeled, his cheeks burning now as he steadied himself on the counter.

"I need to think about it," Finn finally said, his shoulders sinking. "It's... a lot to think about." Not that he'd get much sleep, but the night was wearing on, and he was tired, and he wasn't thinking straight. If he answered Jesse now, he might say things they both regretted.

"Okay. I'll get my friends over here. I don't know, but... no, I'll make them listen. We'll figure out what to do." Jesse's voice wavered again, his eyes wet. "And I hope we can count on your support."

"I'll always support you." That much was true. Finn would never side with Floyd or Rain or any of those assholes.

"I'm glad. Really glad."

Finn drew a breath and reached out, glad that Jesse let him take his hand, at least.

With that, he leaned down for a kiss. A short, simple press of their lips together. Enough to tell him that this wasn't a breakup. "I'll be back. Give me an hour."

"I'll call the guys now." Jesse raised his chin and managed a little smile. "See you in a bit."

Finn let the workshop door close behind him before his shoulders slumped, but his heart was still racing a mile a minute.

It was the choice he'd managed to avoid until now, but he should have seen he couldn't always avoid it.

Did he side with Jesse and start a world of hurt for himself —and the rest of his family—or did he roll over and let the bullies win?

Finn's steps took him not toward his truck, but to the coastal path. Minutes later, with the sound of waves ahead of him and the rock face to his back, he sank to sit on the beach, staring out across the water.

He trailed his fingers through the rocks below, flicking pebbles down one at a time from his handful.

The last one felt smooth as glass, and he glanced down at it. Sea green, polished and yet translucent. He could just about see the moon through it if he raised it to his eye.

Sea glass. As a kid, he'd loved collecting rocks on walks with his grandpa right down to this very beach. Sea glass had been his favorites. He remembered enough to know that Floyd had disapproved, but he'd snuck them into his pockets anyway.

The moon reflected on the water, and his eyes lingered on the path between the beach and the horizon. If only he could set out on it—grab Jesse's hand, take him and walk away. Keep walking until he found somewhere that nobody knew their names.

But Jesse was here, and he couldn't leave Jesse behind. Not ever. And that meant there was only one choice: stand up and speak out for what was right. As much as it stung to admit, Jesse was right: he'd been hiding in this story for much too long.

Although everything was about Jesse, at the same time, none of it was. It began long before he'd walked into the picture. But Jesse was the catalyst. The lighter fluid that had thrown everything into sharp relief again, like the stark shadow of a bonfire flickering along this very rock face.

He slid the glass into his pocket and pushed himself to his feet. It was long past time to take a stand. But how the hell was he going to do that without fracturing an already divided family into irreparable pieces?

21

JESSE

As usual, Jesse's friends' voices preceded them as they unlocked the front door of the gallery. Jesse had only hung up five minutes ago, but they were already piling inside like soldiers called to the battlements.

"—can't believe he'd have the *nerve!*" That was Ezra, furious.

Ross shushed him. "Wait 'til we get inside."

The door banged shut, and someone locked it.

Jesse rushed over the floor toward them and wrapped his arms around Beau. Aaron and Ezra came in for a sideways angle in the hug, and even Ross sidled up to wrap his arms around the whole bundle of them.

"Oh my God. Thank God you're okay. What the hell happened?" Aaron demanded. "What were you doing here? Was it really Floyd?"

Jesse had only given them the bare details on the landline: that Floyd had broken in, tried to mess with the place, and broken his phone. He'd had to try two of their cell phones before someone picked up, since none of them recognized their new gallery phone number yet.

"I waited around to see if the vandal came back. It was definitely Floyd Hart." Jesse pulled away from them, but Aaron and Beau kept a hand on each of his shoulders and steered him toward the back workshop.

Ezra gasped. "No way. I thought I must have heard that wrong."

"Oh, what the hell?" Aaron had spotted the phone, still scattered across the ground.

"I confronted him and tried to record him. I should have called 911. I had my finger over the damn call button, but *no*," Jesse groaned. "I thought I'd be smart and catch evidence of who it was. I panicked and froze. He grabbed my phone and smashed it. And then Finn came in..."

"Where is he now?"

That was a good question. Jesse's heart lurched, and he found his cheeks hot with tears. His chest was so tight that it was suddenly hard to breathe. "I don't know."

"Okay, deep breaths, babe." Ezra steered him to sit at Beau's desk, then crouched in front of him. "Spill."

Tearfully, Jesse recounted a carefully edited version of the last hour: how Floyd had promised he wasn't done harassing them before Finn had scared him off, and then they'd argued about what they were going to do about him.

"And I pretty much gave him an ultimatum: stand up against the bullies or don't stand with me at all." Jesse's heart felt low. That kind of thing never worked out for him. He was offering Finn a choice between his family or Jesse. Who was Jesse to think he was going to win?

"I'm proud of you." Beau took Jesse's hand and squeezed it hard. "We're gonna deal with everything, one step at a time."

"Okay," Aaron said briskly, all business now while Ezra

and Beau sat with Jesse. "First, what do we do about Floyd? Did he break in?"

"I don't know," Jesse admitted. He hung his head. "I forgot to lock it after Finn left. He was here and we argued about... the window display."

"Ah." There were a few moments of uncomfortable silence as his friends looked at each other. Clearly, unspoken words were being exchanged.

Finally, Ezra was the one to speak. He was crouching by the left arm of the chair, looking up at Jesse. "I'm sorry we did that. We didn't think the feud ran that deep. What the hell? Why does it extend to us?"

Jesse drew a breath and let it out, meeting Ezra's gaze. "I know," he said, his lip quirking into a half-smile. "That's what I thought when Finn first told me."

"I really want that juicy T, honey," Aaron gasped. "Whatever the hell happened back then, it must have been *bad*."

Jesse waved the words off. "But what do we do? Call the cops? There's a little DNA on the phone from when he grabbed it, probably..."

Beau nodded slowly, glancing over his shoulder at the ruined phone. "You think Finn's right and that'll make things worse?"

"I don't care." Jesse was taken aback at the ferocity of his own words. "I don't give a fuck if he hates seeing his grandson happy at all, or if it's because he's with another man, or if it's because we're ballsy enough to come in here and help the town. I really don't care what happens. I'm not going down without a fight."

As long as Finn was on his side, that was all true. Without Finn there, well... he'd care a lot more about stuff he shouldn't. He would wilt like a flower in the scorching sun. But Finn had promised his support, and it was a foundation Jesse was starting to trust.

This was not school anymore. He didn't have to hide at home at the kitchen table making ceramics with his mom to get away from the bullies.

At last, Jesse was going to go toe-to-toe with them.

"Attaboy!" Beau exclaimed as he slow-clapped.

Ezra lit up with a grin and leaped up to awkwardly hug him around the shoulders, which sent the chair rolling into Aaron.

Ross looked less convinced, though, pacing back and forth.

"Look, we don't have to make any decisions tonight," Ross finally said. "Let's sleep on it. It's like, eleven now. We'll decide what to do in the morning."

"What if he breaks in again? Or has a key?" Jesse's chest was still tight at the thought: he honestly didn't know if he'd forgotten to lock the door after Finn left, or if Floyd really had let himself in.

"He knows we're wise to him now." Beau's confidence wasn't exactly wise, but it was just what Jesse needed to cling to. He took Jesse by the arm and steered him out toward the front gallery while Aaron locked the workshop door.

Jesse sighed and gave in. "Okay. We'll leave everything as it is and... go home?"

Ross stood over by the window, shading his eyes to peer out. "There's a light on at Cher's. We could always talk this out over a drink."

Until he'd worked things out with Finn, sleep would be hard to come by. Jesse liked that idea a lot better. "Yeah. Let's go."

They all took a turn tugging the door handle once the

alarm was set and the door locked, exchanging smiles that were laden with an unspoken worry.

That was the best they could do. Jesse had been silly to think he could watch the shop 24/7 until the vandal was caught. That was what alarms were for.

And he never would have been in danger tonight had he just listened to reason and gone home with Finn.

They might still be together—in every sense. Now, he wasn't sure where they stood, and nothing in his world seemed stable.

Well, there was one thing: his friends. They surrounded him in a tight bunch, scurrying like a flock of flamingos toward the light that spilled from the closed shutters along the front of the bar.

The door was closed rather than propped open, but there was music playing.

Jesse tried to pull on the door and blinked. The wooden door was firmly locked. "Oh. Shit."

"Maybe it's not open after all?"

"You think? It sounds open, but..." The tables outside were nestled against the building, the chairs upside-down on top of them.

But the door rattled just a few moments later. Instead of welcoming them in, Cher stepped outside, her face fixed in a scowl as she closed the door firmly behind herself.

It was a pretty clear display of exclusion. For half a crazy moment, Jesse wondered if there was some town hall meeting they hadn't been invited to. A meeting about them.

"Yes?" Cher asked, her expression guarded.

"We... sorry, we thought it was open. We were gonna have a drink, that's all." Jesse stumbled backward and gave her an awkward smile and wave.

Her expression softened. "I thought you were meeting Finn. He just came by, looking like a sad puppy. Tracking sand onto my front step and everything." She clicked her tongue.

"Sorry about that." Finn's voice was unmistakable, if quiet, and Jesse spun around to face him. He was emerging from the square, not bothering to look before crossing the street between the square and the bar's front step.

He hesitated as he stood on the sidewalk in front of the bar. Jesse found himself peeling away from his friends instinctively, stepping closer to Finn to find out what he wanted.

"Jesse? A word?"

Jesse swallowed hard, his heart flip-flopping again. He wasn't going to say no to those eyes. Not ever again. He'd done that too many times tonight.

Cher had ducked out of sight behind the door, but she reappeared. "Oh, the rest of you may as well come in, then." She huffed and opened the door, ushering the rest of them in. She eyed the two of them again before letting the door swing shut.

When they were alone, Jesse took a tentative step forward and reached for Finn's hand.

Finn took both his hands and raised them to his lips, pressing his warm lips on the backs of both sets of knuckles. His gaze was sincere. "I'm with you."

Three little words, and Jesse's crashing spirits abruptly reversed course like they were lifted by helium. He caught his breath, a smile creeping across his face. "You... are?"

"You're right." Finn glanced around the square and back to Jesse. He tugged lightly on Jesse's hands and pulled him in. After looping his arms around Jesse's waist, he leaned in for a kiss.

The stress bled from Jesse's body as Finn's lips met his. They were just as solid and reassuring as always.

Several minutes passed as Jesse swayed into Finn, giving him his weight and trusting him to hold it. And Finn did, bracing himself as Jesse leaned into his chest and pressed his nose into his neck.

Perfect. No matter what shit life threw at them, if Finn was willing to face his greatest fears to be with him, Jesse would move heaven and earth to make it work.

"I can't believe it took a stranger to see that," Finn said and gave a disbelieving little chuckle. "But we've been putting way too much stock in this feud. I can't believe my cousins would care about... well, what Floyd cares about."

"And what's that?" Jesse asked, taking Finn's hand. "What the hell is so bad that Floyd won't just leave you alone?"

Finn bit his lip and frowned, looking away. "I only found out pretty recently myself." He spoke slowly. "Apparently... my uncle Roy, who owns the business I work at... he and my dad were pitted against my uncle Monty and Floyd. All because Roy came out."

"Seriously?" Jesse scoffed. Homophobes were *so* last century. He couldn't imagine that really having as much of an impact as this.

"That's how it started, anyway. Then a lot more bad blood developed over any little excuse to fight." Finn shook his head. "Maybe it's not about being gay after all. I can't imagine people our age caring who we sleep with. But I don't know if I can trust them."

The door opened behind them and Jesse glanced back, half-annoyed and prepared to tell his friends off for spying.

But it wasn't them. It was Rain, and he wasn't alone. Just behind him stood Justin.

It was incredible how quickly the veil dropped over Finn's open, honest expression. He was wary now, prepared for any outcome.

And instead of pulling Jesse into him, he was gradually pushing him aside as if he were about to physically put himself between him and Rain.

Jesse let go of Finn's hands and patted his arm. *I'm fine*, he tried to project his thoughts into Finn's brain, like the louder he thought them, the more likely it would work.

"I didn't know all of that," Rain said quietly.

"Listening in?" Finn shot back, his tone cold. "That's not polite, you know."

"Nothing about this damn situation is." Rain snorted. "I didn't realize where it all came from, either."

Finn raised his brow. "Seriously?"

"I mean, I knew they were homophobic. They always used to say stuff. I just didn't realize something as dumb as *that* started all of *this*." Rain gestured around like he was indicating the thick air between them.

Jesse glanced at Justin, who stepped out beside Rain. He was itching to ask if Rain was dating Justin now. It felt like he was watching a strange three-way tennis match.

"Hold on." Justin pointed behind them all. Clearly, Finn was reluctant to turn his back to the others, because he hesitated and raised his chin instead.

Jesse took his chance to look instead, and then his eyes widened.

Flame. Coming from behind their building.

Could it be some bonfire at the harbor? But there was nothing there, just an empty parking lot.

"Shit! Fire! Oh, God, my car's over there!" Rain exclaimed. He took off running, followed closely by Jesse and Finn.

Justin banged on the door and yelled, "Fire!" Then he took off, catching up with them quickly.

Jesse's lungs burned from the quick sprint. It was only a few hundred feet away, but it felt like miles. Within moments, it became clear that it wasn't just something *behind* the building.

It was the back of the building.

"Fuck. Fuck!" Jesse exclaimed. Without thinking, he tried to make a break for the front door of the gallery, but Finn held him back.

To do what? He had no idea. Grab their most valuable pieces? Stop the fire? Grab the fire extinguisher? Or at least they could go around the back of the building and see the fire for themselves.

This was their life's work and business on the line. The last two attacks seemed like nothing compared to the risk that it would all go up in smoke.

And for what?

Jesse fought back tears, and not just from his stinging eyes. He couldn't breathe, and when he tried, the smoke billowing in sheets on the wind made him cough.

It did nothing to clear the weight in his chest, though. Jesse strained against Finn's hold on his hand. He could barely feel his own lips as he formed words. "We can..."

"What, do a bucket line? The firefighters will be here any minute," Finn told him. His voice was solemn but calm. Like a rock that Jesse could anchor himself to. A little *too* solid right now.

"No. We can't just stand here!" Jesse barely managed the words. He pulled against Finn's hand again, his feet slipping for purchase on the concrete.

"Yes, we can. You aren't getting yourself killed over a minor fire."

"It's not minor!"

"Right now it is. There's hope," Finn whispered. His strong arms wrapped around Jesse. Although he struggled against Finn for a few moments, logic kicked in and he went limp.

Finn was right. He'd put himself in danger enough tonight.

"Yeah, on the square. No, nobody's inside. Are they?" Justin was on the phone, gesturing for Jesse's attention. "Nobody inside?"

Jesse shook his head, his throat closing. "No. Nobody is. Thank God."

Finn's expression was dark. "That's no accident."

Of course it wasn't. And there was only one man he'd expect this from. Jesse couldn't breathe, even as Finn took over and started ushering everyone away from the building.

"What the *fuck* did we ever do to deserve this? What did you guys do? That Floyd wants his own grandson's boyfriend to... to... lose everything? And all his friends?"

Finn took both his hands and pressed them to his lips again, then wrapped his arms around Jesse and swayed with him. Sirens were audible in the distance. "I don't know, but I swear I'm going to find out. And we're going to report this. He can't just brush this under the carpet."

Jesse pressed his face into Finn's chest.

His friends' voices—raised again, this time in panic and shock—hit him then.

"What the hell?" Aaron nearly screeched. "Did that motherfucker—"

"Yes." Finn's voice was deadly quiet. He held Jesse

perfectly still and calmly, but Jesse couldn't miss the composed fury burning through him.

Nobody could.

"I'm sorry," Finn murmured.

What? Jesse pulled away to look at him, and he was startled by the wetness on Finn's cheeks. He reached out to cup Finn's cheek. "It's not your fault!"

"Well, it's sure as hell not yours." Finn swiped at his cheek and cleared his throat, looking up at the flames now licking their way along the back of the building.

Shit, it was spreading fast.

"Out of the way." Rain jogged toward them from the parking lot by the harbor. He'd moved his car, apparently, but now he was cool and composed. "Get back." He strode away and the rest of them followed.

They moved as a group around the side of the building, across the street, in front of the grocery store.

Finn's gaze narrowed as they walked, and it was Jesse's turn to clutch his T-shirt like that could stop him from moving toward Rain.

"He didn't do it," Jesse hissed.

"How do we know that?"

Cher stepped between them, still in her bar apron. "I can vouch for him. He's been at my bar for the last hour or two."

"I saw him driving this way." Finn shook his head. "Right before Grandpa broke in. He's hiding something, and I don't know what it is."

"Excuse me?" Rain's voice was icy. "My business is none of yours."

Finn was staring at his cousin, the air thick with tension between them. "It wasn't anyone from *my* side of our family behind this."

"Good for you." Rain's tone was sharp. "Your halo's in the mail."

Jesse twisted his arm around Finn's and grabbed for his hand to keep him rooted to the spot. The last thing they needed as the firefighters pulled up was a brawl.

Besides, the flames licking up the building were chewing at the roof, and a thick smoke was starting to spiral. As the trucks screeched into the square, Jesse gasped for breath.

Even if they contained the fire despite the historic wooden building, the damage to their work would be phenomenal. Pottery, tiny jewelry pieces, canvases— all would be lost.

Please be in time.

"Finn. I need you." Jesse's voice cracked as he sank to sit on the step in front of the grocery store.

The lights flashing from the long red trucks blinded Jesse. His eyes were blurry, his hands shaking once again as his eyes filled with tears.

He was caught in a game of cat and mouse he'd never known about and sure as hell hadn't started. What did he do now?

22

—

FINN

The only thing that could have made him back down from finding out what Rain was hiding was that quiet, insistent tone.

I need you.

Finn gritted his teeth but tore his gaze from Rain's defiant stare. His lover was sinking to the curb, looking ashen and sick.

"Oh, baby," Finn whispered, sinking to his knees instantly and wrapping Jesse up in a hug. He kept an ear out for commands in case they had to move farther away, but right now they all seemed clear of the action.

There were two trucks parked alongside the building and people rushing around in firefighting gear. Above all, he couldn't shake the thick taste of smoke from his nose and mouth.

They were almost ignored, like a bunch of rubberneckers. All they could do was sit and wait helplessly for the flames to be put out.

No, that wasn't true. Not quite *all*. He could try to keep Rain from slinking off.

But when he looked up again, the guy was gone, leaving Finn with a bitter taste in his mouth that was more than just the acrid air around them.

Secrets were bullshit, and he was tired of them. He was about ready to have a blowout fight with Rain if that was what it took to find out what was going on.

"Oh, God. Don't let it all be ruined." Jesse's whispered words brought Finn's attention back to the far more pressing problem: the one he could do very little about.

"We must have caught it right as it started," Finn encouraged him, rubbing Jesse's back. His friends were huddling together, everyone coming together naturally and clutching one another. Finn looked up at them and around to each of them. "It's only the back wall."

"Yeah," Aaron whispered as they listened to the shouted orders, the radios crackling, the cops who were here and directing them to stay back. "What are we going to tell them?"

"The truth." Finn glanced at each of them. "I'm sorry I ever thought otherwise. We're gonna report that scum, and we'll make sure it sticks."

If he had to beg his dad and uncle on bended knee to forgive him for the wounds he'd reopened, he'd do it. But Jesse was right. Even before this low blow, Finn had been ready to report Floyd.

Now, he'd toss him to the wolves.

So the very last person in the world he'd expected to see walking toward him...

"That's Floyd," Jesse breathed out, staring at the approaching man with what looked like horror—or maybe just shock.

"You're *fucking* kidding me!" Beau rose to his feet, fury in his eyes, and Finn had to grab him by the arm before he could throw himself at Floyd.

Aaron and Ezra closed in tighter around Jesse like a protective shield, and Ross stood to help Finn keep Beau back.

"I live here," Floyd insisted, shrugging as he gestured toward one of the roads leading out of the square. And it was true—he did live just a couple of minutes' walk away. "Came to see what was up."

Finn didn't believe that for a second. It was no surprise that Justin and Rain flanked him, like his fucking evil henchmen. He didn't know what the hell was up, but he didn't trust Rain for a second.

"Wait," Rain said the moment his gaze met Finn's.

Finn raised his brow. He didn't even have to say it: *Why the fuck should I wait?*

"Give me a chance," Rain asked, his voice low and urgent. "It's not what you think."

"You'd better not be about to say what I think you're about to." Floyd's voice was sharp and authoritative, like he thought he held any power in this situation still.

Finn turned to skewer him with a look, but it took him a few long moments to realize that Rain was shooting him the exact same look.

Okay. Maybe something *was* afoot here.

"I found Gramps hiding out in a little cove down by the beach."

"Not—" Jesse broke off, staring up at Finn.

Finn squeezed his shoulder. All he had to say was a quiet, "Yes." When Finn searched his memory for the earliest memory he had of that place, it was picking seashells at noon on a town picnic day with his grandpa, stumbling on the little nook.

It had seemed like Narnia to him that day.

"He was the one who told us to feel free to take the old bench down for a bonfire last week." Rain glanced at Justin. "I thought he was replacing it. The lighter fluid's still in my car. Or *was*."

Floyd snarled, "Don't you throw me under the bus, boy. If you try this, you're out. You hear me?"

Rain turned his gaze toward Floyd. "I do. And I'm not keeping silent. There's cops right there, Gramps. You don't want me raising my voice."

The picture of fury, Floyd stared coldly at him, but he stayed deadly silent.

"All I want to know," Jesse said as silence fell upon their group, "is why you did it."

The man—so cursedly familiar, yet as much of a stranger as he had ever been in Finn's life—just glowered at Jesse. "There's stuff you don't understand. You're not from around here; you never will."

"Stuff nobody ever bothered explaining to *me*," Finn interjected hotly. "Because it was all supposed to be dead and buried. You're the one who started it up again. Dad told me why you hate me and Roy so much. And Jesse, and the other guys. It's all gonna come out."

"I don't care what all this shit is about," Aaron snapped. "I want answers. Why hurt *us*? Your own damn building? When people could have died? Are you a fucking lunatic?"

Rain held up a hand, and even though Finn wanted to chew him out for his part in it, he bit his tongue. Silence descended again.

"Look," Rain said when everyone was looking at him. "We all know enough to go to the cops right now. They're gonna come talk to us. And you think they won't investigate this? Connections or no."

Whatever his reasons for suddenly taking Finn's side, Finn was glad. With him as a witness, there was no way Floyd could escape.

Floyd took a step backward, eyes sliding around the scene like he was trying to find another way out.

"But we can also... keep this from spreading to the rest of the town. Because you know Hart's Bay will throw out an arsonist and asshole who'd endanger lives in a heartbeat. So we'll keep the worst of the details to ourselves." Rain met each of their gazes in turn. "Tell the cops what they need to know to investigate for insurance purposes." He shot Grandpa a glare. "Because there *will* be insurance replacing what these young men lost. And that's not all."

"Why would we do that?" Finn burst out. He wanted to call everyone he knew, plaster the news across town, get it on the damn TV. "And how can we trust he'll stick to his side of the deal?"

"Bartenders have all the power," Rain murmured, cracking a smile. "Cher knows everyone in town and their secrets. Nobody would break a promise they make in front of her," Rain said, nodding toward her. "In a day, everyone around town will know if he reneges."

Cher cracked a grin full of teeth. Finn had only seen her use that smile when throwing troublemakers out of the bar. "You betcha."

"I think we can come to a deal. I've been thinking it's time to start passing on those properties you've always promised us." Rain turned to look at their grandfather. "And there are other conditions."

Finn's brain started whirring. "You mean... he stops harassing us, stops sitting on real estate..."

"That's extortion!" Floyd gasped.

As one, Finn and Jesse spoke up while Jesse flung his arm toward the art gallery. "That's arson."

Floyd sucked his teeth and folded his arms. "I don't get a say in this, do I?"

"Nope." Rain popped the *p*, his eyes narrowed as he glared at Floyd.

Finn had never seen that look on his face before, much less directed toward his own family. Like pulling a Jenga piece from the tower, it made him wonder how many other relatives were embroiled in battles of their own that he had no idea about.

His cheeks flushed. Yeah. Maybe he'd been entrenched in one story about this feud for much too long.

Justin sucked a breath through his teeth. He was silently standing by Rain, watching everything unfold. It underscored something Finn still didn't understand.

"What are you doing here?"

Justin cast Rain a quick glance and then looked around at the others. "Apparently witnessing a deal."

"Fine," Floyd barked, fury written across his face. "We call it an accident. They'll find my cigarette butts there, anyway. The insurance will cover your shit." He gestured at Jesse and the other guys.

Rain shook his head slightly, glancing at Jesse. "I think you deserve more than a bone after all of this."

"Never would have taken you for a rat," Floyd muttered.

Rain smiled coldly at his grandfather, which surprised even Finn. "Never would have taken you for an arsonist."

While they talked, Jesse put his head together with his

friends for a quick whisper. Then, Jesse smiled and straightened up. "You sell the gallery and house to us for dirt cheap, which is about what they're worth," Jesse told Floyd. "We're never going to be your tenants again."

Finn's heart leapt as Rain nodded firmly and looked back at their grandfather. "That's the deal, then."

"Fine." Floyd refused the handshake that Rain offered, but his shoulders slumped as he looked toward the cops. "I'd better go 'fess up."

As he walked slowly toward the patrol car, Finn swapped glances with Jesse.

Jesse was smiling at him. He reached a hand out, and Finn took it, stepping close again to sweep him in for a hug.

"Better?" Finn murmured. If he could take away some of those fears his lover held, so much the better.

Jesse nuzzled into his chest, his arms flung around his neck. "Yes. Thank you," he whispered.

Finn rubbed his back for a few long moments before letting go and reaching out to shake hands with Rain. He owed him an apology.

"I'm sorry I doubted you. Thank you."

Rain's gaze flickered to his hand and then back to his face. He took it and shook, his grip firm, but he wasn't smiling. "I'll accept the apology. But there's nothing to thank me for. I'm not doing it for you."

That was about the best reaction Finn could hope for.

As they watched Floyd slide a pack of cigarettes from his pocket and gesture around, hamming it up, a shiver ran down Finn's spine.

"Why'd you turn on him?"

Rain just jerked his head toward his car. "We'll talk one day. I'm going home. Come on, Justin, I'll give you a ride."

The two of them walked off together while Finn shook his head after them.

One by one, after their interviews, their friends dispersed as the smoke settled into ash and the sea breeze began to whip away the thick smell of burning. Finn and Jesse stayed until the very end, until Finn's eyes were warm and heavy and stinging with sleep and not just ash.

There was no question when they reached Finn's house, their clothes reeking of their night together. No question that Jesse might head for his own bed.

No, they nestled together under the covers that night, holding one another tightly as their breath fell into a slow harmony like the evening tide.

JESSE, A MONTH LATER

"Welcome to Seaglass Gallery. Come on in!"

Beau was in his element, taking coats and making conversation with everyone who entered.

And thankfully, there were plenty of people to make conversation with. After all the stress of the past month, seeing lots of people actually show up was a huge sigh of relief for all of them.

Finn and a small crew of guys had worked their butts off to repair the place in time for the grand opening. It had only felt right to rename the gallery as they did so. None of them had been in love with the original name, but this one felt right.

Now that they owned the building, Jesse had been a little bit surprised that Rain had helped to fix it up. That was clearly taking their side, wasn't it? Hell, Finn had said more than once that he was surprised Rain was still on the construction crew. He didn't need to work now that he owned most of Floyd's portfolio, surely.

Floyd was quietly retiring and moving out of the public eye, and nobody around here was asking too many questions.

Rain still hadn't said why he had mediated for them all. In fact, he hadn't said much—he'd just been physically here, working on the building, and that said all Jesse needed to know.

Jesse had a suspicion that he knew why Rain was still keeping his distance, but his lips were sealed. It was for Rain to decide when he was ready to come out, and not a moment before.

"Hi," he greeted Finn's cousin with a smile when he arrived. Unsurprisingly, Justin was with him, so Jesse bit back a little smile as he greeted him, too.

The two of them were cute together, if they *were* together. Rain moved more comfortably around Justin than he did the rest of the construction crew.

"Afternoon. Hope we're not too late."

"Not at all. Just fashionably late," Jesse said with a grin. "The wine hasn't run out yet."

This time, Finn had helped set up the gallery for the grand opening. He seemed to enjoy hanging out with all the guys these days, and they'd easily accepted him as one of their own.

Which was good, since they were going to be neighbors for the foreseeable future. As promised, the five of them now owned the house. Living next door to his boyfriend had its perks, but Jesse was spending more nights at Finn's house than his own. They had more privacy that way, after all.

There was a lull in new guests, so Jesse took the chance to wander the room and chat with people about his new range of ceramics.

He'd incorporated sea glass into a collection of tableware, and they were the hit of the night. Jesse suspected he was going to have to take preorders for the next batch soon.

"Boo."

Jesse smiled at the familiar warm voice in his ear, the warm breath on his neck. Finn's broad hands rested on his shoulders, thumbs rubbing gently into his muscles.

Jesse hadn't realized how much he needed the touch until that moment. A month of stress had gone into tonight, and finally it was underway.

The grand opening was, so far, even more successful than their soft opening had been. Total strangers and tourists had even driven in from nearby towns, as far away as Portland.

And everyone seemed to be enjoying themselves.

The hum of energy in the room was palpable. Ezra stood in the corner, gesturing at his canvases to a small group of onlookers, two of whom were actually taking notes. Beau was helping a small group of women try on necklaces in a mirror, laughing and joking away with them.

There were other pieces in the room, too. They'd found half a dozen other artists who lived relatively close to Hart's Bay and wanted to sell at the gallery. The co-op program was nearly ready to launch so they could share workspace with more people.

The more variety they had in their shop, the better, they all agreed. A rising tide floated all boats.

Best of all, most of Hart's Bay was here. Even Victor, looking uncomfortable in a collared shirt and nice trousers, had come from the newly renovated apartment across the street where he now lived. Gregory had turned up—but only because Cher's bar was closed—and he was chatting with the twins, Darrell and Dan.

Scott, the town newsletter editor, had promoted the event as promised. He was here, wandering around with a notepad, taking notes and interviewing people for a write-up in next week's edition.

Jesse closed his eyes and sighed, leaning back into Finn as

he let Finn's arms snake around his chest from behind. After a few moments, he murmured, "What's up?"

"Hold still." Finn's hands slid up Jesse's chest. For half a moment, Jesse wondered if he was going to feel him up in public. He stifled a giggle, but Finn's hands were busy doing something else.

He glanced down and caught a glimpse of something small and green. Moments later, a thin metal chain fastened around his neck, and Finn's thumb brushed his skin next to the clasp. "What do you think?"

Jesse stepped forward to the mirror next to the jewelry display against one wall. Then, he gasped.

There it was: that piece of sea glass he'd saved from their first time on the beach together. Only now, it was wrapped in wire and threaded onto a silver chain, and it hung around his neck.

"I wondered where that went," he breathed out, touching it and leaning in. He'd hardly been home, but he'd noticed it going missing from his bedside table. He'd just figured it had fallen onto the floor somewhere.

"You like it?" Finn's tone was filled with pride.

Jesse gasped. "Wait. You did this?"

"With a lot of help." Finn sheepishly chuckled. "Probably more Beau's creation than mine."

Nonsense. Jesse picked up the polished glass with his thumb, looking closer at the details. He could see the slight plier marks and twists to the wire that Beau wouldn't have put in.

This was handmade by Finn, and every little nick and lump was precious to Jesse.

The glow of pleasure turned into a raging sun, and Jesse

felt like he was beaming it from every pore. He wriggled in Finn's hold and threw his arms around him.

"Oof!" Finn teased, pretending to stumble.

Jesse stretched onto tiptoe and pressed kisses against Finn's lips, not caring who saw. In fact, he *wanted* them to, as much as Finn tried to keep his gestures of love small and quiet. He'd worked behind the scenes in his old jeans to help Jesse, but he deserved to be in the spotlight today, in his nice suit and at Jesse's side.

"I love you," Jesse whispered.

Finn scooped Jesse off his feet and spun him around once, then set him down and beamed at him like a prized collector's piece. "I love you, too, sweetheart."

Someone cleared their throat nearby, and Jesse cast a glance toward the door.

It was Floyd, dressed in a suit and looking uncomfortable as hell. Cher stood at his elbow. In fact, Jesse might think he was being frog-marched over to them.

When he reached them, Floyd gave them both an uncomfortable nod and then looked at Cher. She raised an eyebrow pointedly.

Floyd sighed and looked back at Jesse for just a moment before picking an invisible bit of lint off his sleeve. "What's your most expensive piece? I'd like to purchase it to... support your endeavor."

Jesse had never heard someone more reluctant to show their support. "Er..."

Aaron swept in like a trained sales hawk. "Right this way. I believe we have a great canvas back here."

Jesse shot a look after them and then covered his mouth. Aaron was leading Floyd straight to that portrait: two men holding hands, standing on the clifftop overlooking Hart's Bay.

Now that he looked at it, it *did* look an awful lot like himself and Finn from behind.

Finn sucked in his breath and took Jesse's hand, squeezing hard. When Jesse glanced at him, he was fighting back a laugh. "I wonder where he'll display that," Finn leaned in to murmur as Floyd got out his wallet.

Cher glanced back over her shoulder and shot them a wink.

"Darling, I love this place."

Jesse turned to see his mom there, in her floaty pale dress covered in sunflowers, unruly curls spilling from the floral headband. She looked like she'd come straight from a commune in the mountains.

"You do? Enough to stick around here?" He grinned.

She winked at him. "Well... let's just say I'm thinking about it. If I have sons living here and the beach on my doorstep, I could handle being farther away from the mountains."

Jesse's heart leapt. He hadn't missed the plural of *son*.

Beside him, Finn stood tall, but Jesse could feel the happiness almost vibrating through him at her quick and simple acceptance.

"We'd love to have you around, Mrs. Stone."

"Oh, please," she chuckled. "That's my mom. Just Laura. Or Mom, to my son's boyfriend." She glanced at Jesse. "He was right—you are a catch, aren't you?"

For once, it was Finn's turn to blush, though Jesse joined him. "Mom!"

She mimed zipping her lips and winked before heading off to talk to Victor. The two of them seemed to be hitting it off.

"Oh. Oh!" Finn broke away from Jesse and strode for the

door, and Jesse turned to watch him, curious who could have caught his eye.

His heart flip-flopped. The cluster of four people who walked through the door all bore a certain resemblance to Finn. Jesse had met them all a couple of times, but never together, as a family unit. His heart pounded.

"Mom and Dad, my uncle Roy, and... that's my brother Dash. Dash!" Finn greeted, ducking around a knot of people by one of the paintings near the door. "Dude! What are you doing here?"

"Surprise!" The man was much shorter than Finn, slender but bright-faced. He had his mom's cute button nose, but the same eyes as the rest of the Harts. Finn swept him up in a hug as they slapped each other's backs. "I got into town yesterday morning."

"How long are you staying?"

"For good."

"Holy shit!" Finn shook Dash by the shoulders like he couldn't quite contain himself. "You're actually gonna be living here? Oh my God!"

"Got a teaching contract and everything." Dash grinned.

Jesse smiled and nodded at Roy, shaking hands. "Good to see you again."

He'd met Finn's uncle a couple times over the last few weeks of construction. The town wasn't so big that he could hide from *all* the family introductions.

Speaking of which... Jesse took a deep breath. "Hi," he said to the man he didn't know. "I'm Jesse." He reached out to shake hands.

Instead, Finn's dad smiled and stepped closer for a hug. "Good to meet you, Jesse. We've heard so much."

"Uh-oh," Jesse joked, smiling before Finn's mom hugged him, too.

Finn finished saying his hellos to his brother and stepped closer to Jesse, wrapping a protective arm around his shoulders. Jesse loved how perfectly he fit under Finn's arm. "Jesse, you met my mom and dad and Roy. This is Dash, my little brother."

Jesse shook hands with Dash, too, and smiled around at everyone. He was strangely dizzy with relief.

"Great place here." Roy looked around approvingly. "I'm glad our boy was able to restore the back wall."

"Oh, me too." Jesse leaned into Finn and smiled up at him. "I don't know what we would have done without him."

"Rain helped, too," Finn pointed out, glancing over at him. "I'd like it if you had a word with him tonight."

Roy and Finn's dad swapped looks, but then Roy nodded. "I'd like that, too. I hear good things about his work ethic."

Finn nodded. "He's been working his ass off."

Jesse was happy to stand back and watch Finn chatter to his brother. But when Roy and Finn's dad approached Rain, Jesse looked past them and froze.

Floyd was standing there, the now-wrapped frame awkwardly balanced in his arms, staring at them all.

A sudden icy chill fell over the place. Shit. He should have kept a closer eye on Floyd while Finn greeted his family.

Jesse strode over toward them, perfectly ready to intervene, but it turned out not to be necessary.

Floyd inclined his chin slightly and headed for the door, flanked by Cher still. He circumvented the others like a spot of mold, while Cher grinned and waved at them all.

As he swept past Jesse, he shoved the frame at Cher as if making a point. "I'm sure you can find a place to put... *this.*"

"I'd be happy to put it up at the bar," Cher agreed.

A frown appeared on his face, but when he looked at Cher, she smiled blandly at him. Jesse bit back his smile as he met Cher's wink a moment later. She knew exactly what she was up to.

Cher was in no hurry to follow Floyd outside. Instead, she gasped at the sight of Dash and stepped in to hug him. Again, Dash told her how he was home for good now.

They hardly noticed Floyd leave. The conversation was loud and enthusiastic again, the air of celebration impossible to destroy. They'd worked too hard on it for any one person to pop the bubble now, especially that one particular persona non grata.

All in all, Jesse reflected as he looked around and finally let himself watch the beginning of something special unfolding all around him... it was a job well done.

2 4

———

JESSE

"That was amazing!"

Jesse was still on a high from the success of their night: several hundred visitors over the course of the night, too many cases of wine drunk, most of their art sold, and two dozen preorders of his very own sea glass pottery.

Finn smiled at him as he sat on the edge of the bed in his boxers, watching Jesse fling his clothes around. "What was the best part?"

Jesse groaned as he thought about that. "Oh, man. Picking one is impossible. All of it!" He'd enjoyed every moment, from the first few guests lined up outside to the reconciliation between some of Finn's family members. Even Floyd showing up hadn't dented anyone's mood.

Cleaning up after the place was closed, joking around with his friends, and laughing about everything as they finished the dregs of the sparkling wine had been wonderful. Dash had stuck around to help a little. Jesse couldn't wait to get to know him along with the rest of Finn's family.

Maybe finding out Mom was thinking about moving here? It would be really nice to be closer to his own family now.

As Jesse tossed his shirt in Finn's laundry basket, Jesse's thumb brushed against the warm glass now nestled just under his collarbones.

No—it wasn't impossible. He smiled, running his finger along the chain as he walked over to the bed. In a few fluid motions, he knelt and straddled Finn's lap.

"Well, hello." Finn laughed, grabbing his ass to keep him steady.

He ground against Jesse, his hand wandering up Jesse's back to cup the back of his head until he pressed a kiss on his lips.

"I have one favorite moment after all." Jesse rolled his hips with Finn's until he found just the right angle to grind against his thigh. He was growing hard at the sheer closeness.

Finn didn't even need to lay a single finger on him to ignite that fire between them. Having both his hands wandering over Jesse's bare torso, his fingers sliding under Jesse's waistband to grip his bare ass...

"What's that?" Finn's touch stopped for a moment as he tilted his head, looking up at Jesse.

As Jesse leaned forward, the necklace brushed Finn's chest. "When you gave me this."

The surprise that flashed over Finn's face was replaced by a warm smile moments later. "I'm so glad you like it. I thought someone would give away the surprise for sure. I hope it's something you'll wear."

"Every day," Jesse murmured, draping his arms around Finn's neck. He tilted his head and grinned. "Hopefully the first of many jewelry experiments."

"I don't know about that," Finn laughed. "I might leave that to the experts."

Ah, he totally missed the hint. Jesse bit his lip to hide his amusement. He had plenty of time to drop hints at what he meant, anyway.

Whether or not Finn knew it yet, one day, this guy would get a ring on his finger and make him the happiest man alive.

Jesse grinned and ran his hands down Finn's chest, pausing to tweak his nipples playfully. A quick glance down at the tent in Finn's boxers told him that he wasn't the only one happy right now.

"In the meantime," Jesse murmured, "I have plans for you."

"Oh, do you?"

"Yep." Jesse beamed at Finn and then shoved him in the chest, hard.

"Whoa!" Finn flopped onto his back on the bed, staring up at him with a grin. "Starting to get some idea what you mean."

Jesse hummed, shifting to straddle Finn's thighs. He walked his fingers down the middle of his stomach to the bulge and then flicked playfully.

"Don't tease," Finn pouted. "That's just mean."

Jesse couldn't restrain his snort. "Says the king of turning me on and edging me for hours."

"You've been a busy man lately." Finn smirked. "I've gotta take advantage of every minute I can get you."

Jesse groaned. "I'm taking advantage of *you* tonight," he informed Finn in a low growl. He shifted to unfasten his own jeans. As usual, it took both of them and a little ungraceful wiggling before he could get his skinny jeans off, though.

"More effective without the sea lion impression," Finn deadpanned.

Jesse gasped at Finn's nerve and then laughed despite himself. "The cheekier you are, the longer I make you watch me finger myself before I ride you."

Finn's eyes widened and his lips parted for just a moment before he clamped them shut and mimed throwing away the key.

"Better." Jesse grinned as he scooped the lube off the bedside table. "Bareback?"

They'd been doing it this way for the last few weeks, since visiting the clinic together and making sure it was safe. It meant a little more spontaneity, which helped during late-night walks on the beach.

"Please." Finn's eyes sparkled as he watched Jesse pulling his underwear off, but he kept his hands off and waited on Jesse's cues.

Jesse loved the heady feeling of being in charge every now and then. Most of the time, he let Finn press him up against the counter, the rock face, the workshop bench, the car hood...

He might have been busy the past few weeks, but they'd found a surprising amount of time for each other. The honeymoon phase was far from over.

As usual, Jesse spread his knees and rolled his head back for a few moments. He moaned loudly as he slid his fingers inside himself. Their sex life was frequent enough that he hardly needed any time to get ready, but he loved teasing Finn.

Jesse loved making Finn watch and wait and want it all the more.

The hard line in Finn's underwear twitched as he watched Jesse's expression as he fingered himself just above Finn's thighs. Jesse kept a hand braced on Finn's chest.

"You're too fucking hot," Finn whispered. He pressed himself up and kissed Jesse, bracing himself on his elbows.

Jesse whimpered against Finn's lips, the world hazy as the crescendo of need climbed within him. "So are you. Especially when you're all dressed up."

Though seeing him peeled out of his good suit was just as gorgeous a sight. Finn's body was hard with need, his muscles taut like he was just barely holding himself back from rolling Jesse over and ravishing him.

The thought made Jesse moan again. Fuck, he couldn't wait another moment. Jesse needed Finn inside him right now.

Finn chuckled, the deep and fond noise reverberating through his chest.

He rested a hand on Jesse's hip and pressed kisses against his neck, guiding Jesse down until he nearly lay flat along his body. The chain of his necklace lay against Finn's skin, the smooth stone twitching as Finn's heart pounded.

Jesse reached behind himself, stroking Finn and enjoying the weight of him in his hand before pressing the tip against himself.

Slowly, he pushed himself back and away from Finn's face as he eased down onto his shaft. Finn opened him up, inch by inch, and filled him to bursting. And God, he was ready to burst already.

"Yes," Jesse gasped, unable to tear his gaze from Finn's. Knowing that Finn was watching him slide onto his cock, feeling Jesse all tight and hot around him, made Jesse twitch and tighten even further. He clamped around that hard cock until he made himself relax and breathe deeply.

"Ride me," Finn growled, urging him on. "I want to see you lose control."

Jesse's thighs burned, so he shifted on his knees, grabbing the headboard as he started to push himself into motion.

Had he ever tasted heaven like this? Jesse couldn't

remember it if so. He brushed his new trinket out of the way so he could claim Finn's lips in a kiss that went from sweet to fierce in three seconds flat.

Jesse's hard cock brushed against Finn's abs, and the harder he pressed himself against his lover, the more the smooth bumps stimulated the sensitive shaft.

But he didn't want to get off yet. He wanted this to last forever.

A flash of heat coursed through him, and his cock jumped between them as Finn smacked his ass. "So hot," Finn whispered, kneading and then spanking him again, bringing more blood rushing to already sensitive nerves.

Jesse whimpered and curled his fingers, nails digging into the headboard, gripping for dear life as he pushed himself more upright. With every rise and fall of his hips, he drove himself onto Finn, enveloping him and taking him in until it felt like they were locked together forever.

He never wanted to be parted from this man—physically or emotionally—ever again.

"I love you," Jesse gasped, his cheeks burning as he stared down at Finn's dark eyes and wild hair. "I love you so much it hurts."

He knew the moment he saw those eyes gleaming that he was getting a cheeky response. Sure enough, Finn winked. "That's not my big, manly cock in your cute little bottom?"

Jesse burst out laughing, his movements slowing for a moment as he lost the rhythm. "That too, silly."

Finn's next words were serious as his palm slid across Jesse's cheek, cupping it gently. "I love you. To the end of the horizon."

Jesse threw himself, heart and soul, into riding Finn. Every grunt and groan he wrung from either of them was only encouragement to keep going. Their bodies were made to fit together. Why else would this feel so right—so perfect?

When every ounce of Jesse's energy was spent and sweat shone on his skin, he started to slow down, his breathing ragged.

But Finn didn't hesitate or make Jesse ask him to take over. He just searched Jesse's gaze and then smiled, firmly gripping Jesse close to him and rolling them both.

With Finn nestled between his thighs, Jesse arched his back, squirming with joy at the weight pinning him to the bed. He wrapped his legs around Finn's waist as he moaned in pleasure.

Finn started moving, driving deeper into Jesse than he could have managed on his own. He seemed to know exactly what angle would make Jesse's gasps turn into squeaks and full-throated moans.

The pleasure built into ecstasy before long, with an edge of desperation that even Jesse couldn't ignore. Finn's thrusts were coming hard and fast now, the bed squeaking under them as they panted for breath.

"I need you," Finn managed, catching his breath as he stared down at Jesse, his eyes dark and hungry. "I need you to come for me. I need to see you explode for me. Would you do that?"

Jesse whimpered. With every pump of that thick length sending sparks flying under his skin, it was all he could do *not* to come on the spot. "Yes, please," he barely managed. "Please, Finn."

One of Finn's big, gentle hands wrapped around his cock, and Jesse cried out, rolling his head back on the pillow. He barely even registered anything besides Finn's weight over him and inside him, and the tight circle of fingers that was jerking along his shaft.

Pulling him over the edge, hard and fast and unstoppable.

The cliff hit, and Jesse's strangled cry of pleasure echoed from every wall as he clutched onto Finn. It was all he could do to wrap himself around that strong body and hang on for dear life.

Every jet of sticky warmth shot across himself and Finn, leaving them a hot mess as he clamped tight around that length. It only made the orgasm feel ten times better—no, a hundred times.

But Finn wasn't done yet. With a growl, he let go of Jesse's softening cock and grabbed his hip, his thrusts hard and fast now. He drove into him until Jesse thought he might send him through the mattress.

"Yes!" Finn panted, low and desperate, near his ear. Jesse knew he was close, swelling within him, ready to claim and mark him as his own.

And Jesse couldn't be happier about it.

"Come, baby," he whispered, trying to memorize every slide of warm skin on skin, every desperate gasp into his ear, every clutch of Finn's nails against his skin.

"J-J..." Finn stuttered before sucking in a breath, his breath short and sharp. "Jesse!"

Jesse ran his palms across Finn's back, enjoying every squeeze of his muscles and shudder of his skin under the touch. He grinned, enjoying more than one kind of warmth inside now.

"Oh, fuck," Finn finally panted when his thrusts slowed, his cock starting to go soft. Jesse still clutched onto Finn, enjoying every last leisurely moment of their bodies together until it was finally impossible and he slid out.

Jesse hummed in contentment. "Damn right." He wrapped his arms around Finn's back and held him close, not planning on letting him get up anytime soon.

"I can't believe how good you feel," Finn whispered, his voice a quiet, sexy rasp.

Jesse beamed. He was still tingling with pleasure himself, the heat sinking into his bones. "I could do that all day long," he murmured. "Every night."

"Do you want to?"

Jesse blinked across Finn's shoulders before he finally let Finn pull back enough to see his face. "What do you mean?"

"You wanna make it official? Move in here?" Finn smirked. "Saves you always having to run next door for clean clothes."

Jesse's heart skipped a beat. The airy joy that swept him up made him twitch his fingers against the comforters just to make sure he wasn't about to float away.

But no, Finn was here to ground him, his weight solid and reassuring against Jesse's whole body. Like an anchor or a rudder, always quietly steering him.

"I'd love to," Jesse murmured. He was smiling so wide his cheeks hurt now.

That same joy spread across Finn's face, and he gave Jesse a big, dopey grin. "Hooray!"

Jesse laughed. "Hooray?" he teased.

"I was trying to figure out how to ask you this whole last week." Finn brushed Jesse's hair back, the touch small and intimate.

Jesse hummed and pressed his nose into Finn's shoulder. "So you decided to lure me in with great sex, huh?"

Finn's eyes were gentle, but they danced with pleasure. "Pretty sure you followed me every step of the way."

"Mmm." Jesse nudged Finn to lie on his side so he could

rest his head on that warm chest. Finn's arm snaked around him, keeping him in place.

Here, by Finn's side, forever.

"I'm pretty sure I did," Jesse agreed, his eyes drifting shut. "And I'm glad."

"Me too," Finn whispered, pressing kisses along Jesse's shoulder. "Me too."

Jesse closed his eyes and held Finn tight. If he stayed just still enough and held his breath, he could swear he could hear the sea.

Or maybe that was the slow wash of Finn's breath across his shoulder, in and out, sweeping him out into his own perfect fantasy land.

A place for just the two of them.

EPILOGUE

FINN

It had been years since the beach had glowed dark orange from a bonfire as the September evening light faded.

Of course Jesse had wanted to bring back the tradition of the end-of-summer beach party. And Finn had been with him all the way, helping spread the word that Hart's Bay was going to see a wonderful night. Little did Jesse know just how wonderful.

Finn smiled as he wrapped his arm tightly around Jesse, casting him another fond sideways glance.

They'd found driftwood and rock benches for seating, and some people had brought deck chairs or thick blankets. Portable barbecues provided the food, and there were plenty of drink coolers so nobody went thirsty.

These gatherings were more common these days—another impromptu party in Hart Square had already happened, and Finn wouldn't be surprised to see more.

"Want another s'more?" Aaron wiggled the bag in Jesse's face. "I know you do."

"I can't say no." Jesse scooped one out and stuck it on the poker, roasting it in the flames. They'd reclaimed fire after the horrible incident a few months ago, turning it into a force for good.

Finn smiled, watching his lover try to avoid making a torch of the marshmallow. He could wait a little longer to say what he needed to say.

It had taken Finn long enough to realize that Jesse was trying to suggest engagement. It wasn't until Jesse had sat him down over coffee and toast one morning a few weeks ago and flat-out told him, "Dude, I'd marry you," that Finn had realized what all the subtle hints about ring sizes had meant.

And then he'd sprung into action.

Darkness was falling, and the moon was peeping over the horizon of the sea. Like they'd planned it, and Mother Nature was joining the party.

"Want some?"

"No, but I want you," Finn teased, waiting until Jesse had licked his fingers clean before he pulled Jesse to his feet.

"Speech!" shouted a couple of their friends, so Finn laughed and patted Jesse's back.

"Thank you all for coming," Jesse spoke up boldly, looking around at them all with one of his blinding grins. "I'm so glad everyone was on board. When Finn told me about this old tradition, I just knew I wanted to help bring it back."

"And you've brought a lot back," Finn told Jesse, stepping away from him just enough to take his hands. The ocean lapped the shore behind him. His cheeks blazed not just because of the heat of the fire that Jesse stood next to, but because of what he was about to say.

"Hope, new opportunities, new residents." Finn nodded at

Jesse's mom, who was sharing a beer with Victor and smiling back at him.

She knew what was afoot, too. He'd asked her permission first.

The ring box was burning a hole in his pocket—metaphorically speaking. Finn had realized quickly that his skill was limited to that necklace that Jesse still wore every single day. He'd recruited Beau's help, along with one of the newer artists at the co-op. That meant that all of Jesse's four former housemates knew.

Finn had walked the length of the cove every morning for three days to gather enough sea glass of exactly the right shade to match Jesse's necklace. It had been crushed into an even band of color laid into a silver ring.

Finn casually slipped his hand into his pocket to grip the box it sat in.

"And I'm so happy that you and your friends chose Hart's Bay to move to. When you walked into Cher's End Table... I don't think either of us expected what lay ahead."

Jesse's smile wobbled. "We sure didn't," he murmured, his eyes shining. Finn could tell that he still had no idea what was up.

Good. He loved surprising his boyfriend... or, with any luck, fiancé. Finn's heart pounded, his hands shaking. Now was the moment.

"Jesse Stone," Finn said, sinking to his knee.

The crackling fire couldn't drown out the murmurs and gasps as everyone suddenly paid attention, the conversations stopping dead.

Jesse's jaw dropped as Finn opened the box, the ring glinting in the firelight.

"I didn't know you were what we all needed to begin

healing these rifts. You sure know how to break a Hart and make him whole. You've worked some kind of spell not just over me, but everyone else here. And I'd be honored until the end of my days if you'd share that magic with me. Would you marry me?"

Tears were rolling down Jesse's nose now, the light from the moon and the fire reflecting on his cheeks. But he was smiling, too, his eyes alight.

He was still the most beautiful man Finn had ever laid eyes on, and everything in Finn's world hinged on the next word Jesse spoke.

Finn couldn't even breathe, couldn't think, couldn't do anything but stare up at Jesse, waiting for those perfect lips to light his way.

"Yes," Jesse whispered, and he nodded jerkily, wiping his cheeks. He laughed and pulled on Finn's shoulder. "Yes, Finn. Oh my God, yes!" His volume only went up with every word.

Then the cheering started, whoops and hollers and applause as Finn stood up and slid the ring onto Jesse's finger.

He didn't expect Jesse to leap at him, but he burst out laughing as he caught his now-fiancé. Not just that, but Finn swept him up into his arms, gripping him tight and close.

"Oop!" Jesse squeaked, grabbing onto Finn's shoulders and waist.

But Finn just smiled, steadying himself as he crushed Jesse against him in the hardest hug he dared.

No way could Jesse throw him off balance now. He was ready for anything. "I gotcha," he whispered.

Jesse's voice was choked, and his nose pressed into Finn's neck as his warm breath tickled his shoulder. "I know."

Finn couldn't wait to celebrate this moment alone with his husband-to-be, but not quite yet. The night was young. They still had dancing, drinking, and congratulations to take in from all around them.

And Finn didn't mind. He had plenty of time to spend with Jesse alone on this very beach in the years and decades to come.

With Jesse in his life, nothing would ever be the same.

Dear reader,

Thank you for reading *Hard Hart*, the first book in the cozy, heartwarming world of Hart's Bay!

It's delightful to finally write a series set in the Pacific Northwest. I grew up scrambling along the coastline, peeking into tide pools and dipping my toes into the surf. I'm beyond thrilled to bring you there, if just for a few hours!

Thanks to Amy, Sandra, Meg, and Kitti for helping make this book the best it can be—any remaining errors are my own, because I'm a constant meddler. My thanks also to several bright stars who know who they are, and who pointed the way on this series. Thanks as well to all the Petals in my Facebook group for your patience, encouragement, kind words, and cheerleading throughout this year.

Last but not least: my eternal thanks and love to the cheesebags for being my rock in every storm, and to the boy for putting up with my mutterings, sudden note dictation, and frequent absentminded stares as this town unfolded slowly over the course of the year.

If you enjoyed *Hard Hart*, you can find the audiobook on Audible or Amazon, brought to life by Greg Boudreaux.

There's lots more to come in Hart's Bay, so be ready to settle in at the town square and meet the locals again soon! The next book in Hart's Bay, *Changed Hart*, is Rain's story, and it's available now.

Make sure you subscribe to my newsletter at edaviesbooks.com/subscribe to hear about freebies and deals; exclusive bonus stories; new releases and preorders; sneak peeks at upcoming books; event appearances; and other exciting news as it happens!

I also have a reader group on Facebook if you want to chat about your favorite parts of *Hard Hart*, see cute bee photos and good news stories, and keep on top of my upcoming releases with a whole bunch of lovely readers: facebook.com/groups/edavies

Last but not least: always be you!

~Ed

NEXT IN HART'S BAY:

CHANGED HART

"Nothing worth having comes easy."

Rainier Hart knows all about hiding. He's ready to burst out of the closet, consequences be damned. His first escape attempt failed, but he's not done fighting. Back in his hometown, all he has are a few worthless buildings and a job on a construction crew. What he needs is a firm hand to guide him—and a family that doesn't look down their noses at him.

Colt Fuller is everything Rain isn't... or is he? Rich, muscular, commanding, and very much out of place in Hart's Bay, he wants more than Rain's run-down warehouses. He wants the surprisingly defiant little twink who owns them, too. The pull between them is too strong to ignore, even with everything that's on the line.

Rain and Colt are perfectly matched: right down to the secrets they'd each prefer to keep buried. Those secrets threaten the very foundations they begin to build a life together on.

Because nothing stays secret in Hart's Bay, including how they really feel about each other. Can they see past the bluster and into each other's hearts?

ABOUT THE AUTHOR

E. Davies grew up moving constantly, which taught him what people have in common, the ways relationships are formed, and the dangers of "miscellaneous" boxes. As a young gay author, Ed prefers to tell feel-good stories that are brimming with hope.

He writes full-time, goes on long nature walks, tries to fill his passport, drinks piña coladas on the beach, flees from cute guys, coos over fuzzy animals (especially bees), and is liable to tilt his head and click his tongue if you don't use your turn signal.

facebook.com/edaviesbooks

twitter.com/edaviesauthor

instagram.com/thisboyisstrange

bookbub.com/authors/e-davies

Hart's Bay

Hard Hart

Changed Hart

Wild Hart

Stolen Hart

Significant Brothers

Splinter

Grasp

Slick

Trace

Clutch

Tremble

Riley Brothers

Buzz

Clang

Swish

Crunch

Slam

Grind

Brooklyn Boys

Electric Sunshine

Live Wire

Boiling Point

F-Word

Flaunt

Freak

Faux

Forever

After

Afterburn

Afterglow

Aftermath

Men of Hidden Creek

Shelter

Adore

Miracle

Redemption

Audiobooks

You can see all my books available in audio here: www.
edaviesbooks.com/audiobooks